I KNOW Y_ _ _ _

DI RITA GUPTA MURDER MYSTERY
BOOK 5

SAM CARTER

Copyright © 2025 by Sam Carter
All rights reserved.
The right of Sam Carter to be identified as the author of this work has been asserted by him in accordance with the Copyright, Designs and Patents Act 1988. No part of this book may be reproduced in any form or by any electronic or mechanical means, including information storage and retrieval systems, without permission in writing from the author. Infringement of copyright by copying.
(1) The copying of the work is an act restricted by the copyright in every description of copyright work and references in this part to copying and copies shall be construed as follows.
(2) Copying in relation to a literary, dramatic, musical, or artistic work means reproducing the work in any material form.
This includes storing the work in any medium by electronic means.
(3) Copying in relation to the typographical arrangement of a published edition means making a facsimile copy of the arrangement.
(4) Copying in relation to any description of work includes the making of copies that are transient or are incidental to some other use of the work.
This book is a work of fiction. Names, characters, places, and incidents either are
products of the author's imagination or are used fictitiously. Any resemblance to actual
persons, living or dead, events, or locales is entirely coincidental.

CHAPTER 1

Andrew Salford hurried along the road, hands stuffed into his pockets, head lowered against the cold. Although it was April, the weather had turned nasty, like it often did without warning in Scarborough. Wind howled in from the North Sea, battering the ramparts of the derelict Scarborough castle walls. The castle had withstood these brutal elements for hundreds of years, and most of it now lay in ruins. Andrew was going inside the castle, although it was late night now, and closed to the public.

He was in the Royal Albert Park, and the castle was easily visible from the park. There were also paths that led up to the main South Gate of the castle, but that massive gate would be locked now. Andrew, like many locals, knew the secret, hidden paths that led up to the castle ramparts and to the old sentry gates that were now disused.

He scaled a fence, and jumped on the other side. He hurried through the undergrowth, although the bushes slowed his progress. Cursing and shoving away branches and leaves, he finally emerged upon the path. Timber slats were fixed on the ground – the wood chipped in the corners, but smooth with human steps from centuries.

He climbed the path swiftly, and by the time he reached the sentry gate, he was out of breath. The rusty iron gate that covered the arched gate was only wide enough to let one person at a time. It smelt of animal urine inside, and graffiti covered the walls. Andrew took out his phone and called the burner phone number. A man's voice answered.

"What?"

"I'll be in position in fifteen to twenty minutes. Are you there?"

"I'll be there." It was a metallic, coarse sound, and Andrew knew the man was using a machine to disguise his voice. The line disconnected. Andrew looked around him once to make sure he hadn't been followed. He had been careful. He couldn't afford to mess this up.

Then he opened the rickety gate, and climbed the ancient stone steps. With one hand, he directed the torch beam downwards, and with the other, he pinched his nose. The stench of rotting vegetation and stale urine was almost overpowering. It became darker as the steps went up the underground tower. Soon, he was enveloped in a cold, still, silence that felt like a grave. He hurried up as fast as the burn in his thighs allowed. Landslides in these old tunnels were not uncommon, and he had no desire to get trapped.

He breathed a sigh of relief when he saw the stars. The stairs ended in a broad landing, and he stepped out on the upper levels of the castle. Grass covered the ruined grounds and the castle ruins rose to an imposing height behind him. Like the skeleton of an ancient ghost, the black tower stared down at him. Opposite, lay the remains of the castle rampart, circling the massive perimeters of the headland the castle occupied. The lofty headland lay between the south and north beaches, and from its elevated position, looked out over the harbour and the North Sea.

Andrew shivered in the gust of wind, which pierced his three layers of clothing, rattled his bones. The moon was out, a generous white sickle that sailed in a spotless sky, studded with diamond stars. As he walked towards the crumbling ramparts, he saw the alabaster moonshine on the North Sea. The dark, restless mass of water moved between the dim outlines of the cliffs that surrendered to the sea, flowing out to join the vast space of the Atlantic. At any other time, the view would be captivating. Now, he had no time for it.

He climbed over the ramparts carefully. These ruins were dangerous, and the public was not allowed here. But he had been here before. He had met with the man who held the key to his life. Or death, he thought grimly. He had to resolve their conflict, that was certain. Andrew couldn't live like this anymore.

With the torchlight, he gingerly made his way across the rampart walls, till he saw the black shape rising in the mid distance. It was a watch tower that had seen better days. Motheaten like an old blanket, riddled with holes through which the wind whined in a banshee wail. The rampart bent around the corner, and the watch tower occupied that angle.

He got there, and heaved a sigh of relief. He leaned against the cold stones, finding a position that offered him some relief from the wind. He wiped his sweaty brow with his sleeve, and panted from the exertion. The crunch of a footstep alerted him of another arrival. He stood, and looked around him.

At first he didn't see the man. Then he walked into the watchtower. He wasn't there, but Andrew saw his outline through the gaping window. He was on the rampart. Andrew came out of the watchtower, and stepped up on the rampart. The wind whipped around him like an angry dragon. Andrew moved forward. The figure watched him approach in silence.

"Just tell me what you want," Andrew shouted. The figure didn't say anything, just watched him. The man wore a jacket, but he seemed to have lost weight. His shoulders were thinner. He wore a baseball cap that came down low over his face.

"Aren't you going to say something?" Andrew shouted. "You arranged this meeting."

He stepped forward when the man said nothing. Something about the figure seemed familiar to Andrew. The person turned and the faint moonlight fell on their face. Andrew gasped.

"What on earth is this?"

He moved forward rapidly. The figure stood still as before. Andrew was within a couple of feet when he suddenly felt his left foot give way. A few small stones loosened, and fell off the rampart, falling to the rocks far below. He straightened himself, but from the corner of his eye, saw the figure advance upon him.

Before Andrew could move, the figure had shoved him to the left, into the open space that fell away into empty air. Andrew screamed, and his hands cartwheeled as he tried to regain his balance. But he couldn't.

He fell backwards, desperately trying to clutch at twigs, stones, anything to break his fall. His bloodied nails ripped from his fingers. His terror bulged out into the lonely night, a scream carried away by the winds. The rocks lay below like the open fangs of a deadly beast, and Andrew fell swiftly to his death.

CHAPTER 2

Detective Inspector Rita Gupta waved when she saw her constable, Maggie Long. Maggie wasn't at work, and they were meeting up socially. Maggie was also twenty-four weeks pregnant, and she looked radiant. They had decided to meet at a café in Scarborough town during Rita's lunch break.
Maggie rose from her seat. She walked over and Rita hugged her gently, taking care not to press on her bump.
"It's okay, you can touch it," Maggie said. "Go on." She laughed as Rita put a tentative hand on it.
"Can you feel the baby kicking?"
"Occasionally, but the doctor said it would get more pronounced in the later stages. But yes, I do feel all sorts of movements."
"Wonderful." Rita smiled and sat down opposite Maggie. They had decided to sit outside and catch the sun. It had been stormy yesterday, but it had died down, like many of the storms that started suddenly over the sea. The sun was out now, and Scarborough town was busy. For Rita it was a fifteen-minute walk from the station.
"How did you get here?" Rita asked.
"My mum gave me a lift. She's shopping now, but will pick me up later." Maggie looked happy, and Rita was so glad for her. She didn't have the easiest time dealing with the unplanned pregnancy, but now

she was looking forward to being a mother.
They chatted for a while, with Maggie talking about how excited Susan was about the new arrival, and so was her dad, Keith. Maggie was an only child, so her parents were overjoyed when she had decided to keep the baby.
Their coffee arrived, and they ordered lunch. A tuna salad for Rita, and a double burger with cheesy potato wedges for Maggie.
"That's one great thing about pregnancy. I can eat what I want. And I'm not missing alcohol to be honest. Not that I was a big drinker to start with."
Rita didn't have any personal experience of pregnancy, but she had friends who had been through it.
"You're young, and you're going to lose any weight you put on after the baby arrives."
"Yes, mum said that too. I won't have time to eat once the baby arrives."
"Boy or girl?" Rita asked.
"Well, the scan at twenty weeks showed it might be a boy, but the scanner wasn't so sure. She also said it's best to wait until week thirty. So we're going to have another scan then."
Rita smiled. "What do you want?"
"A girl," Maggie replied instantly. Then her face clouded over, as if she thought of the alternative. Her face lowered to her coffee cup, and she took a sip.
"But of course, I wouldn't mind if I had a boy."
Rita could see the conflict in her face. A boy would potentially look like the father, and understandably, Maggie had mixed feelings about that. The boy's father was Ed Warren, a convicted killer and child

snatcher.
"You're going to love him or her, and they'll mean the world to you," Rita said, putting a hand over Maggie's. She saw the clouds that had drifted over Maggie, and felt sad. Maggie blinked, then nodded, shaking off her mood.
"Aye, I've stopped wondering about that now, like. It is what it is. My baby will never know their dad, and that's for the best. It's not her fault, is it?"
"Or his," Rita grinned and Maggie laughed.
"Aye, yes." Maggie drained her cup. "How's things at the nick? I heard about the trafficking gang you broke up. Good work, that."
"Team effort. We had to trek up into the Moors at night, that was scary. Yes, glad to get that out of the way."
"Now you can relax," Maggie said. "You're staying now, for good, right?" she added hesitantly.
It had been two years now that Rita had lived in Scarborough. She came to find her mother and never left her hometown. She had always imagined there was nothing left for her in Scarborough. But she had finally given her mother a decent burial. Dozens of people had turned up, much to her surprise. Her mother Clara's disappearance had made waves back then and the town didn't forget, just like Rita. That had moved her to tears. And after that, one case after another popped up. This place had its fair share of serious crime. And so Rita had stayed.
"I think so, yes. I need to go back to London once to get my papers stamped, but then I'm done."
Maggie clapped her hands in delight. "That's amazing. Are you going to buy a place to live here?

Buy near us, in East Ayton."

Maggie lived in a nice village on the A171. Several of them circled Scarborough, and Rita had thought of buying a place there. But for now, she was happy with her seafront flat on Marine Drive. She told Maggie, who agreed.

"That's a great place. You get the best views of the sea and the castle. And it's far enough from the crappy parts of town."

Maggie leaned closer. "I'll tell you what though. I'm getting bored at home. I want to come back."

Rita shook her head. "Best if you don't for now. Active duty will mean you have to drive around, restrain people, not ideal at all."

"But I could help out the researchers. That's only a desk job. I've still got three months to go."

Rita considered it. "Let me have a think about it. I'd hate it if you got involved in something, and then got hurt. Not worth it really, is it?"

"Just a desk job, that's all. Please, guv. I could use the money as well, to be honest. Maternity benefit doesn't count for much, and my salary stopped last month."

Their food had arrived and they tucked in. Rita was famished, she had only had a yoghurt for breakfast after her morning run on the beach.

"You might be able to work from home, if you're only doing research," Rita said. "Let me see if I can arrange that, but no promises."

Maggie beamed at her. "Thanks, guv."

They finished their dinner, and Rita declined dessert. She had to get back to work. She settled for an espresso. She glanced at Maggie, who looked happy and radiant. She didn't want to spoil the mood, but one of the reasons she had met Maggie was to ask her.

"Has Ed 'Kyle' Warren tried to get in touch?"

Maggie froze. She blinked a couple of times, then shook her head in denial. "Thankfully, no. Why do you ask?"

"Just making sure. He's in HMP Full Sutton, which is a Category A prison. He doesn't have the right to contact outsiders. In any case," Rita said swiftly, noting the anxiety now darkening Maggie's features, and regretting bringing Ed's name up. But she had to know. She had fought hard against Ed's lawyers who tried to put him into a less secure prison. She wanted that evil man to be put away for the rest of his life.

"He won't be able to contact you, so don't worry," Rita smiled and gave Maggie's hand a squeeze. "It's going to be all right, okay?"

Maggie smiled back. "I think so too, guv."

CHAPTER 3

Spring was here, and predictably, the weather couldn't make its mind up. Rita was used to the sudden squalls of rain and thunder in Scarborough, but even she was surprised by the sudden cloud cover that blanked out the sun. She smelt rain in the air. She ducked inside the portico of the rear entrance of the police station. Two uniformed constables were on their way out to the car-pool, and they waved at her. Rita waved back – she now knew most of the officers here, and they were a good, hard-working bunch. She walked down the green lino-covered floor, and stopped at the canteen to pick up some biscuits for the lads. Detective Constable Rizwan Ahmed's face lit up when he saw the chocolate Bourbon biscuits.

"Thanks, guv," Rizwan said, wasting no time in opening the packet. Detective Sergeant Richard Staveley, a short, pot-bellied man who was an exceptional investigator, reached for a biscuit, but Rizwan slapped his hand away.

"Get your own," Rizwan said.

Richard glared at him. "I share mine with you. So much for being a team player."

"Boys, please," Rita said, sitting down at her desk.

"How's Maggie?" Rizwan asked, dunking his biscuit in his teacup.

"She's all right. Coping well and looking forward to motherhood. She wants to do some work though – helping out the researchers and so on. I think you two could use a bit of help anyway."

The two men looked at each other and Rita smiled. "Only messing. I know it's been busy since Maggie went on leave, but we've coped, haven't we?"

"Just about," Richard said.

There was a knock on the door, and Jill, one of the uniformed sergeants, poked her head in; Rita waved her inside. From Jill's expression, Rita knew it wasn't good news.

"IC1 male found on the rocks underneath the castle ramparts near South Beach. A dog-walker found the body twenty minutes ago. We've set up a perimeter and informed Shola." Shola Adebayo was the head of forensics, or scene-of-crime.

Rita liked visiting a crime scene when it was fresh; even the uniformed officers, despite the care they took, trampled over valuable evidence.

"Were you at the crime scene? Any obvious cause of death?"

"Yes, I've just got back," Jill said. "The victim's body is in a bad way – broken in several places. I'm no expert, guv, but he's basically smashed to pieces."

"How old does he look?"

"Not young. I'd say in his thirties or forties, maybe?"

"Probably a drunk who tried to climb the walls," Richard murmured.

"Let's go and find out," Rita said, standing. "No time like the present."

Scarborough Castle occupied the headland that split the long beach into the North and South sections. As the car drove down the Sea Wall Heritage Trail, Rita looked out at the sea. The waters were a dark blue, and the grey clouds remained, brushing idly against the cliffs on either side of the bay and on the horizon. She looked inland, to her left. The ruined hulk of the castle, and the hill which it occupied, now blocked her view of Marine Drive North, where she lived. She had such beautiful views of the castle and the sea from her living-room window. That panorama comforted her eyes every morning she flung the curtains open – a sweeping visage of blue sea and green hills she would never get tired of.

Police cars had cordoned off part of the Heritage Trail road, and a couple of disgruntled motorists were questioning the uniformed sergeant on duty. Rita didn't see anyone wearing a suit, camera round their neck, lurking by the blue-and-white crime-scene tape. No reporters then – not as yet, anyway. She knew they would be around soon.

The Heritage Trail lay just before the rocks that formed this part of the beach. Some of the rocks were man-made, and used to protect the Heritage Trail, which had motor access as well as pedestrians. Two dog-walkers had joined the motorists, and five of them were hanging around. All eyes turned to Rita as she got out of the car. The sergeant came up to her, leaving the constables in charge of manning the cordon.

Rita pointed to the end of the road, not visible from here as it curled to the left, hugging the bottom of the green cliffs that rolled down to the sea.

"Is the South Beach access also closed?"
"Yes, ma'am." The man, whose name badge said Cleverly, wore a chest rig and a peaked cap. He pointed up the cliffs. Rita saw the desiccated yellow-brick ruins perched on the edge of the slopes. "We think the body fell from there, rolled down to the grass, then ended up on the rocks at the bottom. You can't see it for the trees. There's a path on the right, but you have to climb over the fence."
Cleverly meant the yellow sandstone-brick verge that formed the boundary of the road. Rita saw a uniformed constable standing there, hands behind his back, looking around.
"Aye, no problem," she said.
The bank of trees just after the dip of the land beyond the fence blocked her view initially, but when she looked closer, she could see shapes moving. She knew right away moving the body wouldn't be easy; there was no vehicular access there. Next to the two patrol cars blocking the road, she spotted an ambulance. A paramedic was leaning against the driver's door, talking on the phone.
Rita, Rizwan and Richard – the Three R's, as Maggie liked to call them – crossed the road and easily climbed the waist-high brick fence. The land sloped down gently from there, and they moved carefully, avoiding the puddle that had formed in the ditch at the bottom. Then it was a shallow slope upwards to the line of trees.

It took them about ten minutes to cross the bank of trees. Blue-and-white tape had been tied across the trunks. Some rocks were strewn on the green grass, remnants of a landslide from decades ago. The body lay between two rocks. A figure in a white spacesuit crouched by the body; Rita could only see the victim's shoes. A white scene-of-crime tent was in the process of being erected by another white-coated figure and two uniformed constables.

The crouching figure in white stood as Rita got closer. It was Shola, the head of SOCO. She lowered her mask and her chestnut-brown eyes crinkled at the corners as she smiled.

"Cometh the hour, cometh the detective," Shola said.

"Looks like forensics trumped the detective," Rita smiled back. "Well done getting here so quickly. Did you fly?"

"Yes. The helipad on the castle, then paragliding down the slopes. Try it sometime."

"Not a high-flyer like you," Rita said. "What have we got?"

Together, they looked at the body. PC Jill had been correct: the body was smashed up. The legs were bent at an unnatural angle, as were the elbows. The chest had caved in, dark blood congealed among multiple broken ribs. The left side of the face had also taken a battering, and the left eyeball protruded. The man had come to rest on his back, eyes staring up at the grey skies in disbelief.

Rita noted the stubble on his cheeks, the short brown hair matted with blood. His clothes were casual – a dark-blue windproof jacket and a grey jumper underneath. Blue jeans on his legs, and black trainers on his feet. Rita walked round to the head of the body. She sat on her haunches and examined the top of the head: swollen and depressed in places, denoting skull fractures. The left shoulder seemed to be lifted from the green grass, but she realised it was actually broken.

She looked behind her, to where the strewn rocks gave way to the green cliffs that rose dizzyingly to the castle walls. The ramparts were crumbling here, most of them succumbed to wind and rain. But the castle walls were vast, and she knew sections of the rampart had withstood the years well. She wondered why the man had been here last night – or this morning.

Rizwan stood next to her as she scanned the ramparts. "Can't see owt up there," he said. "But there is that watchtower, eh? Not much of it left, mind."

The once-tall watchtower, occupying the corner of the rampart before it curved to the left, was now almost gone, but the shell still remained, looking like a decaying mouth missing most of its teeth.

"Well spotted," Rita said. "Get someone up there, only to block pedestrians – the castle grounds are open now. Tell uniforms not to venture up there: looks like a death-trap."

"Why on earth would he be up there?" Rizwan shook his head. He trudged off to speak to one of the uniformed sergeants. Rita saw Richard leaning over a rock, inspecting something. She turned back to the victim.

He had fallen, hit the rocks, then finally rolled to rest here. It was a miracle that he was still as well preserved. She sat down again to inspect him. His clothes were not expensive – cheap, in fact. Or was it the weather-beaten edges of the jacket and his sleeves that swayed her opinion? These clothes had seen harsh weather. The man's hands were large and calloused – a working man's hands. A builder? Or sailor? A sea-going man couldn't be ruled out. His nails were yellow-tinged with nicotine.

A voice behind her spoke. "Detective Gupta, I presume?"

CHAPTER 4

She looked up to find the slim, neat figure of Dr Das. His white hair was swept back from his forehead, and his ash-grey suit was well pressed as usual. His shoe-coverings were muddy from walking. He adjusted the silver-rimmed spectacles on his nose. They gave him a scholarly look. His shaven cheeks were as smooth as marble. Dr Das looked more like an accomplished university academic than a veteran pathologist. But Rita knew very well he was definitely the latter, and not the former. He had a sharp and analytical mind that loved to tease out secrets from dead bodies.
"Guilty as charged," Rita grinned. "How are you, doc?"
"All the better for seeing a dead man first thing in the morning. But at least I'm out of the morgue, eh?" He put his briefcase on the ground.
"Count your blessings. I'll let you get on, shall I?"
"Any background on our victim?"
"None so far. A pedestrian saw him. I assume he's that man over there." Rita pointed to a rock where a civilian sat, flanked by Richard and a uniformed constable. "We think he fell from the ramparts. The injuries indicate a fall from a great height, and that's the probable cause of death. But you're the expert."
"If you say so," Dr Das smiled. He was a modest man, despite his decades of experience as a forensic pathologist. Rita loved that about him. "So we don't have an ID as yet?"
"Not yet. But I'm hoping we get one, soon."

Rita left Dr Das to speak to Shola, and walked over to the witness who found the body. The man was old, and a lovely cocker spaniel sat by his feet. Rita liked that breed. The dog raised his head as Rita approached. Then he put his head between his paws, and blinked a few times.

Rita turned her attention to the man. He looked tired, with bags under his eyes, and shoulders stooped. Richard turned to Rita. "Mr Deakins was out walking his dog this morning. There's a path that leads to here from South Beach. He does this route a few times every week. First time he's seen this, obviously. Normally it's a quiet stretch."

Mr Deakins was staring at Rita. She stepped closer, and the lovely dog at his feet looked up at Rita. She smiled at it, then looked back at Mr Deakins.

"What time were you here?"

"Around lunchtime. Just after midday, I'd say. I park in the South Beach car park, then walk down here. I was chucking his ball around," he indicated the dog. "He went behind the rock and started barking. I saw the feet first and then…" He stopped speaking, and a stricken look appeared on his face. Breath left his lungs slowly, like a balloon deflating.

"And you called 999?"

"Yes, I did." He passed a hand over his face. "Can I go now?"

Rita glanced at Richard and he nodded, which meant he had the old man's contact details.

"Yes, you can. But please don't leave Scarborough. We might need to speak to you again. By the way, did you see anyone else here today? Or anything unusual?"

Mr Deakins frowned, then lowered his head in thought. "No, can't say I have. It was just me and Lucky." He indicated the dog, who clearly recognised his name. He looked up expectantly, pink tongue lolling out. Rita resisted the urge to scratch his head. She wanted a dog, but with her work schedule, and living alone, it was well nigh impossible.

Rita went back to the body, and joined Dr Das and Shola. Henry, Shola's scrawny and tall assistant, was kneeling on the grass, picking up something with tweezers. He noticed Rita and nodded. How Henry fitted into a sterile white suit Rita would never understand. The fabric was stretched to almost breaking point at his head, and ended several inches above his ankles.

He put the tiny white object into a specimen bag. "What was that?" Rita asked.

"A tooth, I think." He held up the bag for Rita to see, and she agreed. "Probably from our victim's mouth. Have we found anything else – like a wallet or phone?"

"No wallet, but three twenty-pound notes in his right jeans pocket. We didn't find a phone. If it was in his jacket pocket, it could've fallen out anywhere. Uniforms are doing a search." Henry pointed, and Rita looked at where the hill slopes levelled out flat. A line of uniformed officers in high-visibility jackets were moving slowly, eyes fixed on the ground.

"We need a drone up there," Rita pointed at the sky. "Can you please arrange that?"

"Speak to the boss, please," Henry indicated Shola.

Rita nodded. The white tent had been erected around the body now. Rita lifted up one of the flaps and went inside. Bright halogen lamps lit up the interior with garish brightness.

Rita asked Shola about the drones.

She agreed, and made a call to the Tech Lab to release the drones at the correct location.

Rita thanked her, aware the visual footage from a drone could be crucial in a case like this. She crouched by where Dr Das was putting away the probe of the rectal thermometer.

"Time of death, doc?"

"Body temperature is twelve degrees below the ambient. He's a slim guy, no water around here, so loss of temperature would be about one degree per hour. So I would say about ten to twelve hours ago. It's half two in the afternoon now, so between half twelve and half two in the morning."

"Thanks, doc. And cause of death? Just your rough idea, that's all."

"Well, it's difficult to know if there was previous trauma to the body – as in, if he got into a fight. His neck and chest don't show any obvious marks."

He showed where he had cut into the clothes with a pair of scissors to expose the chest and abdomen, and the upper legs.

"The ribs, pelvic brim and long bones of the leg are broken in several places. There's a lot of bruising, which is disguising any other trauma. On his face and neck I can't see any obvious fingerprints."
He pointed at the swollen eyes, and the strangely protruding left eye.
"That eye is probably the result of a fall on that side, as opposed to a crushing blow. The eye socket is in pieces, as is the side of the skull." He shrugged. "I might have a better idea when we open him up."
"Thanks, doc. We need some answers, ASAP."

CHAPTER 5

Melanie waved goodbye to two-year-old Carla at the nursery gates. Carla turned and smiled, then pulled at the teacher's hand. Carla had a different look on her face, and Melanie thought she looked sad. The teacher stopped, and turned towards Melanie.

"What is it, darling?" Melanie said, leaning over the nursery gate. "Are you alright?"
Carla enjoyed her nursery. Melanie didn't understand what was bothering her. Carla stared at her with huge blue eyes that dominated her face. With her strawberry-blonde hair tied up in a bun, she was the picture of cuteness. She uttered a single word as a question.

"Daddy?"
The dread returned to stab Melanie in the chest. Andrew didn't return from work last night. He wasn't answering his phone, either. She didn't want to think about it too much. He was under pressure, but he stayed in touch with her.
True, he came home late from the fishing at night, but yesterday he'd been out in the afternoon as the tides were up. He went to the pub sometimes, but he should still have been back.

"He'll be here soon," Melanie reassured Carla.
"When?"
"Soon," Melanie smiled at the little one's presence of mind. Children never ceased to amaze. Carla was two years and one month, and already she had started to speak some words.
"Daddy will be at home when you get back."
"Promise?"
"Promise."
Carla waved again as her teacher led her away. Melanie waited till the door was shut. Then she took out her phone and called Andrew. Again, it went to no reply. She left a message. Then she walked back into Filey town, which was about ten minutes. She decided to check in at the coble landing on the beach, which was small, and Andrew didn't normally moor his fishing trawler there. He moored it in Scarborough, where the Fishing Quay had better facilities for larger boats like Andrew's.
She walked briskly, head down against the sudden wind that had struck up, fresh from the sea. There was no break from the sea here, and the wind hit her like a body blow – a gentle one, but still cold for April. Melanie wrapped the coat around her and hurried on. She could see the white, blue and black boats bobbing up and down on the mild swells of the water. The tide was halfway, the beach was still walkable. Some pre-school kids ran on the sand; dogs chased seagulls. Filey didn't have a harbour. The jetty on the slipway off the beach, and the small landing, had a few small boats tied to the wooden posts of the jetty.

But all the big boats had gone, and, due to the roughness of the sea, Melanie knew they didn't stay here for long.

She thought for a while. Scarborough wasn't far, only twenty minutes up the road. She could check at the harbour and then get back within an hour. She walked back home quickly. Filey was a small town on the beach, and she was home at their pretty little cottage within fifteen minutes. She took Scarborough Road, then joined the A165 that went up to Scarborough town.

Melanie parked in the South Beach car park and got out. She checked the car park for Andrew's car. It was an old, beaten-up Ford Fiesta from the nineties. Melanie drove the main family car, and Andrew's car was ready for the scrap-metal yard, but they couldn't afford anything else right now.

The wind grew stronger as she turned into Foreshore Road, the main promenade on the beach. The harbour lay to her left, and she walked briskly in that direction.

She walked down and got to the Bluewater Sea Cruise stall on the harbour front, the company that Andrew owned. He used his trawler to fish in the autumn and winter, and then revamped it the best he could to arrange tourist sea-fishing tours. He made more money in the summer than he did from fishing – a fate that had befallen most fishermen since the advent of giant trawlers that dredged the seabeds, and the big corporations that owned them.

Melanie went to the boat first. She had a pass for the harbour, and, as she pressed her fob key to the gate, it swung open. She walked in and saw the kiosk where the harbour-master sat was open. He was called Jonty, and he glanced at her through the glass window. Then he opened the side door and leaned out.

"Hello, luv," Jonty said. Melanie knew him well. She looked up at the sky, and her eyes met the CCTV cameras that looked down upon the marina.
"I'm looking for Andrew. Did he come back last night?"
"Ah, yes," Jonty said. He came down from the kiosk. "The Merigold did return." He took out his phone and scrolled to a screen. "Yes, at 21.48 hours. Why do you ask?"
"Andrew's not back home and I'm worried."
"Oh," Jonty frowned. "Well, the boat's back. I wasn't here that late last night, but I can take you to the boat, if you want. I'm sure he was in the boat, right?"
"Yes, he was. I mean, he should be. I spoke to him after he left. He still had reception. But he didn't answer after that."
"Come on then," Jonty said. "I'll take you to the boat."
They went down the marina, past all the boats with the sails folded, standing still. A couple of fishermen were mending their nets, and they looked up to wave. The Merigold was a thirty-six-foot fishing trawler. It was black and gold in colour, and it was in good condition. Melanie knew the boat went far out to sea. It could carry eight crew members, including the captain.

Jonty stood in front of the boat and called Andrew's name. There was no answer. He went on board, and Melanie followed. The plastic see-through cover that protected the deck was zipped up, and he unzipped it. The deck and cockpit were empty. Melanie went downstairs; she had been here before and knew her way around.

The kitchen, galley and the two small bedrooms were also empty. She saw cups in the sink, and an empty plate. Andrew had been here, she was certain. But where was he now?

"Sorry, luv," Jonty said. "Looks like he ain't here."

Melanie gulped, swallowing the heavy weight at the back of her throat. "Yes. Thanks for coming along."

"Any time, luv," Jonty said, as they made their way back outside. Jonty helped Melanie step off the boat. His old eyes searched Melanie's face.

"Could he have gone anywhere else? Like his parents' house?"

"I don't know. I'll ring them, thanks."

She went back to the shop, which stood on the road that led to the harbour. A blue-and-white sign above the door said Bluewater Sea Cruise. The shop was closed. Melanie looked in through the glass window, cupping her hands over it. The office was empty, she thought, because the blinds were drawn and she couldn't see much through the gap at the sides. She knocked on the door and tried the handle, calling Andrew's name.

There was a café next to the shop, which was owned by an old sea dog. Dean also ran boat trips in the summer, but his boats were as old as he was. His café, run by his daughter, did far better than his old boat trips. Dean wasn't in, but his daughter Corrie was, checking the tills at the counter. She looked up as Melanie bustled in. She was confused at first, but then smiled uncertainly, recognising Melanie. They didn't know each other well, but had said hello in the past.
"Have you seen Andrew?" Melanie got straight to the point. "He went on a fishing trip yesterday afternoon, and he returned at 21.48, according to the harbour-master's log. I've just seen Jonty."
Corrie bent her lips, frowning as she thought. She knew what Andrew looked like.
"Pretty sure I saw him yesterday afternoon. Around midday? He was here in the shop. He didn't say hello, he was busy. I saw him go out to the marina."
That made sense, Melanie thought. "Is that the last time you saw him?"
"Aye. I didn't see him come back. But I left around six p.m. and he would've been back later, like you said. He must've gone to see his folk?"
"No," Melanie sighed. "I mean, I haven't asked them yet. But they live in Bridlington. Thanks, anyway."
She walked away, head bowed in thought. It took her a while to get back to her house in Filey. She didn't call Andrew's parents; she didn't want them to worry. She sat in the living room, staring at the carpet. Her hands twisted on her lap, and voices whispered in her mind.
What could she do?

CHAPTER 6

"Be careful!" Rita called out as she moved up the steps to the castle rampart. Richard and Rizwan were running up the steps, which were old and crumbly, like this section of the ramparts.
"Yes, go slow, old man," Rizwan said to Richard. Richard was shorter and chubbier than Rizwan, who had youth on his side. Hence, Richard was making a point by racing up the steps.
"I'm ahead of you," he called back. "Catch me if you can."
"Speed up then."
Rita watched in alarm as Richard got on to the rampart, the wind lifting the lapels of his coat. He strode forward with purpose, not looking back.
"Slow down," Rita called out. Rizwan stopped at the top, looking a little sheepish.
"Right then," Rita said. "Let's move a little slower."
Richard had halted as well, looking out at the blue expanse of the sea ahead of them. The sea stretched out beyond the broad bay shaped by the cliffs, its distant blue merging with the horizon. The wind was sharp against Rita's scalp, pushing her hair back. She moved forward, her eyes scanning the crumbling rampart walls and the green grass of the old castle yard below.

Not many people came here. The ancient watchtower was way behind them, the one that every tourist came to see. Most of the castle was in ruins, certainly the part they were visiting now.

The stone fence of the rampart was in poor condition and had completely given way in places. The drop from here was dizzying, steep, all the way to the rocks and trees far below. Rita didn't want to look for too long; she didn't have a head for heights. She gritted her teeth and followed behind Rizwan and Richard. The two were chatting away, oblivious to her discomfort.

They came upon the curve in the rampart, and the smaller watchtower that Rizwan had seen from below. The men huddled inside the watchtower, but their gaze was fixed on the floor. Rita joined them. The wind whined above and around them, slicing in through the gap that was once the window.

They didn't find anything. And yet, when Rita steeled herself, held on to the wall of the watchtower, and forced herself to look down, she saw the high-visibility jackets of the uniformed officers far below. They were so small they looked like ants, and she might've missed them were it not for the jackets and the flashing sirens on the road.

"He fell from here," she said, turning back to the lads. Richard had already looked out.

"I think so, too. That's why we were looking for signs of a struggle. But there's nowt here."

Rita checked the worn-out, uneven stone floor herself. She went out of the watchtower and walked along the rampart slowly. The side fence had completely fallen off here, and she didn't dare go too far on the left. The fall led to oblivion.

The men followed slowly behind her, aware of the danger. Rita saw something lodged against a stone that had lifted from the earth. She put on gloves and knelt. It was a brown button, the kind found on a coat. She bagged it in a specimen bag.

"Boot prints," Richard announced. He was on his knees too, inspecting the ground close to the edge.

"Here as well," Rizwan followed. He was close to Richard but facing towards Rita and the castle ground. Rita went closer to have a look. The ground wasn't wet, but moisture in the air, and the soil between the tarnished stones, had kept some shoe marks. The marks by Rizwan were smaller than the ones Richard had found.

"Size 9 over here, and about 11 by the edge," Rita said. "Men's shoes, both of them?"

"I think so, guv," Richard said. "Looks like there was a scuffle here. Our victim might've been pushed over the edge."

"Or they could be marks from a random tourist," Rita said. "We need to keep an open mind. But these boot prints are fresh. And it seems like a struggle did take place. So yes, it could be the crime scene we're looking for."

She pressed her lips together, thinking. "Let's get Scene of Crime up here. Cordon this place. But let's keep looking for now."

They walked up and down the rampart for a few metres more. They didn't see any more boot prints, or anything else of interest. After about twenty minutes, Rita was frozen to the bone. The wind whipped around her like an angry beast. She shivered. She couldn't imagine what it would've been like last night. Why would the victim be up here? And who did he arrange to meet?

If he was up here, she cautioned herself. Well, he had to fall from somewhere. As she looked around, at the dangerous edge a few feet away, and felt the wind buffeting them, she realised it wouldn't be long before rain and wind would destroy whatever fragile evidence lay here. She pulled out her radio and called Shola, who answered.

"You want me up there? What for?"

Shola wasn't best pleased. She was a methodical woman and liked to take her time—one of the reasons she was so good at her job. Rita felt bad for disturbing her, but she didn't have much choice. Shola and Henry were the only two SOCs on the job.

"Send Henry up here," she said. "I can show him the scene, and we'll take it from there."

"Alright."

"Have the uniforms found a phone down there? One that might belong to the victim. It might well be in pieces."

"Not that I've heard," Shola said.

"I think the victim had a phone. He met up with another man here. He'd have kept a phone to stay in touch with him."

"I'll ask again. And send Henry up. Don't ask for much, do you?"

"Thanks, Shola."

Rizwan stayed back to show Henry around, while Rita and Richard made their way down the derelict, and frankly dangerous, stone steps. Rita sighed with relief when she got to the green grass. Once, this greenery had been covered by the castle buildings. She imagined it as it had been almost a thousand years ago – huge stone domes rising hundreds of feet above, like the crumbling watchtower in the main castle green. Well, time and nature made a mockery of man's ambitions.

They walked to the south gate, which was big and well maintained. This was one of the main tourist gates, and the paved stones on the wide path gleamed as if they were polished. At the crime scene, Dr Das had already left, and so had the ambulance, with the body. Rita knew she'd catch up with Dr Das first thing tomorrow, when the Post Mortem would be done, with any luck.

Bob Chandler, the old, bearded Highlander who was also the forensic gait analyst, had turned up.

"Och, aye, our kid," he rasped in greeting to Rita. "Ah dinnae ken you're gonnae find none prints down 'ere. That poor wee bugger didnae walk down 'ere, did he? More like flying."

He belched out a wheezy laugh at his own joke, and then dissolved into a vortex of coughing. He put hands on his knees and hacked up phlegm into the grass. Rita closed her eyes. Bob was still a chain-smoker, and it was best if she didn't think about the alcohol she could faintly smell on his breath. Despite his fondness for smoke and booze, he was remarkably good at his job.

"As I was sayin'," Bob stood and heaved air into his lungs. "Ain't no boot prints down 'ere."

"Yes, but we found some up on the ramparts," Rita pointed upwards, and Bob followed her line of vision. She looked critically at Bob, but with sympathy. "Sure you can make it up there?"

Bob's bushy eyebrows did a dance, and a frown rippled across his face. He slapped his knee and then winced. Rita smothered her laughter, and Richard giggled. Bob glared at him.

"There's life in me old limbs yet. I used to hike all the way up Arthur's Seat without stopping in the old days."

"Be careful here," Rita cautioned. "The steps are dangerous and I don't want you to fall."

"Away with yer," Bob waved a hand. He stomped off in the direction of the castle gates. "I'll have yer report ready by this evening. Ciao!"

CHAPTER 7

It was half five by the time Rita got back to the office with Richard. Her inbox was full, and she spent some time responding to emails. Nicola Perkins, her boss—or Dragon Woman, as Rita liked to call her—had heard about the victim and asked for a report. Rita did the best she could, given what little she knew. Luckily, Nicola was out of the office currently; she was in Alverton Court in Northallerton, where North Yorkshire Police had their HQ.

Richard got the coffees while Rita settled down to finish her reports. An e-fit photo of the victim's face was already up on the NYP website, and the Media Liaison Officer had sent it to Crimestoppers to ask for information. The cat was out of the bag, in other words. By first light tomorrow, if not tonight, reporters would swarm the crime scene. It was good, Rita thought, that the site wasn't that easy to get to. The Heritage Trail Road would be closed for a while, and that would fan even more curiosity.

Rita needed to find a positive ID without delay. She rang Dr Das, who didn't answer, which meant he was in the morgue. The morgue was in the basement of Scarborough General Hospital, and there was no phone reception there. She tried through switchboard and was rewarded with the pathologist's voice.

"How can I help, Rita?"

"Any preliminary findings?"

Dr Das chuckled. "You don't give up, do you? Well, so far I can only comment on the time of death. Given the state of rigor mortis, colour change, body temperature, I think I was almost right the first time. I'd say he died between eleven and one a.m. last night."

"And cause of death is the trauma from the fall?"

"Yes. He's got multiple organ rupture—I've just opened up the abdomen. Pelvic crush fracture as well. Like I said, it's virtually impossible to find specific injuries, given the smashing the body received. But no signs of him being strangled, and no lacerations or knife wounds."

Dr Das paused. "I've seen a few other things that might help you. I'll prepare a report tomorrow, unless you wanted to come down and have a look tonight, while I do the PM?"

Rita thought for a few seconds. She knew the victim's body would hold important clues. It was the lab analysis that really helped, but that wouldn't happen till tomorrow, unless Shola had been a wonder woman.

"Where are his clothes and shoes?" Rita asked.

"With Shola, in the lab."

Rita glanced at her watch. It was close to six p.m. "How long will you be there for?"

"Another hour, at the most. Only doing this for you, Rita. I should've been home by now."

Rita didn't hear any reproach in his voice, only a smile. "I'll buy you a coffee on my way over. Thanks, doc. I'll be there in the next twenty minutes."

The door opened and Rizwan came in. "Uniforms didn't find much else," he said. "It's dark now so they've gone home. Bob's taken the boot prints. We looked around on the castle grounds just below the ramparts—no more prints or anything else."
Rita had handed the button she had found to Shola. "Alright. I'll go and see Dr Das; I think he's got something. Can one of you please see Shola and ask if she's uncovered anything so far? Unlikely, I know, but worth asking."
"I'll do that, guv," Rizwan said, heading for the door.

Rita pointed at Richard. "Go home. You don't have the kids this evening, I take it?" She knew Richard had to leave early on the days he had his children; he shared their care with his ex-wife.
"No, guv. But Charlene has her chemistry exams and wanted to run something past me."
Charlene was eleven and Rita had met her a couple of times. She was a cute little redhead with a mass of freckles on her nose. Rita had become friends with her.
"Tell her hello from me," Rita said. "And go home now."
She left the office and asked at the front desk if there was a patrol car available to give her a lift to the hospital. One was just leaving in that direction, and Rita took a ride with them. In the hospital mortuary, Dr Das's assistant, a Chinese woman called Shen, opened the door for her. Rita changed into crocs and pulled a sterile plastic apron around her, with a mask and gloves.

Dr Das was by a gurney, staring at the feet of the now-naked victim. The skin was a lemon-yellow colour, but most of the body was racked with large areas of black and blue bruises. Bones in the pelvis, ribs and legs that were jutting out had been cleaved off with a saw. Rita saw the bone fragments in a bucket as she got closer.

Dr Das straightened as Rita approached. Behind his silver-framed glasses, his brown eyes looked tired.

"Thanks for staying back to do this," Rita said.

"No problem," he pointed at two gurneys on the left, both containing zipped-up body bags. "Now that I've done yours, I can get to those two tomorrow."

The pathologist walked up to the victim's head. He pointed at the clean line around the circumference of the skull, where the saw had sliced through the bone, allowing him to take out the brain and examine it.

"No clots or haemorrhages in the brain matter itself, which means only that he didn't have a stroke. But plenty of blood clots under the skull—where it literally bounced along the ground after he fell."

"Not a nice way to go," Rita said in a grim tone.

"No. Those large clots pressed on the brain matter, and he would've lost consciousness, which is a blessing, as he wouldn't feel too much pain then."

Dr Das moved down to the face. "Look at the deep crow's feet around the eyes and the lines on his forehead. See how leathery the skin is. Go on, feel it." Rita did so, glad she had put the gloves on. She tried not to look at the protruding left eye, still bulging out of its socket. It was black with blood, ghoulish. The forehead skin felt tough and stretched.

"Weather-beaten?" Rita asked. "Too much exposure to sun?"

"Exactly. Which means he had an outdoor job. Could be various things—mountaineer, sailor." Dr Das now had a twinkle in his eyes.

He moved to the shoulder and asked Rita to come over to his side. On the left shoulder there was a tattoo: dark blue, in the form of a fish jumping out of water. The letters SMM were visible on the fish's body. The tattoo was faded but still readable.

"Was he a fisherman?" Rita frowned. "What does SMM stand for?"

"Well, while I was waiting for you, I did a little digging around," Dr Das smiled. "I can't be sure about this, but there used to be an old fishermen's society called the Seagoing Mariners' Mission. It doesn't exist anymore, but I found it mentioned on the Scarborough Maritime Heritage Society site. Maybe this tattoo refers to the same Mission?"

Rita was genuinely impressed. She nudged Dr Das with an elbow and he grinned. "Doc, you've been busy. Thank you. You didn't have to do that. It's my job."

"Well, it's the reason I asked you to come down here. Thought I might as well have a look myself."

"Thanks anyway. So it seems this man was a fisherman?"

Dr Das raised a hand and moved lower down the body. Rita followed. The seasoned pathologist indicated the left hand. Rita had already seen the yellow-stained nails.

"He was a smoker?" she asked.

Dr Das didn't look convinced. "Look at his lips. They don't have the dark stain that a smoker's lips have." He lifted the hand. "Rough and calloused palms. Nails are cut short, but stained yellow."

He raised an eyebrow at Rita; the doctor was trying to engage her in a quiz. She didn't mind. She had come to realise his quirky methods, which were actually helpful.

"I don't know," she confessed. "But could the rough skin on the palms be from pulling nets?"

"Exactly," the older man beamed. "And salt water and fishing-net chemicals actually stain the nails yellow. Fishermen keep their nails trimmed so they don't catch on the nets. Notice his muscular forearms and shoulders. Fishermen need strong arms to lift nets out of the sea."

Rita looked at the arms and nodded slowly. "So he was a fisherman?"

"The signs seem to indicate that," Dr Das said. "You didn't find any ID on him, did you?"

"Nope. Only forty pounds in banknotes. No phone as yet, but I'm hoping it fell out of his pockets." She rocked back on her heels, eyes on the rest of the body. "Anything else, doc?"

"The toxicology reports will be back in a couple of days. But there's no evidence of high alcohol content in his bloodstream. There are some food remnants in his stomach, which means he ate about an hour before his death. On his fingernails, I didn't find any white powder like cocaine or amphetamines. So far, I don't think he was under the influence of drugs or alcohol. But the tox report will be more thorough."

Dr Das paused to clear his throat. "The DNA matches will be back tomorrow. Sodium chloride—salt crystals—underneath the nails, which indicate sea water. Also bleach and industrial chemicals. I think this man definitely handled nets and went out to sea."

"Hence his weather-beaten appearance as well." Rita took out her phone and snapped photos of the tattoo. "This is great, doc. You've got us moving."

"Pleasure is all mine. I hope you find out what happened to him."

Rita thanked him and left. On her way out to the car park to wait for the taxi she'd called, her phone pinged. It was Rizwan.

"Shola's found some interesting stuff, guv."

CHAPTER 8

"Shola and Henry have analysed the clothes," Rizwan said. "The jacket was scuffed and worn-out. The edges were crusted white and yellow. They took scrapings and looked under the microscope."
"Salt and bleach?"
"And sodium nitrate, often used to strengthen fishing nets. Same chemicals from his shoes. The shoes were steel-toe-capped, hard leather—the type worn by fishermen. The jacket was made by Almondy and Sons – a well-known fishing-gear supplier in Hull."
"That makes sense, given what Dr Das has found." Rita explained Dr Das's findings. "Seems like our victim was a fisherman. An active one, I think—one who has been to sea recently. Those callus marks on his hands were fresh. The nails were recently trimmed."
"You think he was out at sea yesterday?"
"Or recently, in the last few weeks." Rita's knowledge of fishing was rudimentary. Scarborough had a small harbour, and its fishing fleet had dwindled over time – that was about the extent of her knowledge. She asked Rizwan, who didn't know much either.
"Richard once said his uncle used to be a fisherman, back in the day. Uncle's dead now, and the new fishermen are clamouring for a modernisation of the harbour. Parts of it are old and scabby."

Rita had heard about the new, planned development of Scarborough Harbour, including the creation of a deep-sea port. That would transform the region's economy. Scarborough had become a deprived town, its main source of income the tourists who flocked every year in the summer. Reviving the town's fishing industry by creating a port would transform the place.

Rizwan said, "But it's not going well. The council scrapped the funding, and the fishermen are campaigning against it. They're calling the council corrupt. They didn't deliver on their promises."

Rita wondered how the death of a fisherman would affect the current conflict between the council and the fishermen. Was there another angle to this?

"Anyway," she said. "We did well today. Thanks to Dr Das and Shola. Tomorrow we get cracking with the Seagoing Mariners' Mission. They might not exist any more, but we need to find the old members."

"We'll get cracking first thing tomorrow, guv."

Rita hung up. Her taxi arrived, and she went home to her apartment block on North Marine Drive. Her flat was on the second floor, and the views out to the harbour and castle were stunning. She sat down with a glass of wine and responded to some texts from her father, Jay. He lived in Wales with his second wife and their adult son. Angela, her mother's friend, had also called. Rita rang her back.

"How are you, love?" Angela said. "Not heard from you in a while."

"All good. Just been busy with work and that. How's you and Derek?"

Angela was Clara's oldest friend. Clara, Rita's mother, used to leave Rita with Angela when she went to work. Angela knew the secrets of this town, and she had carried them all these years, until Rita came back asking questions. She had tried to protect Rita, but both of them ended in a dangerous situation precisely due to those secrets. Rita and Angela had made amends, and she was like family to Rita.

"Derek's good. He's always travelling with work. But he's here this weekend. Would you like to pop round?"

"Yes, maybe." Weekends when she wasn't on duty were slow for Rita. She met up with Jack Banford sometimes, her old sweetheart. But apart from that, her free weekends were times when she sometimes felt lonely. And it had been worse the last few weeks. She knew why.

"Next Tuesday is the 15th," Rita said softly. "Mum's birthday."

"Yes, love, I know."

15th April was the hardest day for Rita. It was her mother Clara's birthday—the mother she'd lost when she was eleven years old. A loss that left her mind and soul empty for ever, a chasm that would never be filled. But at least she had found her mother's remains and given her a proper burial. She visited the grave often, when she walked by the hill cemetery next to the church near the castle. The cemetery had a lovely view of the sea. Clara would've loved it.

Rita said, "I'm going to arrange a little get-together at my place. A couple of people from work, my friend Jack, you and Derek, of course. And Mum's friends – Jo and Lauren."

"Oh, that'll be good. Yes, I can call Jo and Lauren as well, if you don't have time." Angela paused. "How's Jack Banford these days? He's your age, isn't he? His solicitor's office did well."

Angela didn't miss a trick, Rita thought. Angela had been like an aunt to her after her mother vanished. She knew about Rita's life as a teenager.

"Oh, he's fine," she said briefly.

"How often do you see him?"

"Once in a while."

"Oh." Angela paused. "He's divorced, isn't he? Heard it didn't go well for him. But he's got the business. He's doing all right. His office has opened up new branches in Leeds and York, right?"

Nosey parker, Rita thought, with a smile on her lips. Angela was clearly digging for dirt. "I guess you can ask him when you see him."

"Are you still good friends with him?" Angela asked, innocently. Who was she kidding, Rita.

"Yes," she sighed. "I'd better go now."

"Okay, love. I worry about you, you know? Living alone, and that. I hope you don't mind me saying. You need some company."

"Do I?"

"Well, everyone does, don't they?" Angela coughed once. "Look at me and my Derek. We've been together for thirty years now."

That reminded Rita. She had a vague memory of Derek working in the harbour once. "Angie, can I ask if Derek worked on a boat, ever?"

Angela stopped to think. "Aye," she said slowly. "He was a fisherman's apprentice as a young lad. That's when I met him, actually. He wasn't a fisherman for long. Even back then, the fishing stock was taken up by the big trawlers owned by companies. Individual fishermen were struggling. He gave up to become a plumber. Why do you ask?"

"I might have to pick his brains about a fishermen's society. It's called the Seagoing Mariners' Mission. Would you mind writing the name down? Please ask Derek when you see him."

"He's back tomorrow. Okay, hold on."

Rita heard pen scratch against paper as Angela wrote.

"I'll let you know what he says, love. Good night."

Rita had a shower after finishing her glass of wine. She had a pasta bake in the fridge and ate that with some salad. She was about to go to bed when Jack rang.

"Hello, stranger," Jack's warm, sonorous voice came down the line. Rita was tired and wanted to go to bed, and she tried her best to ignore the warm tingle that ran down her spine when Jack spoke to her.

They had been old sweethearts, but now they were just friends, right?

Right.

"It's not me who's always away with work. Which city are you setting up an office in now? Edinburgh?"

"Very funny. I was only in York last week. Came back and rang you but you didn't reply. Busy social life?" She didn't miss the hint of reproach in his voice. She had been out with Jack a few times now. They went to Filey, Bempton, Bridlington—the nice towns and villages that dotted the eastern coast. They were firm friends, but was there something more? The tug of her heart gave her an answer that she wasn't comfortable with. Not just yet. The soft, hazy ball in her belly spread to the rest of her body as she lay down.

"People to see, things to do. You know me." She smiled, and felt Jack do the same.

"Ever since you arrived, Scarborough heated up. Looks like the crimes followed you."

"That's not fair. I only came here to look for Mum."

"I know," Jack sounded as though he regretted his last remark. "Only joking. All I'm saying is that the town's different since you got back."

"In what way?"

Jack was silent for a long time. Then he spoke before she could. "For me, anyway. It's… it's nice to have you back."

The silence flowed back again, like the waves lapping on the shore quietly on a low tide. Her heart beat a little faster, and a current of warm blood splashed against the lonely corners of her heart.

She didn't know where it would lead to, and the last thing she wanted was to lose Jack's friendship.

"Is that why you stay out of town so much?" she teased. She turned on the bedside lamp and pulled the duvet to her chin.

"Who's being unfair now? I had business, like you do, I guess. Anyway, I'm calling to make amends. I've got a court hearing, but will be at the station later. Buy you lunch?"

"I've got a new case. Fisherman, found dead at the bottom of the castle. Doesn't look good. I think he was pushed."

"See what I mean? Trouble follows you around, DI Gupta." He laughed. "Only messing."

"Trouble's my middle name. So don't mess with me."

"Seriously, though. You think it's murder?"

"Well, we think there was a scuffle on the ramparts, and his body lies on the grounds way below. But I could be wrong. The boot prints we found could be random. Somehow, I doubt it." Rita explained what they found, and Dr Das's discoveries.

"Why would a fisherman be up on the worst part of the castle ramparts that late at night?"

"To meet someone who didn't want to be seen. Or he was drunk, or on drugs. So far, there's no evidence of that."

"You might be right, then."

"I think I am. Wish I wasn't, though. Anyway, good night. I need to get some sleep."

"See you tomorrow," Jack said before she hung up.

CHAPTER 9

Rita was up at five a.m., before the alarm. She had slept well, falling into a deep sleep as soon as her head hit the pillow. She got up and realised she had enough time to go for a morning run. The weather was also fair – a pink sky slowly rising to yellow with the morning sun. Not a cloud on the horizon. The sea was a calm blue, the cliffs a dull green.
Rita got ready in her running gear and also took her warrant card. She would be jogging past the harbour. Fishermen were up before the crack of dawn and chances were the harbour was active. She could potentially ask some questions of any seafaring men she met.

She stretched, did a slight warm-up, then hit the road. She jogged slowly, enjoying the bracing morning air. There was no wind today, only a light breeze that brought in the tang of sea salt. Sea gulls hovered high above, and the sun glinted on the waves. Rita reached the harbour and slowed down. She was sweating profusely and was glad she had decided to wear shorts, not full-length Lycra. It was already getting warm.
Scarborough Harbour was in the shadow of the castle, which loomed on the hill to her right.
It was also on South Beach, the stretch of beach favoured by fishermen and tourists alike.

She saw a couple of fishing trawlers making their way back through the mouth of the harbour. One of them tooted its horn, presumably to warn the other trawlers. Rita watched the boat make its way through the West Pier and sail slowly to the Fish Quay on the inner side of West Harbour.

The harbour was big, and opposite the Fish Quay there was the East Pier, where a number of commercial and pleasure vessels were moored. In the middle lay the Old Harbour, which dated back hundreds of years.

On the Fish Quay, close to where Rita stood, men hovered on the marina, some pulling nets and stowing them on board, and others checking their boats. Rita stopped at the gates and waved at the bearded man standing outside the harbour-master's cottage. There was a kiosk next to the cottage, which was locked. The white-bearded man looked at Rita curiously, wondering, no doubt, what a woman in shorts and a running vest was doing here at this hour of the morning. Can't women be fishermen? Rita asked herself. Of course they could.

She waited while the bearded man reluctantly came over to her. He was wearing a high-visibility jacket and a peaked cap.

"Are you the harbour-master?" Rita asked.

"Aye," the man said gruffly. "Who wants to know, like?"

Rita unclasped her phone from the armband, which also had a compartment for cards. She showed the man her warrant card.

"DI Gupta of North Yorkshire Police. Please excuse my appearance, but we need to make urgent enquiries about a man. What's your name?"

"Oh, aye? My name's Jonty Stanforth."

Rita scrolled to the e-fit photo of the victim on her phone. She showed it to Jonty, still outside, and had to pass her phone through the grilles of the marina gate.

"Can you please let me in?"

"Of course, sorry." Jonty bustled to the side of the long gate and pressed a buzzer. With a grating sound the gate slid open. Rita walked in and stood next to Jonty, who was inspecting the phone screen.

"He does look familiar. What's happened to him?"

"We need to find him," Rita said. "It's part of a current investigation, so I can't say a great deal more right now."

"Is he in trouble?"

"Sorry, but I can't comment any further. But it is very important that we find him as soon as possible."

Jonty's bushy eyebrows hiked upwards and he removed his cap.

He scratched the few straggly hairs on his bald pate, frowned, and looked down at the screen again. When he looked up, Rita saw trouble in his eyes.

"Come with me," Jonty said. He was an old man, but he walked with purpose, and Rita had to half-jog to keep up with him.

Jonty stopped a fisherman in blue overalls, showed him the photo, and they had a hushed conversation. The fisherman looked Rita up and down, then back to the screen. Slowly, he nodded. Jonty turned back to Rita.

"I think we know who this is. He's a man called Andrew Salford. His wife was here yesterday, looking for him."

"Right, I see," Rita tried to hide her excitement. This was a real stroke of luck – now she had a positive ID. "Are you sure?"

Jonty looked at the other fisherman, who hailed one of his friends on a nearby boat. He came over, and the three men looked at the screen and nodded slowly.

"Yes," Jonty said. "This is Andrew. What's happened to him?"

"Like I said, I can't comment on that right now. Can you give me his details, please? And his wife's name and address."

"Yes," Jonty cleared his throat. "He runs a sailing company called Bluewater Cruises. His boat's called the Merigold. It's docked at the Fish Quay, over here."

Rita had taken the phone back from Jonty and was writing down the details. When she looked up, she saw the two men who had joined them were walking away.

"Excuse me," Rita called after them. They didn't stop, so she ran after them, telling Jonty to stay where he was. The man in blue overalls turned; the other man, shorter and wider, in black overalls, didn't stop.

"I need your names and contact numbers," Rita said. "We need to ask you about Andrew Salford." She looked at the shorter man first. He was fidgeting, and Rita didn't like his restless movements. He was itching to get away.

"What's your name?"

"Matt Yardley."

"Are you a fisherman here?"

Matt looked lazily up and down Rita's body, and she felt heat rising in her cheeks. Perhaps she should have planned this better.

"Yes. Who are you, love?"

"Detective Inspector Gupta of the NYP," Rita thrust her warrant card close to both men. The incipient smile on Matt's face vanished.

"And you?" Rita looked at the man in the blue overalls.

"Daniel Ashman."

Rita took their phone numbers down. "We will be contacting you soon. Thank you. How long will you be here for?"

Daniel said, "Well, I just got back from being out at sea all night. I need a rest. So I'm going home now."

Matt said, "Yes, me too."

Rita glanced at both of them. "Did you know Andrew Salford?"

Daniel answered first. "Yes, I did. He used to work with his dad, but the old man died a few years ago. Andy ran a tourist boat in the summer, like I do. And he fished in the other months, same as me."

"When did you last see him?"

Daniel frowned, his weather-beaten face crinkling at the forehead and eyes. "Last week, I think. Yes, that's right. Early in the week, he was coming back from sea, early morning, like now."

"Did you notice anything unusual about him that day?"

Daniel looked surprised. "No. I mean, not that I noticed."

Rita looked at Matt. "How about you?"

Matt shrugged. "I didn't know Andy well. Seen him around, that's all."

"You also have a boat here?"

"Aye. I fish and sell it on the wholesale market." Matt lapsed into silence and looked away. Rita didn't like his attitude. Something about him told her he knew more than he was letting on.

"When did you last see Andrew?"

"Can't remember. Been a while." Matt had a stony, impassive look on his face. Rita got the impression he wouldn't talk any further.

"We will contact you again later today. Perhaps in the afternoon?"

Both men nodded, then trudged off. Rita also walked away, aware of the other fishermen staring at her. She jogged back to the main gate, where Jonty still stood in front of his cottage. The kiosk was now open.

Jonty went inside and came back with a clipboard in his hand. A car had arrived at the gates, and Jonty walked through a side gate and spoke to the driver. Then he opened the gates and the car drove through slowly.

Rita caught up with Jonty as he walked back to the kiosk. "Thanks for your help," Rita said. "I can't really interview people now, but I'll be back with my team later on. Can you gather as many contact details as you can for people who knew Andrew Salford?"

"Aye, I'll try." He hesitated, peering at Rita through his bushy white eyebrows. "What's he done, like?"

"I'm sorry, but I can't discuss that right now."

"Does this have owt to do with the police on the Sea Wall Heritage Trail Road?" Jonty asked. "The police have shut down the road, haven't they?"

Clearly, the old man didn't miss much. Rita smiled at him. "Thanks for your help," she repeated and checked her watch. It was half six. She needed to get going.

"Please stay on site. We will be back in a couple of hours at the latest."

CHAPTER 10

Rita ran back home, and called the duty uniforms team on her radio. She got showered and changed quickly, then took a taxi to the station.
She rang the lads on her way to the station, and Rizwan answered.
"I've got a positive ID," Rita told him. "Get to the nick ASAP. I need a full disclosure on Andrew Salford. Inform the researchers. His wife has been asking at the harbour for him. Find out if she's filed a missing person's note."
"Bloody hell, guv, you've been busy. Sure, no problem."
Rita was on the back seat of a taxi. She checked her watch; it was half seven.

"Ask Dr Das or Shola – they should have a name from the dental records. See if it matches Andrew Salford."
"Will do right now."

"Contact the wife and ask her to meet us at the nick. Send a police escort to pick her up. Once all that is sorted out, meet me at the harbour-master's office. I've informed the duty uniforms team – they'll be arriving at the harbour in ten minutes. The victim was a fisherman, and he has a boat on the marina."

"Mooring fees aren't cheap. He must've been doing all right to have a spot."

"Yes," Rita said slowly. The thought hadn't occurred to her. She hadn't seen Andrew's boat yet. "Inform Shola as well. I want the boat treated as a crime scene, given that the victim was on the boat shortly before his death."

"No worries. Shall I ask HMCG if his boat was on their watch-list?" HMCG was the abbreviation for His Majesty's Coastguard.

"Excellent idea," Rita smiled. "Glad you had your Weetabix this morning."

"Frosties for me, guv. I need the sugar rush. HMCG, and anyone else you can think of?"

"Maybe the RNLI as well, in case the boat needed to be rescued at any time. It'd be good to have that data." (RNLI – the Royal National Lifeboat Institution – was the search-and-rescue charity that undertakes most civilian rescues near the coast.)

"Got it, guv. I'll coordinate that with the researchers, and see you at the harbour."

Rita thanked Rizwan and hung up. When she got to the harbour, she didn't go in.

Instead, she walked down Foreshore Road, the broad avenue that overlooked the expanse of the beach. She had the address of the Bluewater Sea Cruise company, and it was a short walk from the harbour.

It was closed. Rita turned the handle but the door was locked. There was a café to the right and a fishing-gear shop on the left.

The café was open, so Rita went in. A woman was making coffee, and a few customers sat waiting in the front area. An old man was at the till and he looked up when Rita entered.
"I'm looking for Andrew Salford," Rita said. "He owns the business next door to you." She pointed.
"Oh, aye," the old man said. "Not seen him for a few days. Hang on." He turned and called for the woman. She was much younger than him, and she came over, wiping her hands on the apron.
"Yeah, I saw him the day before yesterday, when he was going out to the harbour. Just said hello, that's all." The woman frowned. "His wife also came yesterday to ask for him. Is he all right?"
"Melanie Salford? Is that who you mean?"
"Melanie, yes. Sorry, I'm Corrie by the way. This is my dad, Dean."
"Ah right," Rita nodded. "Hence the name, Dean's Café. Did either of you know Andrew well?"
"Not particularly," Corrie said. She looked at her father. Dean turned his aged eyes to Rita; the deep-set lines around his eyes crinkled.
"What is this about? And who are you?" Dean asked.
Rita showed them her warrant card and introduced herself.
"What's going on?" Dean asked.
"We need to speak to Andrew urgently with regards to an investigation. Can you tell us a bit more about him?"

Dean said, "He's been around for a while. I set up shop before him, but he and his dad moved in about ten years ago. His dad was Michael; he's gone now."

"What do you know about Andrew?"

"Well, he was a fisherman, obviously. So was his dad, and three generations before him. Fishing runs in the family, you see. I used to be one myself. Andrew also did the sea-fishing expeditions as well. All of us do it now. We lost our fishing rights to the European Union, and then came the days of the dredging companies. No need for line-caught fishermen like us any more."

Dean stopped and breathed heavily. He was clearly tired from his rant. Corrie put a hand on his back. "Sit down, Dad."

He did as told, pulling up the chair next to the cash counter. Rita said, "Did Andrew look worried or concerned when you last saw him?"

"I didn't see him much. He was running around. I last spoke to him maybe a couple of weeks ago. He seemed like his usual self. Cheerful."

"How is his business doing?" Rita asked the question to both father and daughter. Corrie shrugged. Dean stared at Rita, and she suspected he knew more.

"Life isn't easy here, Inspector. I don't know how long you've lived here. But the fishing business pretty much folded years ago. We have the tourists, but they only come in the summer. The rest of the time this place is deserted."

"And Andrew's business?" Rita prompted, trying to get the man back on track.

The dark look was back in the old man's eyes. Rita knew his brief rant on the local economy was a preamble to something else. And she could guess what it was.

"It's doing as good as anything else these days," drawled Dean.

"Was Andrew in debt? Was he in financial trouble?"

Dean's dull eyes slid to the left, and then back to Rita. "I don't know."

"Did anyone come asking for him, like I have?" Rita glanced at Corrie, who had gone still, watching her carefully.

"No," Dean said. He shuffled in his chair, then stood. "We have to be getting on. We've got work to do."

He tried to walk away but Rita stood firm. "This is a serious matter. I wouldn't be asking otherwise. If you know something about Andrew or his business, please tell us now."

Dean stopped and glared at Rita. "I don't go around poking into other people's affairs. But I know that his business had slim pickings. He asked to borrow money once. I didn't have any spare."

Rita considered that. "Did he not ask a bank for a loan?"

"You need to ask him that. I can't speak for him."

"Do you think he had tried other banks and they refused him?"

"How would I know?" Dean frowned. "Look, you need to leave us alone now. We have work to do."

"Did anyone else come to see him?"

Dean went silent and shrugged.

Corrie was listening, and she caught Rita's eyes. "A man did come once. Andy wasn't here. He left a message – ask Andy to call Jack when he came back."

"Jack? Did he have a last name, or a phone number?"

"No."

"Can you describe him?"

"In his thirties, I'd say. About six feet, average build. He wore a brown leather jacket and dark glasses. He took them off when he spoke to me. He was clean-shaven. Had a brown matching shirt on, and dark-blue jeans. Black shoes, I think. Yes, black shoes."

"Any tattoos or other identifying marks?"

Corrie thought for a while, then shook her head. "Not that I recall." Then her eyes brightened. "Oh yes. His left earlobe was missing a portion. Like it'd been bitten off – I mean, I'm sure it wasn't, but it looked like that. Weird, I guess." Corrie smiled and shrugged.

"Thank you. And you've only seen this man once?"

"Yes."

"You said he took his glasses off. Do you remember anything else about his face? Eye colour, for example? Any moles on his face?"

Corrie put a finger to her lips and her head sank lower as she thought.

In his corner, Dean huffed. "Get busy, lass," he growled.

Then he fixed Rita with a glare, which she ignored.
"Aye, Dad, just wait." Corrie waved a hand at the old man. She glanced at Rita. "Grey eyes, I think. Good-looking bloke he was." She smiled and Rita grinned back.
"Thanks. That's very helpful. Do you have a CCTV camera here?"
Corrie's face fell. "We do, but it's not working. Dad, did we get it fixed?" She looked at Dean, who shook his head.
"Technician should be coming next week."
"Let us know if you think of anything else," Rita said. She left her card for Corrie and walked back to Andrew's office. She looked in through the windows but couldn't see a great deal. She walked round the back, through the narrow alley that separated the office from the café. There was a small backyard with two derelict office chairs and a rubbish bin. The back door was also locked.
Rita went out and walked to the harbour. She saw two police cars parked outside the gates, and one of the uniformed sergeants speaking to Jonty, the harbour-master.

CHAPTER 11

As Rita approached the gates, Jonty opened them, and the two squad cars swept in. Rita walked up to Jonty and the uniformed sergeant. PS Thomas, his name badge read. He was a burly, black-bearded man. He wore a peaked cap and chest rig. He touched his cap when Rita approached. Rita caught Jonty gaping at her, evidently surprised by her change in attire.

"Morning, ma'am," Thomas said. "Any orders?"
"Yes. We want to question everyone here before they leave. We can't keep them too long as they might well be knackered from the night's fishing. Take details of those who've left already and chase them up later today. Ask them about Andrew Salford – the usual questions."
"Aye." Thomas nodded and left to update his team. Rita turned to Jonty.
"Did you find anyone else who knew Andrew well?"
"I asked around. To be honest, all the old muckers know one another. Some of the lads are tidying up on their boats. I can show you them, if you like?"
"My men," Rita pointed at the uniformed officers, "will ask the questions. What happened to Daniel and Matt, the two men I saw this morning?"
"Not sure. You can ask at their boats. They both have fishing hands, or boat crew. Not sure if they're around either, though."

Jonty walked with Rita to the boats. As before, the fishermen looked on curiously. Rita was very glad she was now in her official black suit. Daniel's and Matt's boats were empty. They were good-sized fishing trawlers, and no one replied to Jonty's call. "Where's the Merigold?" Rita asked. She wanted to be the first one to look at Andrew's boat, but then Jonty informed her Melanie, Andrew's wife, had already been.

Rita wished they hadn't trampled around what could be vital evidence. She stopped in front of the Merigold. Running footsteps came behind her. She turned to see Richard, his cheeks red from the effort. The sun was casting a warm glow already, but the sea breeze was still cool. So far, it was a much nicer day than yesterday.

"Sorry, guv," Richard said. "I came as soon as I could. Rizwan updated me. We've got the dental-records data. Shola checked them late last night. Yes, the records belong to an Andrew Salford. He lives in Filey."

"Good," Rita nodded grimly. It was anything but good. But at least they now had a confirmed ID. She turned to Richard. "Thanks for coming in early. Did you have the kids to drop off at school?"

"No, guv." Richard smiled, looking embarrassed. "Just got up late. The victim's wife is arriving at the station soon. Uniforms are going to her house as we speak."

"OK. Let's have a look at the boat. It belonged to the victim. Is Shola on her way?"

"She's sending Henry."

Rita nodded and got on board. Jonty wanted to join them, but Rita stopped him.

"We'll take it from here."

"Are you sure?" Jonty looked doubtful. "I can show you around."

Rita wondered what he meant. True, she wasn't adept at sailing or around boats. But it wasn't difficult to look around a moored vessel. While she didn't enjoy the stench of old fish, she had a mask, and could easily have a look around.

"I think we'll manage," she told Jonty. "Forensic officers will be on this boat soon, so I don't want anyone else to step aboard."

"Forensics?" Jonty raised his bushy white eyebrows. "They only get involved if there's been a crime, right? Not that I know much about what you lot get up to."

Rita gazed at him. "Thank you for your help, but please let us do our job. If you can tell the other fishermen and boat owners to stay away from the Merigold."

"Aye, no problem, like."

Jonty slouched off. He stopped to speak to a group of fishermen and pointed at the boat. They looked at Rita and Richard. Rita could see the uniformed officers fanning out, stopping the fishermen they came across to ask them questions.

"This is a tightly knit community," Rita said quietly. "I doubt we'll get much out of them."

Rita and Richard got on board the Merigold. The large fishing trawler swayed gently in the water. The marina was protected by the outcropping of the harbour, and it was crested by a Second World War anti-aircraft gun. Rita glanced around the deck. The trawlers and boats around looked empty, but opposite, she could see docks with inquisitive faces on the decks of boats.

Richard said, "You got that right, guv. The fishing lot are famously tight-lipped. They keep themselves to themselves. Their jobs are risky, and even now, some trawlers are lost in storms at sea. In the old days it used to be a lot more. They look out for each other; it's almost a genetic trait."

"Then they wouldn't kill one of their own, would they? And presumably, they'll do all they can to help us."

"You would think so," Richard said, joining Rita as she walked around. "But they'll want to know what happened first."

Rita had walked around the captain's cabin and looked down at the oily waters below. The grey, opaque waters looked back at her. Richard lifted the seats screwed on the deck and checked the nets and fishing gear inside. Rita joined him. They didn't find anything unusual.

They went inside the captain's cabin, which was large enough for three people to stand at the front windscreen. The compartments and drawers held some maps, a torch, a couple of hooks and instruction manuals for the engine.

"SMM," Rita said. "Seagoing Mariners' Mission. That was the tattoo on the victim's arm. Do you know anything about them? Rizwan said your grandfather came from fishing stock. Is that true?"

A gentle swell moved the boat as a trawler came in from the sea, blowing its whistle. It headed for its berth in the opposite marina. Richard and Rita braced themselves by holding on to the dashboard.

"Aye. My grandad was from Grimsby actually. It's still a fishing port, albeit small. But he didn't carry on fishing; he joined the Navy and sailed around the world. He was proud of being a fisherman though. Told us stories of going out on his dad's boat when he was a teenager. They used to leave at night and come back in the mornings. They caught lobster, shrimps, cod, haddock, shark, octopus – all sorts."

Rita smiled. "Made an impression on you, it seems. You loved your grandpa, right?"

"Yes. For a while I wanted to be a fisherman as well. But I'm here instead."

"Well, let's keep going. I want to interview Melanie Salford as soon as I get back."

They searched the boat up and below deck, in the cabins, but found nothing. Rita knew Henry would take samples of the cutlery in the sink, so she left them where she found them. One of the bedrooms had a man's boxer shorts in the bed, and she took that in an evidence bag.

Outside, they walked to the canteen in the harbour, which still had some punters. They were all men, dressed in waterproof, animal-skin jackets, and similar trousers. They had heavy black boots on their feet, whiskers and beards on their jaws. Their eyes were laden with mistrust as they watched Rita and Richard.

Rita walked up to the woman at the counter, the first woman she'd seen in the harbour. She was in her late thirties to early forties, with brunette hair up to her shoulders. She wore an apron that said: Girls can also be sailors.

Rita went up to her. Conversation had stilled when she and Richard entered the canteen, and it had slowly picked up again but the earlier buzz was absent.

"DI Gupta and DS Staveley, from the NYP," Rita said, showing her warrant card. "What's your name?"

"Gillian."

"Hello, Gillian. We are here about a man called Andrew Salford. Do you know him?"

Gillian shrugged. "No. Should I?"

Richard took out his phone.

He had Andrew's passport and driving-licence photo, which the researchers had provided.

Gillian looked at the photo closely.

A younger woman came up to the counter, opened the fridge door, and served a customer.

Gillian showed the woman the photo on Richard's screen. They had a hushed chat, then Gillian handed the phone back to Richard.

"Aye, seen him around, like. What do you want him for? What's he done?"

Rita ignored the questions. "Can you tell us a bit about him?"

"Nowt to say, to be honest," Gillian shrugged. "He's a fisherman, innit? Does his job and goes home."

"Did you know him?"

"Not really. Just seen him around."

"When was the last time?"

"Can't remember." Gillian turned to the younger woman, who had vanished behind the curtained door and appeared again, carrying a tray of coffee and bacon sandwiches. She put the tray down on the counter and Gillian spoke to her. She shook her head and went away.

"We can't remember," Gillian said. "But I think I saw him a couple of days ago."

"Was he alone, or with someone?"

"With another bloke. I've seen him around too. Matty, I think he's called. Matt Yardley, but people call him Matty. Don't know him either, mind. I work here, then go home."

Gillian frowned. "Andrew and Matty were having an argument that day. I don't know what about, but Andrew had his finger up in Matt's face. Matt stormed off. That's why I remember."

Rita exchanged a glance with Richard. "Have you seen them around before?"

"Yes. They sat here and had breakfast. Maybe they were in business together. I don't know."

Richard asked, "Is there a pub around here the men go to? Like a fishermen's pub?"

Gillian shrugged again. "I'm not from fishing stock myself. But there's the George on West Pier. I've heard some of the lads drink there."

"The George Inn?" Rita said. "The one with the lights out front and the green sign? Opposite the West Pier, near the Old Harbour."

"That's the one."

Richard looked at Rita and nodded.

CHAPTER 12

Rita left Richard to coordinate with the uniforms in questioning the remaining fishermen. From the sullen looks she got, she doubted she'd get much from them. But she had to try. Later today, she'd head down to the George Inn. If Andrew drank there, chances were someone would know him. One of the squad cars gave her a lift back to the station. She called Rizwan on her way.
"Any sign of Andrew's car?"
"The old Ford Fiesta? Not yet, guv. The South Beach Car Park has CCTV, but Andrew's car wasn't there. I think he parked in one of the side streets near the harbour. We can't find it on ANPR, but traffic are still looking."
"OK, tell Traffic to look further out, on the A roads and motorway as well. If someone's nicked his car, they might be driving it around."
"No worries, guv."
"Matt Yardley," Rita said. "He was evasive when I spoke to him this morning, and he had an argument with the victim in the days before he died. Have you got his details?"
"Is he a fishy fisherman, guv?"
Rita grinned. "Nice one, Riz. Unfortunately, you're not a comedian. Have you Mr Yardley's address?"

"Aye. He lives in a small village called Gristhorpe, according to his council tax returns. Will go and knock on his door. The victim's wife is here."

"That's why I'm on my way back. See you soon."

Rita got herself a coffee and yogurt from the canteen, and a packet of biscuits and coffee for Rizwan. He rubbed his hands together when she put them on his desk. He wasted no time in dunking his chocolate bourbon biscuit into his coffee, as Rita looked on with distaste. She couldn't bear to dunk her biscuits in her tea or coffee. Rizwan relished it.

He spoke after taking a sip. "I contacted the HMCG. They don't have the Merigold on their watch list. They did say there's been a lot of night traffic on the north east coast. Boats coming up to Scarborough and Bridlington from Hull, and down from Hartlepool."

Hull and Hartlepool were two large ports in the northeastern coast of England. Rita tapped an unpolished but manicured nail on the table top.

"They've been monitoring the traffic? How do they know there's more boats at night?"

"They have radar systems on shore, and also on patrolling boats. They monitor maritime traffic for security reasons. We have Denmark straight to our west, and Holland in the south. Norway to the north. All friendly countries in the North Sea. But with the recent war in Ukraine, security patrols on the North Sea are tighter. And those patrolling boats have noticed more traffic closer to the coast."

"Have they stopped any of the boats? I presume these are British boats if they're sailing on our coast."

"Yes, they're UK boats, but no, they haven't been stopped. Some traffic is permitted as the port in Hartlepool especially is huge, one of the biggest in the country. They often carry small containers and industrial products up and down the coast, but HMCG also said the main transport is via road and inland."

"So we don't know what this increased sea traffic on our coast is about, correct?"

"It would seem so, guv. But HMCG are monitoring it." Rizwan clicked on his keyboard and glanced at the screen.

"I looked up the Scarborough Fisheries Office, where all fishing boats over ten metres length have to be registered. It's the same system all over England. And I found the Merigold's registration."

"Good work. Anything interesting?"

"As it happens, yes. There's a whole bureaucracy about registering sea vessels – you know how much us Brits love ticking boxes and filling form, right? Well, a fishing boat has to be registered, then issued with a Carving and Marking certificate, then enrolled in the Survey – the list goes on. But what we're interested in is the certificate of incorporation, which only happens if a corporation owns the boat."

"Like Bluewater Sea Cruise – the company that Andrew Salford owned?"

"I'll get to that later, that company so deep in debt its not made a profit in years. I don't even know how Andrew was making the company work, to be honest. But no, his boat, which was twenty two metres in length, actually had a mortgage on it, and it was owned by another company. Andrew paid the lease, and the boat was his, but only as long as he paid the lease."

"So like owning a house but paying mortgage to the bank."

"Exactly. The company owns a lot of boats, as it happens. It's a boat financing company, and it does the mortgages. It's called Poseidon Ventures or PV for short."

"Nice name after the Greek god of Sea. So PV owns a lot of boats around here, it seems. Who's behind the company?"

"That's where it gets interesting. I had to ring around, because the board of directors have also formed a company. So there no names. PV is owned by Dartmoor Holdings – and they are the holding company, so to speak. Even Dartmoor Holdings doesn't have any named Directors. They're also owned by a company. This time, it's an offshore company, based in the Isle of Man."

"An onion," Rita said. "Common practice for the ultra rich and criminals to hide their money from the tax man."

"Precisely, guv. All perfectly legal, of course. Anyone can form a company, and then form another to own the first one. Anyway, I managed to get hold of the bank account via our colleagues at the forensic accounting section, and hence got the name that signs the cheques."

Rita clapped her hands. "Well done, our kid. What did you find?"

"A man called Damien Salt is at the head of the board of directors. He's the effective owner of the company, and the CEO."

Rita thought for a while, the name buzzing around her brain like a busy bee. She didn't like the last name. Then her eyes opened wider, as did an old, creaky door at the back of her mind. A cold, freezing wind blew over her body, and she shivered.

"Salt?"

Rizwan was quiet now. "Yes, guv. I'm sorry. Damien is Edward Salt's brother."

CHAPTER 13

Rita could feel her heart shrinking, her fingertips turning to ice. She stared at Rizwan. When she spoke, her voice was dry, thorny as a desert cactus.
"Edward Salt?" she whispered. "The man who …"
Words failed her then. The slow thud of her heart was cannon-balling against her ears, the sound muffled but raging, like a stormy sea dashing against the rocks.
"Yes, the businessman. The one who owned Blue Rise Holdings."
The names were like sledgehammers to Rita's heart, fracturing her inner peace like a sheet of glass. She closed her eyes briefly and swallowed, fighting to regain control.
"Ed Salt is out of prison now, right? I didn't know he had a brother."
"Neither did I. It seems they have a family business. Ever since the investigation, I guess they moved the company offshore but kept their business interests intact here."
Rita sat back in her chair.
Her mind was like a jungle, creepers and vines crawling out of every corner.

Ed Salt was one of the masterminds behind her mother's death. He had been involved in the scandal that had ultimately cost Clara her life. Rita had interrogated him and later arrested him. She would never forget him, or his cronies.

She got up, trying to shake off the clawing fingers reaching out from beyond the grave, scratching at her heart.
"Back in a minute," she told Rizwan. She walked fast down the corridor and went out into the rear car park. She turned left, where there was a bike shed and a couple of mature trees with seats under them. She sat down and tried to think.
When she investigated Edward Salt and his business—which was extensive across the North-East—she had come across his family. They were of no relevance to the case involving Clara Winters, her mother. She didn't even remember the Salt family that well. Edward's business associates, like Lord Northallerton, were much more important. But that was in the past. Edward had ended up in jail, like Alfred Northallerton. Unlike Northallerton, Edward was now out, courtesy of his expensive lawyers. But he kept a low profile and Rita had never heard o fhim again.
So who the hell was Damien Salt? She could only imagine he was the brother who had remained beyond the veil and had now emerged to take control of the empire Edward once commanded. They had hidden the family name very well—behind a series of holding companies.

Rita strode back to the office with renewed purpose. Rizwan looked up as she stood in front of his desk.
"Tell me about Damien."
"No PCNs or police record. Never had a brush with law enforcement, apart from a couple of council parking tickets. I checked the electoral roll—he's registered to vote. He lives with his family in Harrogate."
"Nice and posh. Makes sense." Harrogate was a lovely town near the bigger city of York.

"Yes. Poseidon Ventures is one of the companies the Salt family owns. Damien has a sister called Natalie—she lives in Weybridge, Surrey, way down south. More importantly," Rizwan dropped his voice, "Damien Salt's name has come up in connection with the Scarborough Harbour Regeneration Project."
"He's a donor?"
"A big one. As you know, guv, the harbour is long due a facelift. The fifty-five-million-pound, six-year project was scrapped last year as the council couldn't come up with all the money. Damien has now stepped in and said he'll help."

"I bet the council love him for that. Anything else?"

"PV is actually one of his biggest assets. They pretty much mortgage all the fishing and commercial vessels in Scarborough, Whitby, Bridlington, Hull, Immingham—you name it."

"Immingham's a big port, isn't it? Near Hull, by the mouth of the Humber," Rita said.

"That's right, guv. It's one of the largest container ports in the country. If PV owns boats there, they must be big."

Rita went up to the map on the wall. It showed the north-east coast of England, from Edinburgh in Scotland all the way down to Grimsby in North Lincolnshire. Rita traced a line on the sea with her forefinger.

"So you come out of Immingham and sail straight up the coast to get to Scarborough, Whitby and Hartlepool."

"And many other stopping points along the way," Rizwan said, joining her. "There's Bridlington, Filey, Bempton Cliffs—those are the named ones. The fishermen know lots of small coves that are isolated but, I think, have road links. The only problem is landing on these beaches, because the rocks and North Sea currents make it dangerous for boats to get in and out."

Rita glanced at Rizwan, then back at the map. "So HMCG has seen increased traffic all along this coastline. I wonder why that is."

"And our victim's boat could've been one of them," Rizwan said.

Rita's brow furrowed as she looked at the map again. Somehow this was important to Andrew Salford's death, but she couldn't place it yet. The distant hum in her mind grew louder, like the engine of a phantom car.

CHAPTER 14

Melanie Salford didn't ask for a lawyer and nor did she need to, as she was not a suspect of any crime. She was alone, sitting with her head bowed. As Rita and Rizwan came in, she looked up, her eyes red-rimmed, a haunted, desperate look in them.
She wore a sky-blue cardigan. Her blonde hair was tied up in a ponytail. She had no make-up on. Rita knew she had a toddler, and she looked like a mother who had just done the morning drop-off and was off to do some shopping. A normal day. Only, in this case, the normality had morphed into a nightmare. Rita also knew the uniformed Inspector, David Botley, had sat down with Melanie in her living room and broken the news to her. She had questions, and she now expected Rita to answer them.
Melanie didn't move. She remained rigid, only her eyes scanning Rita's face before switching to Rizwan. Her hands moved continuously on her lap. Shallow, jerky breaths moved her chest.
Rita introduced herself and Rizwan as they sat down. "Would you like a glass of water? Or some tea or coffee?"
"No," Melanie blurted out. The tip of her nose turned red and tears brimmed in her eyes. "Just tell me what happened."

From previous experience Rita knew that family members wanted clarity. They needed the facts, and often they had to be repeated.

"Andrew Salford was found dead at the base of Scarborough Castle, in the southern section of the Sea Wall Heritage Trail road. He had fallen, it seems, from a considerable height. We think he fell from the castle ramparts."

Melanie looked as if someone had slapped her. She knew this already, but hearing it from Rita's lips seemed to shock her again.

"How do you know it was him? It could be anybody. How do you know?" Her voice rose into a wail, ending in a stifled sob.

"We did the dental records and that showed a match. We also have witnesses in the harbour who recognised his photo." Rita kept her voice low and gentle. "We would also like you to identify the body."

Melanie's head lowered, and her shoulders shook. Rita nudged Rizwan, who pushed the box of tissues across the table. Rita got up, went to the water-cooler and poured water into a plastic cup. They were in the interrogation chambers, and Rita didn't like that. She should have been able to see Melanie in the family rooms upstairs.

When Melanie recovered and took a sip of water, Rita spoke again.

"I'm sorry for your loss. I understand you were looking for your husband yesterday. Why didn't you report him as missing?"

"I looked online. The advice said most missing people come back home within a day or two. That's also why I didn't tell his parents. Also, Andrew's a fisherman, and sometimes they can be out at sea the whole night. They come back in the morning."

"But the night before last was different, is that correct? The harbour-master, Jonty Stanforth, said Andrew's boat returned at 21:47."

"Yes, that's right. I went to see Jonty yesterday. We had a look on the boat. It was empty. I just thought he'd spent the night at one of his mate's houses. I rang around, but no one had seen him. I still thought he'd be back. But he didn't. I called the police this morning. I was waiting when the police car turned up."

Melanie lowered her head again. Rita knew – when the police turned up, they gave her the news. She thought Melanie had been very brave to wait for Andrew to return. She didn't panic. She was an astute woman. Most people would have panicked and called the police the next morning, only to be told to wait for a day or two.

"You have a daughter," Rita said softly. "Where is she now?"

"At home, with my friend. There's also an officer at my home. A woman called Emily."

Rita nodded. Emily Thornberry was the family-liaison officer.

She knew Melanie had to get home soon. The toddler was probably playing now, but would be asking for her mother soon.

"Once you identify the body, you can go home. Is it OK if I ask you a few questions about Andrew?"
Melanie nodded.
"Has he ever done anything like this before? Stayed away for the night without informing you?"
"Like I said, often fishermen go out for the night."
"That's not what I meant." Rita kept her voice gentle, but she saw the shadow pass over Melanie's face. "Was everything all right between you two? Was your relationship stable?"
Melanie's forehead muscles contracted. "Yes. Of course. Nowt wrong with us. Andrew loved me, and our little Carla."
She was a grieving woman, and Rita knew her emotions were all over the place. And yet, she didn't know if she fully believed Melanie. Her statement seemed a little too forceful.
"How long have you been married?"
"Eight years." A sad smile flickered over Melanie's lips before fading swiftly.
"And when did you have Carla?"
Melanie looked puzzled at the question. "Well, she's almost two, so it was two years ago. Eighteenth June. Carla will be two in two months."
Rita smiled. "Thank you." Her smile was wiped away when she thought of the poor child growing up without her father. Rita knew that life only too well. She kept a lid on her emotions, sending them to the dungeons of her heart.

"Tell us about Andrew's business. How was it going?"

Another shadow flickered across Melanie's face. She hesitated before replying. "Not great, to be honest. It's hard to make ends meet from fishing alone. Too much competition from the wholesalers. And the tourism market can be fickle. He still put food on the table and paid the rent. That's all we had, really."

"Did he try anything else? To earn money, I mean?"

Melanie blinked a few times, dabbed a tissue to her nose. "Not sure what you mean. He was a fisherman, so that's all he did."

"His boat is mortgaged to a company called Poseidon Ventures. Was he meeting the monthly payments? He had the rent to pay as well."

"I work as well," Melanie said, a touch of irritation in her voice. "I do part-time receptionist work at the local GP surgery. Ours is a small community, and the money's not great, but it's better than nowt."

"Of course. I meant if you knew whether Andrew was doing another job."

"No, I don't."

"Was he in debt? Or in financial trouble?"

Melanie took her time to answer, and Rita knew the pause was significant. "It weren't easy for us. It never is, with a family. We had moved to a house from a flat, so the little one could play in a garden. So yes, money worries were constant. Last month, Andrew had to take a loan to make the rent payment." Her head lowered again. "We're already two months late on the rent. The landlord's asked us to leave. We couldn't afford another month of not paying."

"Sorry to hear that. Was Andrew looking for more work? Or you?"

"Aye. Her childcare would wipe out anything I earned, even if I was a full-time receptionist."

"So what was Andrew doing?" Rita was trying to get to the point, and it seemed to her Melanie was stalling. Melanie looked down at her lap, where her hands were twisting again.

"He wouldn't tell me," she finally said. "But a couple of dodgy-looking people came to the house once. Andy was talking to them. They shut the door but I could hear them. They were asking Andy if he could move gear in his boat."

"What sort of gear?"

"I don't know. I heard them say Hull and Teesside."

Rizwan said, "By Teesside you mean Hartlepool?"

"Yes. They said there's heat on the roads—stop and search. So they wanted to move gear in the boats."

"You overheard all of this?"

"Yes. I put my ear to the closed door of the living-room. That door's not thick. I heard most of what they said. Carla was asleep."

"What else did the men say?"

"They wanted to know if Andy could do it. He said yes. The more gear he took, the more he got paid. They said a grand for every five kilos. So if he took a load of twenty kilos, he could make four grand in one trip. Andy asked them this, and they confirmed. Then they were quiet for a while. One of the men said if they could trust Andy, then they would send him up to Glasgow and Aberdeen as well. He could earn a lot more then."

Rizwan asked, "What did these men look like?"
"One was tall and burly, in a black leather jacket. Shaven head. He looked like a thug. The other was shorter, with brown hair. I heard Andy say his name. Matt. I've heard Andy say that name before, when he speaks on the phone."

Rita hid her excitement. "What's Matt's last name?"
"Sorry, I don't know. But I saw his name on his phone's screen one day, when I handed the phone to him. They were talking about the tides, and a beach where the low tide exposes the rocks. I think this Matt might be a sailor. Or even a fisherman, I don't know."
"Matt Yardley. Does that name mean anything to you?"
Melanie frowned and narrowed her eyes. "The name sounds familiar. Not sure why. I don't know anyone called Matt, but Andy clearly did."
"How about Daniel Ashman?"
Melanie nodded. "Do you mean Dan? Yes, I seen him once. At the George Inn pub, near the old harbour. Andy used to go drinking there. I went with him once or twice. I seen Dan there. Seems like a good bloke."
"But you never met Matt, until he turned up at your house that day?"
"Nope. They came a few weeks ago—end of February, I think. It was still cold out."
Rizwan asked, "Did either of the two men have any distinguishing features? For example, visible tattoos or rings? Or did they walk or talk a certain way?"

Melanie thought for a while. "The big guy had an earring in his left ear. I remember that because he kept touching it when he walked in. He was scary." Melanie shivered. "I didn't like either of them, to be honest. I did ask Andy what they wanted, but he wouldn't tell me."

"Did he know that you had eavesdropped on them?"

Melanie closed her eyes. She touched her forehead and was silent for a while.

"Yes. We had an argument. He stayed out a couple of nights on the sea. He told me he was fishing. But he smells different when he comes back from fishing. He didn't, those nights, so I kept askin' him where he'd been. That's when I told him. He was angry, but also worried. He told me not to tell anyone."

Rita said, "And you didn't, did you?"

Looking miserable, Melanie shook her head slowly.

"One last thing," Rita asked. "Where were you on the night of 6 April?"

Melanie looked surprised. "You mean the night …" Words failed her.

"Yes. The night Andrew didn't come home—so, night before last."

"I was at home."

"I see," Rita said.

"Thank you," Rita said. "Please stay local for the next few days. We will want to get in touch with you again."

CHAPTER 15

Rafik Khan parked his car two blocks away from Luna's house. Luna was Edward "Kyle" Warren, the convicted murderer and child kidnapper's sister. Ed was also the father of Maggie Long's soon-to-be-born child.

Rafik had been a key member of a human-trafficking gang that Rita had just dismantled. The head of the gang was now in prison, and the other members were dead, but Rafik had managed to escape. He had changed his name and used cash for all his financial needs. Luna had helped him because she believed he was innocent.

Rafik had shaved off his beard and he now wore glasses. He stepped out of his car and looked around him carefully. He couldn't see anyone sitting in a car, watching him. He walked to the end of the road, then took the back alley to get to Luna's block. He knocked on her door and she opened it.

"Hiya, love," Luna trilled. She had bright-red lipstick on her dermal-filler duck-lips. Her fake eyelashes were so long they brushed Rafik's cheek. She stank of cheap perfume and cigarette smoke. A five-year-old boy clung to her legs.

Rafik followed Luna into the living room, where a baby was playing in his play-pen. Luna picked him up and started to breastfeed him. Luna had five children in all, from three different men. None of the men were around any more. That was OK with Luna. She had no trouble finding men, and she knew the babies were a great source of income, because she got the house, bills, food, holidays abroad – all for free.

The eldest was over eighteen, but he still stayed at home. The house was busy, to say the least. Rafik sat down on a toy, which squeaked loudly. He cursed and moved it from under his buttock.

Rafik said, "I heard a man died outside the castle. The cops have blocked off the Sea Wall Heritage Trail road. I hope that keeps them busy and they stay off my case."

"Yes, love," Luna said. "Bloody pigs. Ain't got nothing better to do, have they?"

"No one knows I'm here, right? You've not told your mum? Or any of your friends?"

"Relax, babe. I barely speak to my mum. You know what she's like. And my mates only know you as Matt. It doesn't matter."

Luna stopped and looked at Rafik. "

There's one thing, though. You know you told me about that Detective Inspector – Rita Gupta?"

"Yes," Rafik said slowly, a wary look in his eyes. "What about her?"

"Well, she was the one that arrested Ed as well. That stupid cow actually prevented his transfer to a less-secure prison. As if our Ed would harm a fly. Ridiculous, really. Do you know poor Ed can't even have a hot drink? They don't let him—"

"Hang on," Rafik interrupted. His eyebrows were lowered, jaw tight. "What did you tell Ed?"

"Well, he told me about this DI Rita Gupta. The same copper you told me about. He wants to speak to you about her."

The baby stopped feeding, and Luna put him on her shoulder and patted his back. The baby burped and then slowly fell asleep. Luna put him in his cot. Rafik was standing, shoving his hands in and out of his pockets. He was agitated. Luna put her flabby arms around him and kissed him.

"Relax, love. Ed thinks he can find a way to sort this Inspector out."

Rafik angled his head, suddenly interested. "Really? What do you mean?"

"Well, he knows where she lives, for starters." Luna sat down on the sofa with Rafik. "Ed's met her; he knows what she looks like. She came to Ed's school to talk to him about that missing boy. Anyway, Ed thinks you can do something for him."

"Like what?"

"He thinks you could keep an eye on her. See who she meets up with. She might have a weak point. Here, he wrote this note for you."

Luna stood and made sure they were alone in the room. She shut the door, then smiled at Rafik. Standing in front of him, she lifted up her skirt. From her knickers, she pulled out a folded piece of paper. "Ed wrote this in the loo and hid it in his shoes, where the guards wouldn't find it. He passed it to me under the table in the meeting room. I'm searched when I go in to see him, and also on the way out. That's why I hid it in my knickers."

They kissed again, then Rafik read the note on the paper. It had been written with a ball-point pen:

Find out who she cares about. If it's a child, we can abduct them. If it's an elderly person, we can do the same. Then we pressure Rita Gupta into dropping the case against you and me. I think she has a boyfriend called Jack Banford. He's got an eight-year-old daughter. I can provide more details. Let me know if you're interested.

Rafik looked up at Luna, his eyes shining. "Yes. Tell him I'm definitely interested."

CHAPTER 16

Bob Chandler, the forensic gait analyst was on the phone to Rita. "Och, aye, I agree there's several boot prints clustered on that edge of the rampart."
"Are there are any hits on the forensic boot print database?"
Bob coughed, then wheezed. "I cannae see none, tae be honest. But on that rampart, there was a wee scuffle, like. Ah ken two blokes from the boot sizes. And the wee prints aren't that old. Nae rain last night. Ah reckon these prints be fresh."
"So two blokes had a fight, and that happened last night. Just above where we found our victim. That can't be a coincidence," Rita said. Her hunch had been right.
"Ah cannae be sure, but yer gotta point. Yer ken he was pushed, and he didnae fall?"
"I think so, Bob. He was pushed." Rita thought of the round, brown button she picked up. She needed to ask Shola about that. She thanked Bob and hung up.
Shola answered on the first ring. Rita could hear sea gulls squawking, and the sea-breeze.
"You're on the Merigold, is that correct?" Rita asked.
"Thanks to you, yes. We've just finished. Taken samples of everything. Not much to see, but have you checked underneath the floorboards?"

Rita paused, thinking of what she'd discussed with Rizwan about the increased traffic from in the coastline, and what Melanie had said. The two strands of her thinking entwined perfectly, creating a snake with sharp fangs. Rita sighed, and touched her forehead.

"We think the victim might've been transporting contraband up and down the north east coast. I don't know exactly what as yet. What have you found underneath the floorboards?"

"Nothing as we haven't looked. Henry's found panels however, screwed onto the floor. They can be unscrewed, and lifted. But we don't have the tools, like a drill. You might want to have a look."

Rita nodded slowly. "Thanks Shola. That's really helpful. Did you find anything else on the boat?"

"Nope. We've taken swabs of all the surfaces, bedsheets, and samples of the few clothes. All men's garments. The engine works, as does the satellite phone. There's also a radar interceptor, and infra red sensors. Are you sure this is just a fishing trawler? The technology on display is quite high tech."

A distant storm was breaking over the horizon of Rita's mind. The rush of ideas came with gusts of bad omens. She didn't like the sound of what Shola just said. "What do you think the tech was used for?"

"Well radar is basically to check for surrounding vessels on the sea. The infra red is more interesting, as it looks for heat signals on the water. It's used by marine biologists to search for whales, for instance, or to discover human heat signals in the water."

Rita thought aloud. "Why would a fisherman need that?"

"My sentiments precisely. Oh, and he also had an ultrasound depth probe – which is used to scan the bottom of the sea bed. These machines are not cheap. They're used by university departments that study the ocean floor."

Rita was silent for a while, her mind running loops. "Thanks Shola. Is there anything on the boat that might point to why these machines were used?"

"Not really. In the captain's cabin, there's all these high tech gear on the dashboard. Henry fired up the engine and we looked through them. A friend of mine is a marine biologist, and I go diving with him. He explained these machines to me. He's very good at his job."

Shola paused and something in her voice suggested to Rita this man was more than a friend to Shola.

"Can you ask your friend," Rita said the last word slowly. "If he can shed any light on your recent discover?"

"I can ask, sure."

"Thanks, Shola. Let me know if there's anything else."

Rizwan and Richard were sat opposite Rita, and were listening to the conversation. They looked up expectantly, and Rita explained what Shola said. Richard said, "Now that we have Andrew's address, we can use CCTV to see these men. We might find a match using facial recog software on HOLMES, if these two have prior records."

HOLMES or the home office large major enquiry systems, was a massive supercomputer that contained one of the world's largest crime and terrorist database. It was housed in Whitehall and stored video, audio and any files for every single criminal in the UK.

Rizwan had written down the dates that Melanie had given him, although they were approximate. He was busy examining his laptop screen and looked up at Rita soon, eyes flashing.

"We have CCTV from last night, guv. I think the researchers found Andrew."

Richard and Rita crowded around Rizwan's desk. His laptop screen showed a man walking on the street, his features hidden under a cap. He was medium height for a man and he wore a blue jacket that matched what Rita had seen on Andrew's body. The CCTV images were in colour. Rizwan zoomed in on the man's face as he walked under a streetlight. Even with the close up, the face wasn't clear, but it was enough for them to recognise Andrew.

The time was ten thirty at night, and the date was yesterday 6th April.

"He's walked down Foreshore Road," Rizwan said, "Then he goes up Castlegate." He fast forwarded the tape, and they watched the solitary figure of Andrew, back bent against the wind, as he hurried down Castlegate – so called as it led to one of the gates of Scarborough Castle. Andrew stopped as he came upto the Royal Albert Park fence. There was a gap in the iron rods of the fence, it seemed, as he stepped through them with some difficulty. Then he vanished.

Richard said, "The Royal Albert Park leads into the castle. Bring up the map, Riz."

Rizwan did as requested, and Richard pointed to the relevant section where the park butted up to the south gate of the castle.

"Lots of different paths lead up to the castle walls. Not all of them are well known, and some have secret entrances. These were the old sentry entrances and some of them have tunnels. Adventurous teenagers have fallen into holes that formed the old tunnel exits."

Rizwan pulled up photos of the castle walls. "If that was Andrew's direction of travel, it makes sense he climbed the ramparts here. We visited those ramparts. Here's that sentry wall," Rizwan tapped his finger on an old crumbly edifice on the ramparts that Rita recognised as the spot they had just visited.

"Okay, well done," She said. "Andrew was alone on CCTV that night. Whoever he met up with was already inside the castle. Has CCTV checked all the roads leading up to the castle ramparts?"

Rizwan turned in his seat. "Yes, guv, they have. There's a couple of cars, and ANPR shows they belong to civilians with no police record. We are reaching out to them to see if there are any witnesses for Andrew, or anyone else."

"But no one else was seen walking down to the castle?"

Rizwan shook his head. "It was a windy night and you know what its like. Everyone stays away from the castle on those night."

Rita did know. Scarborough Castle was a famous tourist attraction, but it was also old and crumbly in many places. On a dark and stormy night, parts of the castle were death traps.

"Lets keep looking for this other person that Andrew met inside the castle", Rita said. She stood and drained her coffee mug. "I'm going to the morgue with Melanie. She's going to ID the body. See you soon."

Rita went out to the rear car park, where the squad car was waiting for her. Melanie had gone ahead with a friend. She didn't have any other family. Her parents were elderly and lived in Hartelpool, and she was the only child.

When Rita arrived at the morgue, Melanie was in the changing room. She introduced Rita to her friend.

"This is Sarah, my friend and neighbour."

Rita shook hands with Sarah, and the three of them walked out to the main chamber, where Dr Das was waiting. He was wearing his white coat over the blue scrubs he normally wore. He had solemn expression on his face as she shook hands with Melanie, and then Sarah. Melanie and Sarah held hands, and Rita watched Melanie stiffen and go rigid as Dr Das uncovered the victim's face.

Melanie broke down, covering her face in her hands. Rita and Sarah helped her to a nearby chair. Rita let Melanie be for a few minutes. Sarah sat next to Melanie, an arm around her shoulder. Rita checked in with Dr Das.

"We got a positive ID. You were right, he was a fisherman."

"Yes, I heard," Dr Das said softly. "Well done. It's such a shame, he's got a little girl." The pathologist shook his head mournfully. "I hope you get to the bottom of this soon."

"Me too. Did you send off the DNA?"

"Yes, all done. We should have results back by tomorrow at the latest. That includes the DNA on his clothes, and under his nails. If he had a physical fight with his attacker, then there will some skin cells under his nails." Dr Das gazed at Rita contemplatively. "You think he was pushed, don't you?"

"Yes, definitely."

Rita went up to Melanie and crouched by her chair. "I know this is very difficult for you. I'm sorry to ask, but did you recognise the person on the gurney?"

"Yes," Melanie's voice broke. Her face was colourless and white as a bone. "That's Andrew, my husband."

"Thank you." Rita glanced at Sarah. "You can go home now. Please stay at home, and make sure you're not alone."

Sarah said, "I'm staying with her. I live next door, and our children go to the same school. They're the same age. We'll look after her."

"Thank you," Rita said. She rose as Sarah helped Melanie to her feet. The poor woman could barely walk. She shuffled forward somehow, and Rita walked behind them. No matter how many times she saw this, it never got any easier. The dead had departed, but the weight of grief they had left behind was like an iron cloak that Melanie would wear forever.

Outside the morgue gates, Melanie turned to Rita. Her sunken, gaunt eyes had a wild look in them.
"Find out what happened to my Andrew. Please."
Rita grasped her outstretched hand. "I will. I promise."

CHAPTER 17

"A drill, guv?" Rizwan raised an eyebrow.
"Yes, Riz, an instrument that builders and homeowners use. Have you never used a drill before? Or done any DIY?" Rita took a long sip of her coffee. She had returned from the morgue half an hour ago, and spent her time responding to emails and sorting out paperwork.
Rizwan looked sheepish, and Rita suspected he had led a pretty sheltered life, living with his parents. He had moved out only recently.
"I know what a drill is, guv, but I'm wondering why you need one."
Rita pointed at the bare wall next to the large map on the wall. "I thought I'd hang a photo of our supreme leader, DS Nicola Perkins."
Rizwan coughed into his coffee, spluttering. He wiped his lips and grinned. "For a while I thought you were being serious. Honestly, though, why a drill?"
Richard walked in, interrupting their conversation. "Uniforms are back with their questionnaires." He held up a tablet device. These days, police didn't carry papers to fill in their forms; it was cheaper for them to do the same forms on a mini-tablet.

"Anything interesting?" Rita asked.

"I spoke to David," Richard said, referring to Inspector Botley, the veteran uniformed inspector. "Several fishermen said they knew Andrew, but not very well. He was a quiet man, apparently. Worked hard, according to some of his colleagues. Often spent long hours at night out at sea."

"Catching fish, eh?" Rizwan raised an eyebrow.

Richard looked at him questioningly.

Rizwan said, "HMCG has seen a lot of nocturnal traffic on the seas, up and down our coast. They can't all be fishing boats."

Rita said, "And Shola found Andrew's boat to be very high-tech. Its depth-sonar machine, radar— all sorts. I don't think a fishing trawler would need those."

Richard frowned. "So, what was he doing?"

"That's why we need a drill."

"A drill?" Richard echoed Rizwan's earlier question.

"Yes. Can one of you please get one and come with me to the harbour? We need to take apart Andrew's boat, the Merigold. I need a hand."

"Sure thing," Rizwan said, getting to his feet. "I'll ask in Equipment, but if there's none, I can always get my dad's."

"It's time you did some drilling, Riz," Richard said.

"Hey, I've used a drill before," Rizwan said, as he went out of the door.

Richard turned to Rita.

"How was it at the morgue?"

"Tough, as expected. Melanie's in pieces. She doesn't have any family around here. Andrew's family aren't close by either. She's got good neighbours, luckily."

Richard sat down. "She hasn't lived in Filey for long. Before that, she and Andrew lived in Runswick Bay."

"Where's Runswick Bay?" Rita frowned, racking her brains.

"I have heard of it, but never been. It's a small fishing village, which has its own little harbour. They still have a fishing community there. It's north of Whitby, about fifty minutes' drive from here. The Salford's were there for about four years. They've only moved to Filey two years ago."

"That wasn't on Andrew's file, was it?"

"I don't think his wife mentioned it. Not surprising, given what she's going through."

"Yes, poor thing," Rita sighed. "So where did they live before Runswick Bay?"

"That I'm not sure of. Andrew's family is from Runswick Bay. They're mostly fishermen there. Inspector Botley told me, by the way. His sergeant spoke to one of the neighbours in Filey during the door-to-door."

"So they might have lived in Runswick Bay most of their lives," Rita said. "If Andrew's from there, I mean. We should do a door-to-door there as well, or at the very least ask around for Andrew's parents. Are they still alive?"

"That I don't know, guv. Need to check."

"Please do that. I think it's important. The more we know about Andrew, the better. I'll speak to Melanie, as well."

"Another thing," Richard said. He took his phone out and showed the screen to Rita. It was a contract and Rita saw the name of Matt Yardley. The contract was from Poseidon Ventures, and Matt had signed it. He was employed by PV as a commercial fisherman, and they owned his boat, for which he paid a lease.

"It seems Matt worked for PV," Richard said. "Andrew didn't, by the way. Andrew only had his boat lease with PV."

"But Matt actually signed a contract with them. Can you get his work file from PV?"

"I tried already. I rang their human-resources department and asked for it under the Freedom of Information Act, but they refused. Then I asked for it for the police and they said they'd get back to me."

"Let me guess," Rita sighed. "You're still waiting to hear back from them."

"That's right, guv. I'll keep chasing. PV is definitely dodgy."

"I've half a mind to bring Damien Salt in for questioning."

Rizwan breezed in through the door, right hand behind his back. He grinned. "We're in luck. Equipment do have a drill, and they're willing to lend it to us." He lifted the drill with a flourish. "Ta-daa! Look what I've got."

"Like a kid with a new toy," Rita said. "Come on then, you two. Show me who can use the drill better."

Richard drove, and they reached the harbour car park soon. Jonty was at his kiosk and hurried over to open the gate. Richard parked, and they walked over to the Fishing Quay marina. Rizwan clutched the small case with the drill and bits, a spring in his step.

"Looking forward to this," he said to Rita. "Been a while since I did a bit of DIY. I've got the hammer and wrench as well."

"Good," Rita grinned. "We're going to need the wrench to lift up the floorboards if they're stuck, even after we take the screws out."

Her eyes fell on some empty berths on the marina. Boats had been berthed there, but now they had left—presumably on business, although it was afternoon and fishermen usually departed in the evening when the tides were higher.

Then her eyes alighted on the spot where the Merigold had been. It was empty. She ran forward and looked around. The boats on either side were the same ones she had seen earlier.

The Merigold was gone.

CHAPTER 18

Jonty, the harbourmaster, wasn't at his kiosk. Rita asked a passing fisherman in blue overalls where he was.
"Haven't seen him," came the casual reply. The man walked off but Rita ran after him.
"Where could he be? I'm DI Gupta of the NYP. This is urgent."
"Sorry, love, no idea." The man slouched off, and Rita fumed at his incompetence and casual sexism. Rizwan was with her, but Richard had popped into the canteen. Rita went to join him. Richard was speaking to a couple of the fishermen. Rita walked up to the counter, where Gillian, the woman she'd seen before, looked up at her. She had a wary look on her face as Rita stalked to the counter and stopped.
"Where's Jonty, the harbourmaster?"
Gillian looked from Rita to Rizwan. "I don't know. Has something happened?"
"Yes. There's a boat missing and it belongs to the man we're investigating – Andrew Salford. The boat's called the Merigold. I had placed express orders no one was to board the boat. And it definitely wasn't supposed to leave the fishing quay."
Rita was furious, and her voice was raised. The canteen was very quiet all of a sudden. Gillian looked puzzled. Rita whirled around so she was facing all the men inside the canteen.

"What happened to the Merigold?" She demanded in a loud voice. "Who knows where it's gone?"
Richard hurried over to her. "They don't know, guv. I've asked around. Two men said they arrived a couple of hours ago and they saw the boat was gone."
"And where's Jonty?"
Richard scratched his neck. "They don't seem to know."
Gillian spoke from behind. "He might've gone to the George. He likes an afternoon pint with his lunch, which he normally has there."
"Perfect," Rita ground her teeth together. "That was going to be our next stop anyway. Thanks Gillian." She strode out of the canteen. "Call uniforms," she ordered the lads. "Tell them to get back here, and put the place on lockdown. No one leaves, or gets in, and no boat leaves either."
"We can stop people from leaving," Richard said, "But we can't stop the boats. That's under the jurisdiction of the HMCG."
"Well then call them and find out what happened to the Marigold."
"Ok, guv."
Richard was on his radio as Rizwan took the wheels and drove them to the Old Harbour, which sat between the east and west sides of the harbour piers. The George Inn was a nice looking pub.
Several garlands of yellow bulbs were festooned across the front, giving it a festive appearance.

The green and white frontage, with the green painted windows looked charming. The pub occupied the corner of a little elevation, and faced the quaint old harbour and sea. Rita walked up the stone flagged steps and entered the pub. Richard and Rizwan followed behind her.

The pub was warmly lit inside as well, with same yellow bulbs in the corners. Brown panelled wood covered the walls, and red leather sofa and armchairs were strewn across the interior. Rita walked up to the counter, where a young, acne scarred man was wiping glasses with a towel. She showed him her warrant card. Richard and Rizwan fanned out without a word, checking the other rooms inside the pub.

"I'm DI Rita Gupta of North Yorkshire Police," Rita said, showing her card. "I'm looking for a man called Jonty Stanforth. He's the harbourmaster. He drinks here regularly. Have you seen him?"

The man gaped at Rita, frozen while holding the glass in his hand. He put it down slowly on the counter. He went to speak, but his lips moved without sound. Then he cleared his throat.

"Er..uh...

"Let me make this easier for you. This is an urgent police investigation, and if you are hiding anything, you could be arrested." Rita raised an eyebrow, and speared the young man with a glare. His cheeks turned pale, and he blinked.

"He's here, I think. In the back room. But I'm not sure if he's still there. He ordered lunch and one of us gave it to him about ten minutes ago."

"Thank you. Where is the back room?"

"Down your left, and through that corridor."

Rita hurried down the stone hallway, her rubber soled feet not making any sound. She came across another section of the pub that faced the sea. A few punters were at the tables, clutching the golden beer in their afternoon pint glasses. Rita scanned them, and saw Richard speaking to an old man by a corner table. "Come with me," Rita said. She walked through the corridor, and came across an open doorway that led to another section of the pub.

This place was smaller, with an intimate, lounge feel. Two men were sat by a window that overlooked the harbour and sea. One of them was Jonty Stanforth. The other was Matt Yardley. Rita quickly checked if there was another entrance to the room. There wasn't but the window next to the two men was large, and it was half open, allowing the sea breeze to filter in.

Matt saw them first, turning his head. Rita and Richard advanced. Matt shot up like he had a rocket under him. He grabbed the window sill, and before Rita could even utter a word, he had jumped through the open window. He was a short man, and incredibly agile.

"Stay here," Rita told Richard. She brushed past him, and ran to the front of the pub, where the young lad at the counter gaped as she ran across. She came outside, and saw Rizwan standing in the front beer garden, speaking to a woman. He was taking notes on his phone.

"This way," Rita shouted as she ran past him.

"Suspect escaping on foot."

Rizwan joined her. "He went that way," Rita pointed to the left, where a slope of grassy land led to a road, and beyond that, the harbour.

They saw Matt, running down the road. Rita and Rizwan set off in pursuit. Rizwan was younger and faster. But Matt had the advantage of being ahead already. Rita saw him zoom down the road, which was long and straight. She could see the west pier ahead, with its array of private and commercial boats. Matt jumped over the barrier separating the road from the grass verge. Rita shouted at Rizwan.

"He's making for the harbour. Stop him if you can."

She was pumping her legs as fast as she could, sweat pouring down her face. Rizwan jumped down to the pavement of the road. Up ahead, she saw Matt climbing the fence on the quayside, that separated the boats on the marina from the road. Rizwan couldn't get there on time. He was trying his best, running faster than Rita ever could. She pulled out her radio, and called for support.

Rizwan got to the fence, and started to climb. But Rita couldn't see Matt anymore. He had vanished between the boats, his figure no longer visible between the jetties and masts. She caught up with Rizwan just as he scaled the fence and landed on the other side.

Rita put her hands on the fence railings. It was tall, two metres high, and not easy to climb. She had to jump up to grab the horizontal rail over her head, and then pull herself up in a dead lift. Rizwan had managed it easily, but she struggled. She managed to push up with her feet against the railings, and finally scrambled to the top. She could clamber over the top, but the drop down was suddenly a long way. She closed her eyes and jumped.

There was no grass on the other side, only solid pavement. Her ankles jarred with pain as she landed, and she rolled over. She stood and found she could move. She ran towards the boats. Rizwan veered to the right ahead of her, heading down a jetty with boats bobbing on the water on either side. She heard the roar of a motor engine and her heart sank.

She raced down the jetty, to where Rizwan was standing, hands on his hips. A small motorboat was on the water, with Matt Yardley at the helm. He didn't look back. The motor scythed through the water, and Rita watched in frustration as the boat sped down the harbour, then out of the east pier.

Rita pulled her radio out and asked for switchboard to connect her to HMCG. She gave them a brief update, and the sergeant she spoke to promised to start a search.

"Right," Rita said, her chest still heaving with the effort of the chase, sweat pouring down her forehead. "Let's get back to Jonty."

CHAPTER 19

Richard was waiting in the pub, standing next to Jonty. The harbour-master sat patiently, sipping from his pint. He looked as if nothing had happened and didn't care that Richard was only a few feet away, watching him like a hawk. The window was shut now.

Jonty looked up as Rita and Rizwan walked in. They took a moment to confer in whispers at the end of the room, keeping an eye on him. The old man ignored them and sipped his drink. Richard and Rizwan then left the room. Rita walked over and sat opposite Jonty.

"Now then," Jonty said – the familiar North-East greeting. He stroked his white beard. "Can I go home?"

"Soon," Rita replied. Jonty hadn't tried to escape, and he hadn't called for a solicitor. Richard had already briefed her: Jonty insisted he knew nothing about Matt's dash through the window – in fact, he knew little about Matt at all.

"What happened to the Merigold?" Rita asked.

Jonty shrugged. "It left about three hours ago. The boat's owners wanted their property back. Don't ask me why. You should really be asking Andrew. Where is he, by the way?"

Rita suspected he was trying to deflect. No one could be this calm after observing a friend flee the police.
"He's dead," Rita said, locking eyes with him. That got his attention. The ruddy cheeks paled, eyes widened; he licked his lips.
"He was killed," Rita went on. "We have suspects already, and we'll find out what happened. One suspect is Matt, obviously. You told my sergeant you don't know much about him. If that's true, why were you having lunch together?"
Jonty raised his hands, then lowered them to the table. "I've known all these lads for years. They were fishing with their dads when they were kids. We come from the same villages. I've known Matt, ooh, twenty-five years, I reckon."
"And yet you've no idea why he ran?"
"If he'd told me, I'd be tellin' you now." Jonty wiped his beard with his sleeve. "Hang about – what happened to Andrew, then? How was he killed?"
"I'm asking the questions. Matt is now a suspect in Andrew's murder. So are you, frankly."
The leathery forehead furrowed.
"Eh? What did I do? I was just havin' me lunch. Not my fault if that idiot's up to owt and runs from you lot. What am I meant to do about it?"
"Have you seen Matt and Andrew together?"
"They talk now and then, I suppose. Like the other lads on the quay. I don't keep tabs on them, so I don't know when they last met."

"They were seen arguing in the canteen the day before Andrew died. Now Matt's done a runner, escaping on a boat. The Coastguard's looking for him. Are you still sure you know nothing? Because if you're hiding anything, that won't look good."

Rita withheld the fact that Matt had visited Andrew's house with another man and tried to recruit Andrew into their illicit business. Matt probably realised the CCTV would show him going to Andrew's house – hence his dash.

Jonty reached for his pint, then paused and set his hands in his lap. He stared at the dregs, then out of the window at the sparkling sea.

"I don't know what Matt's up to now," he said quietly. "But that lad's been in bother before. He was a grafter – sold drugs and that. That's what I heard. I knew his dad, from my village up in Ravenscar, so I have a pint with Matt now and then. But he doesn't tell me owt."

"Has Matt ever been in prison?"

"I think he might've. He was gone a couple o' years. Said he'd worked abroad, but rumour was he'd left the country to dodge trouble."

"Who told you that?"

"Word gets round. You know what it's like – or maybe you don't if you're not from round here."

"I am from round here," Rita said. "Grew up near Scalby."

"Aye, that makes sense. Thought I heard some hidden Yorkshire under your southern tongue."

He smiled but Rita did not. The smile faded.

"Who took the Merigold out? I'd ordered that no one touch the boat."

"When the owners come, we've no choice."

"And why did they come? We haven't put anything in the press."

That had bothered Rita the moment she saw the empty berth. Whoever moved the boat clearly knew something had happened to Andrew.

"Who are the owners?"

"Poseidon Ventures. Bloke who drove it off said the boss had ordered him direct, to take the boat now."

"And who's the boss?"

Jonty shook his head. "I don't know."

Rita didn't need him to say it. She already knew the name: Damien Salt.

CHAPTER 20

Poseidon Ventures was housed in a glass and metallic building that suited its grandiose name. It was in an industrial park ten miles south of Scarborough, sandwiched between the town and Eastfield.
Retail giants had warehouses here, with large logos blazoned across the front of the squat, hulking buildings. Poseidon had the only office like structure. The guard at the gate looked bored, but snapped to attention when Richard showed him warrant card.
Rita was on the passenger seat, her eyes scanning the office complex. There was a garden in the front, with a waterfall. Trees lined the courtyard, surrounding the building. It was on three floors. Windows were open on all floors save the ground floor. The scene was calm and tranquil, just as the owners of the complex would want it to be.
Richard parked in the car park and they went inside. A young woman at the reception looked up as they entered. The two guards at the gates watched them in silence. They were burly, with biceps straining at their suit sleeves. More like nightclub bouncers, Rita thought, than office security. That would make sense as well, as Ed Salt, Damien's older brother, had, or used to have, a collection of nightclubs and hotels across the towns of the north east coast.

That was before Rita cracked down on Ed's past, and sent him to jail. Rita knew he was out on bail after a short sentence in the low security HMP Wakefield. But she knew his business empire had crumbled. Rita looked around at the metal shards of the post-modern chandeliers hanging low from the tall ceiling, and the contrasting, expensive white marble of the floor. It seemed like the Salt family had found other ways to make money.

She showed her warrant card to the young woman, whose smile faltered, then became forced.

"I want to see Mr Damien Salt," Rita said. "Please tell him DI Gupta of the NYP needs to see him about a vessel that is under investigation."

"And we know he's in the building," Richard added. Rizwan had already spoken to Damien's secretary, who had confirmed, albeit unwillingly, that her boss was in a meeting at the office.

"Do you have an appointment?" The woman flicked her eyes to Rita.

"No."

"Please take a seat, and I'll be with you in a moment."

"I don't think you understand," Rita said. "This is an urgent matter, and it cannot wait. Which floor does Mr Salt have his office in?"

"Third floor. But you must have an appointment."

"We have tried without success, and we can't wait any longer."

The woman opened her mouth to speak then decided against it. She picked up the receiver of a phone in front of her. Rita moved across the marble floor, towards the lifts on the left. Richard followed. The secretary was on her feet, raising her voice.

"Excuse me, you can't go there."

The guards moved quickly, but Rita and Richard were at the lift doors already. The doors slid open, and they were about to step inside, when a big hand landed on the dial, stopping the doors from closing. Rita sized up the two guards, who dwarfed Richard and herself in size.

One of them was slightly taller than the other. His cheeks were puffy with what Rita suspected might be overuse of steroids. His small, beady blue eyes flicked from Rita to Richard.

"No one's allowed upstairs without permission."

"I don't need permission to arrest you." Rita reached behind into her pockets and pulled out a pair of handcuffs. "For blocking a murder investigation." She dangled the handcuffs in the man's face. "Would you like that?"

The man stared at her, then to his colleague, standing behind Richard.

Rita said, "More forces will arrive as soon as we call them." She glanced at Richard. "Radio?"

Richard pulled out his radio and twirled the black knob on the top to the right. The sound of static filled the silence.

Rita looked pointedly at the muscle-bound gimp facing her. His barrel chest was heaving, and the collar of his tight shirt was digging into his neck.

Rita said, "You've got two choices. Let us go upstairs and speak to your boss. Or explain to your boss how you created an emergency situation, got arrested, and got reported in the media as well."

The man cleared his throat. "You've got no right to arrest us. We've not done anything wrong. It's you who's treapassing."

"Yeah," his colleague drawled. "We're just doin' our job, innit?"

"So are we," Rita said. "At the moment, you're actively impeding a murder investigation. We have a right to question the suspects. But you're stopping us. Hence, we have the right to arrest you."

The men looked at each other again, and the guard didn't move his hand from the dial on the wall.

Rita grabbed the hands of the man in front of her. He flung her away easily, and Richard spoke on his radio.

"All units alert. Serious incident at Stonehouse Industrial Estate, Poseidon Ventures building. Police officer assaulted. Repeat –

"Mate, let them go," the man behind them said. He removed his hand from the dial. Rita glared at the man facing her, who had backed off. He pulled out a phone and spoke on it. Richard pulled Rita inside the lift, and pressed the button for the third floor.

CHAPTER 21

A woman was waiting for them upstairs. She was older, her hair grey and white, with nervous eyes behind her glasses.
"Sorry, who are you?"
Rita showed her warrant card. The woman blinked as she looked at the card closely. She wrung her hands together.
"My name's Jackie, I'm Mr Salt's secretary." Her voice became firm. "What do you want?"
"We need to see Mr Salt. Right now." Rita had enough. She pushed past Jackie. The carpet was nice and deep, her feet sinking into the warm pile. Tasteful modern art hung on the walls. Jackie tried to keep up with Rita, but she was faster.
Damien Salt's door had his name in silver letters, with CEO engraved under it. Rita rapped her knuckles on the door, loudly. When there was no answer, she turned the handle. It was open.
The office was spacious, with a glass wall behind the desk, that looked out to the green land beyond. A slim man with short blond hair sat at the desk. He wore a navy-blue shirt, crisply pressed. He removed the glasses from his eyes. A handsome man, Rita noted, with sharp green eyes and high cheek bones. She could see the resemblance with his older brother.
Damien Salt stood, an inquisitive expression on his face. "Are you the police inspector who was demanding to see me?"

His manner seemed to suggest he was astonished by Rita's temerity. He couldn't believe someone like Rita would have the guts to walk into his office. Rita walked forward till she was face to face with him, separated by the table. Damien's green eyes searched her face, then slid to Richard, who stood behind her.
"Yes, I am. I need a few minutes of your time, and it cannot wait."
Rita kept her voice steady, but it wasn't easy for her. Now that she was here, in front of Ed's brother, dark shadows had separated from the dungeons of her mind, and floated up her spine. Grim memories were reaching long, rakish fingers into her heart, spilling blood.
She took a breath to ground herself, exhaling slightly. She sat down without being invited. She gestured for Richard to do the same.
Damien stared at her, and a shot of irritation creased his forehead. He sat down slowly, then pressed a button on the desk. A lock clicked on the door.
Rita got straight to the point. "Your company owns the fishing trawler called Merigold. It was leased to Mr Andrew Salford. Is that correct?"
Damien's eyebrows lifted. "We have many boats, Inspector…
"Gupta."
"Thank you. We're a large organisation, Inspector Gupta. It's not possible for me to be aware of all the lease holders."
His accent was southern, polished home counties. "May I ask what this is about?"

"Mr Salford was found dead yesterday. His death is being regarded as suspicious." Rita watched Damien closely. He remained silent. Not a muscle twitched on his face.

"His boat, the Merigold, is a crime scene, and needs to be investigated. However, before we could complete our investigation, the boat was driven out of the harbour this morning. Apparently, the order came from you."

Damien stared at Rita like she had two heads.

"Excuse me? I gave the order to have a boat removed from the harbour? Which harbour, exactly?" He raised a hand before Rita could reply. "I haven't given any such order, in any case. As I mentioned, I do not get involved in the minutiae of the business. My management team do."

"Well, someone in your organisation drove the boat out this morning. Who was it? If you didn't give the order, you must be able to find out who did so?"

Damien shook his head once, then waved his hand like he was trying to get rid of a fly on his nose.

"Yes, I suppose I can. But why would I need to? We often need to tow boats back to the yard for maintenance, and sometimes we sadly have to even repossess boats when the lease holder cannot keep up with the payments. We have hundreds of boats, up and down the coastline, in various harbours. I really couldn't tell you what happened to this particular boat."

That was a good answer, Rita thought. Damien was as sly as his brother. Flies wouldn't slip on his marble smooth cheeks. If Andrew Salford, the victim, had money trouble there was every chance he had missed his monthly lease payments.

Damien senses Rita's hesitation. "So, as you can see, you've been misinformed. I personally didn't order any boat to get towed out of Scarborough." He spread his hands, and an arrogant smile touched the corner of his lips. "I'm afraid you wasted your journey."

Rita pulled out her phone, and scrolled to the document that Rizwan had sent her. It was the lease that Andrew had signed with PV. She handed her phone to Damien, who looked through it briefly. Rita took her phone back. Damien shrugged.

"I guess you knew that already. It doesn't change anything, does it?"

"It proves that Andrew Salford signed the lease and so did you. That's your signature next to his, correct?"

"Yes," Damien said slowly, like he was speaking to a child. "So what? Many of these documents have my signature, and many of these boats are inspected by our team of engineers. I suspect that's what happened in this case."

"Andrew Salford is dead. He was murdered, and his body was discovered yesterday."

That wiped the smile out of Damien's face. Rita said, "And the day after, one of your men take his boat back, when I gave orders not to do so. Can you see the problem here?"

Damien recovered his composure. "If you want to see the boat again, that's not a problem."

"Yes, we would. I also want you to check Mr Salford's file. Not later, but now, please."

Damien opened his mouth to say something then seemed to think the better of it. His lips pressed firmly together and he clicked on the wireless keyboard on his desk. The screen to his left came alive, but Rita couldn't see it well. Damien stared at the screen, then nodded.

"Yes, I have his account here. Would you like me to send you the details?"

"Yes please." She turned to Richard, who gave Damien the CID email address.

"He hadn't paid three months lease," Damien said. "That could be the reason why his boat was repossessed." His eyes narrowed. "I hope you can see there's no other connection between us and Mr Salford."

Rita felt a touch deflated. The boat would now be wiped clean of all the evidence she wanted. And Damien had his defence ready. But she wasn't letting him go that easily.

"The Merigold had state of the art, maritime surveillance equipment. It had a radar, an ultrasound sonar system, equipment not normally found in a fishing trawler. Do you know why that might be the case?"

Damien shook his head slowly. "What the leaseholder does with their boat is not our concern. When the lease expires, we want the boat back in its original condition. That is all."

He had an answer for everything, but Rita could see her last question had rattled him. His teeth ground together, and his nostrils flared. She stared back at him, letting the silence stretch out.

"You've got a lot of boats, haven't you, Mr Salt? From the Teeside harbours in the north, to Hull and Immingham in the Lincolnshire coast."

"Yes, and?" Damien inclined his head, looking askance at Rita.

"Nothing. It's just that the coastguards have seen a lot of maritime activity at night, up and down that north eastern coastline. I wondered if you knew why."

"I'm sorry Inspector, I have no idea. You need to ask the Coastguards. Look, I'm sorry Mr Salford has died, but it has nothing to do with us. I will send you the details of how to examine the vessel at the boatyard. Now, if you'll please excuse me, I have a meeting to attend."

He stood, indicating the meeting was over. But his earlier smoothness now had cracks in it, and they were growing. There was an urgency in his movements. He clicked the remote on his desk, and the lock snapped back. He walked to the door and held it open.

Rita paused on the doorway and looked back at him. "Please don't leave this area. I want to speak to you again." She gave him a stare and he met it without flinching. He nodded once.

***

Damien shut the door after Rita left and made sure it was locked. He glanced at the small TV screen next to the door, which showed the CCTV camera screen. He watched Rita and Richard get into the lift.

He walked to his drawer and pulled out a fob key. He removed a picture frame from the wall. There was a safe behind it, recessed into the wall. He pressed the fob key against the digital keypad and the metal door swung open. Inside, there was a collection of passports, bundles of bank notes, and three phones. He took a phone out, then locked the safe, and put the picture frame back. He turned the phone on and rang a number.

A male voice answered. It was his brother, Edward. "All okay?"

"No. That detective Rita Gupta was back here."

"What? She came to your office? Why?"

"A fisherman's dead. We used him. I got the boat back in time, luckily. But she's sniffing around."

Ed swore under his breath. "I thought if I retired, she might leave us alone. Looks like I was wrong. How did this fisherman die?"

"I'm looking into it now. It doesn't look good. A gang land revenge killing, I think. I'm going to make the killer disappear, and hopefully this will die down."

Ed was silent for a while. "Does she know about us?"

"Yes, I think so. I saw it in the way she looked at me." Damien swore. "I could rip her head off. That bitch. Can't believe she's come back."

"You need to stay in control. Don't fall for her pressure tactics. That's what she wants."

"I know." Damien was silent for a few seconds. "We need to sort her out once and for all. She can't keep coming back like this."

"Yes." Ed sighed. "Okay. Listen to me carefully."

CHAPTER 22

"Apples don't fall far from the tree, guv, do they?" Richard said, as they drove towards the boatyard in Bridlington. "The man's as slimy as his brother."
"Yes," Rita stared out of the window. The green hills dipped and rose, the blue sea winking in between. The sun was out and the sky was suddenly spotless, the North Sea weather having changed in the blink of an eye.
Rita's mind was churning. She pulled out her phone and called Rizwan. "Did Shola take photos of the equipment in the Merigold?"

Rizwan's voice crackled over the loudspeaker on the dashboard. "Yes, guv."

"Track down the manufacturer and see if you can get receipts for the sale. They should all be digital. I don't think we'll get anything from the boat now; it's going to be scrubbed clean."

"Do you want me to meet you at the boatyard?"

"No. Richard and I can manage. You stay there and coordinate the search for Matt. Any sign of his boat?"

"HMCG are on the case. They haven't seen the boat yet. That means he's probably gone to a wild beach nearby. They're mostly rocky coves around here, and they're dangerous when the tide's up. But he'll know a spot, being local. If he's done that it might be tough to find him, guv."

"Tell HMCG to keep looking. Put out an APB with his name and photo. He can't get far without someone spotting him."

"I'll do it now."
"And put a squad car outside Melanie's house. I want her safe. Anything more from the door-to-door in Filey? Or any CCTV footage?"
"Nothing from uniforms so far. No one's been up to Runswick Bay, where Melanie and Andrew lived before they moved to Filey. I'll sort that out—don't worry. I'll also speak to Melanie."
"Good. We'll see you back at the nick soon."
Bridlington town soon came into view as they descended from the hills. It was a beautiful town nestled in its own bay. Personally, Rita loved the tiny village of Flamborough. Angela, her mother's best friend, had a cottage there, and Rita remembered spending many summers at the rocky-yet-sandy beach where the waters were calmer than elsewhere. But Rita also liked Bridlington. It hadn't become run down like Scarborough had.

Richard drove through Bridlington, heading for the harbour. Bridlington felt more up-market than Scarborough; the council had spent more on its upkeep, and the Spa drew tourists all year. The town also had a thriving local market and artisanal centre. They found the boatyard with some effort—near the lighthouse on the sea-front, not in the harbour as Poseidon Ventures' secretary had claimed.

The warehouse in front of the jetty was busy, men working on boats. Richard spoke to a man in greasy overalls, who pointed to another inspecting an engine. "Hello, are you the manager?" Richard asked, showing his warrant card. The man wiped his hands on a rag, inspected the card, and nodded warily. He was a tall, big man and something about his watchful eyes bothered Rita. He spoke softly.

"Yes, the boss told us you were coming. This is about the boat we got from Scarborough this morning, right?"

"Yes. We need to see it." Rita observed the man. "What's your name?"

The man hesitated for a while. "David."

"Ok, David. Show us the Merigold, please."

They followed him into a quieter section. Larger, newer boats stood on hoists. The manager led them to the Merigold, now up on a platform. He went up the steps and stood aside, but did not leave. Rita accepted Richard's hand and stepped aboard, then glanced down.

"Could you give us some privacy? We'll see you downstairs."

Reluctantly, he descended. Rita and Richard donned gloves and shoe-covers. The equipment Shola had photographed was all present—Rita scolded herself for overlooking it earlier. She tried the engine, but there was no power.

Below deck, on all fours, she and Richard thumped every plank, listening for hollows. After half an hour they had covered the floor. Rita, sweating, wiped her forehead.

"If there was anything under the floorboards, it's gone now. These boards are solid."

Richard, still kneeling with the drill, tried a screw. "These boards are new, guv. Look at the layout—vertical, not the horizontal planks we saw last time. And the pieces are smaller."

"Yes, I see," Rita muttered, teeth clenched. "Let's take swabs for fingerprints. I want to know if the engineers show up on IDENT-1."

She went to the railings and looked down.

David, the manager was talking to some workmen; they glanced up. Rita descended to confront him. The knot of men melted away, leaving David alone. He had that same cautious look in his eyes, and something told Rita this man was dangerous.

She couldn't put a finger on it, but she wondered if he had trouble with the law in the past.

"The deck boards have been replaced," she said. "When was that done?"

"Not sure. They were worn out and needed changing. The boat's being refurbished for sale later on."

"That boat is not being sold," Rita said, stepping closer. "It belonged to a murdered man and it's a crime scene. Understand?" Her eyes blazed at David, who gulped and blinked a few times.

"Really?"

"Yes, really. My team will be back to examine the vessel. If it's sold before they arrive, you will be arrested. Are we clear?"

David nodded slowly as if he was digesting the information.

CHAPTER 23

Ruth Hodgson heard the ticking of the clock on the wall. Apart from her own breathing, it was the only sound. The armchair she sat in was deep, and she could smell the faint trace of leather upholstery. Opposite her, the man sat still and relaxed. He wore a shirt without a tie. His eyes were fixed on her, but Ruth wasn't looking at him.

"I need to make amends," Ruth said. "I can't live otherwise." She saw the psychiatrist stir. Dr Patel was his name. She trusted him. He had been there from day one, and he was the only one she trusted—apart from her mother. Sometimes more than her mother, because after what had happened she felt their bond had weakened. Ruth couldn't blame her mother for that.

She spoke quickly, aware of what her words signified. "I didn't mean it like that. I mean I'd find it very hard to live my life without making amends."

She saw Vik relax. That was his name, Vikram Patel. He insisted she call him by his first name. They met twice a week in his Scarborough Hospital office.

"So, you don't have suicidal thoughts?"

"No."

"How about self-harm? Have you cut yourself recently?"

"Not for the last three months."

Ruth now had the strength to look down at her wrists, at the old scars that ran like lines on a page. Once, that pain had numbed the poison inside her. The pain of the knife had stilled her screams. She didn't hear those screams any more; they didn't possess her. She felt like a new woman. She lifted her eyes to the sunbeams slanting through the windows.

She lifted her bare ankles—she had come in slippers; the weather was mild enough for the ride in the car. Her ankles also bore scars, and they too were old.

"See?" she said. Vik nodded.

"Thank you. You know what to do if the thoughts come back?"

"Talk to my mother and call you."

"Exactly. Don't keep the thoughts running in your head."

Ruth was quiet for a while. The clock ticked away, barely audible, like water melting from an ice cube. Time had faded for her, dissolving into nothing, taking the darkness with it.

"I want to make amends," she repeated.

"What does that mean?" Vik was staring at her, but Ruth closed her eyes.

"I've been back to the place where it happened," she said softly. "I go there often now. I walk up and down. Yesterday I drove along the road following the sea. I think I know what happened."

She could feel Vik's discomfort. He said, "How often do you go there?"

"Daily." She looked at him then. "You told me to face my fears when I was strong enough."

"Yes," Vik said slowly. "And you feel strong now?"
"You know that."
"It's for you to know, and feel. You will know when the time is right."
"That's why I'm telling you. The time has come for me to go back there and find out what happened."
Vik sighed. "There's a problem there. You'll have to get specialist help. It's not something you can do alone. Do you know someone who can help?"
"My uncle knows the currents and tides well. He used to be a fisherman. He's older now, but yes, he'll help."
Vik stared at her for a while. A gentle, benevolent gaze, but she knew he was still assessing her. His voice was soft when he spoke.
"What do you think happened?"
"You know." She glanced at him and, this time, held his gaze.
"Tell me again. From the beginning."
She did. It wasn't easy. Flashes of the screaming, the pain, the knife-like slashes of torture came and went like images in the shutter of a clicking camera. Then she was silent, her breath like the waves of the North Sea at low tide—slowly in, slowly out. She felt much calmer when she controlled her breathing. Prāṇāyāma yoga: her mother practised it and Vik had reinforced it. Her breaths controlled her soul now. She felt in balance with her inner core. It wasn't wishy-washy rubbish; she actually felt it. She could bear the pain. But the immense sadness remained—the knowledge of what she had endured. Tears blurred her eyes; she sniffed and wiped them away.

She was glad Vik didn't speak. She took her time to compose herself. Then Vik said, "They never found it, though, did they? I know they looked everywhere."
"I know. But I also know that she's alive."
That got Vik's attention. A frown creased his forehead and his spine stiffened. "How do you know that?"

"Someone told me."

CHAPTER 24

Rita was exhausted by the time she got back. The sun was leaning on the horizon, tired like her. A golden shimmer flowed from the melting sun into the sea, turning the dark blue waters into sparkles of orange and gold. Rita watched out the window as Richard drove. Her mind moved from the Merigold, to Damien, then to his brother, Ed. Finally, her thoughts cloistered on Clara, her mother.

Edward Salt had been Clara's lover once, and he had ruined her life. Not just him, but also two other evil men, both of when were now behind bars. Edward got off with a lighter sentence, his historical crimes were harder to prove. He had moved out of Scarborough, and she knew the Salt family had homes dotted around the North East.

She had heard from an officer colleague in Harrogate that he was living there with his family. Rita felt the bitter bile rise in her throat. The burning resentment she felt against Edward for getting away scot free would never abate. He should spend his life behind bars for what he had done to Clara.

What he and his friends did to her.

Motherless from the age of eleven.

Her father had gone years before that. The succession of care homes.

Angela had looked after her the best she could. Rita had been one of the lucky ones. She didn't have a bad foster parent. The last couple were elderly and childless – and they treated her like their own daughter. But she would always miss Clara. The mother taken away from her by men like Edward Salt. Rita closed her eyes, the memories washing over her like sea water over rocks, the saline stinging the old wounds that never died.

She forced her mind to the investigation. Damien had been evasive. She felt it in her bones. He couldn't wait to get rid of her. And the Merigold had been tampered with. There was also no doubt about that. Rita called Shola, and the head of forensics answered.

"You're lucky you caught me. I'm on my way out of the office."

"This won't take long. The Merigold was driven out of the harbour this morning, despite my orders. It's now in a boat yard in Bridlington. The owners have tampered with it and in my opinion, removed valuable evidence."

"Given the state-of-the-art surveillance gear on that boat," Shola said, "there's a high chance there was more on that boat than we found. I think you're right."

"What was all that gear for? They were looking for something out at sea, right?" Rita frowned as a thought struck her. "Do you think they were sailing without any lights so HMCG couldn't watch them."

"HMCG can still track the larger vessels with radar. I think the Merigold was looking for other boats, and maybe something in the water."

"Like what? It can't be big fish, for that they need to go really far out in the ocean."
"Aye. I don't know. Your job to figure out, innit?"
Rita felt Shola smile. "Anyway, chuck," Shola said, "I'll send Henry and Emily out tomorrow first thing to check the boat. Not that we'll find much, from what you're saying."
"We might get some fingerprints of the engineers. Worth a try."
"No worries. See ya. Don't work too hard."
"Enjoy your evening."
Rita hung up and rested her head back on the seat. She rang Rizwan. "Any sign of Matt?"
"Not as yet, guv," Rizwan's voice crackled on the radio. "I spoke to Melanie though. Do you want to see her?"
"It's going to have to wait till tomorrow. See you soon."
It was half six in the evening by the time Rita and Richard got back. Rizwan wasn't in the office, but he returned with a smile on his face and waving a pencil storage disk.
"Uniforms found Andrew Salford's car. It's a little Fiat, and it's worn out with use. It was locked so they broke into it. There was nothing inside, they checked under the chassis as well. The car's now in the forensic garage, and they'll let us know if they find anything."
"Excellent," Rita said. "There was nothing in the dashboard? No hidden compartment under the seats, or in the wheel well in the boot?"

Rizwan shook his head. "Nowt. They were thorough. I've got the photos here." He opened up his laptop and showed Rita and Richard the images – the car was indeed a rust bucket, ready for the scrap heap. Uniforms had taken apart the seats, and the cavities underneath only had old springs, normal for car seats. The photos showed a thorough check, and Rita knew the car didn't have any visible secrets.

"Time for this now," Rizwan said, holding up the pencil disk. He inserted the disk into his laptop, and Rita sat down next to him.

The CCTV footage was from the Filey and Eastfield Police Station, Rizwan explained.

"The street where Melanie lives doesn't have any CCTV, unfortunately. But the main road outside her house does. We have footage from there. A car registered to Matt Yardley was seen coming out of her street on 12th December, last year."

Rizwan played the CCTV, and they saw the car. It was a black Ford Fiesta. The car moved down the main road, and the cameras tracked it till reached the A165, the large artery that connected many of the coastal towns in the north east.

"Matt's not at home by the way. He lives with his girlfriend, and she doesn't know where he is," Rizwan said.

"Where does he live?"

"Watch," Rizwan pointed a finger at the screen. They saw the car take the exit for a small village called Gristhorpe. It was on the way up north towards Scarborough, from Filey. Rita had never heard of it.

They caught up with the car again as Matt parked up outside his house. It was a bungalow, and lights were on inside. Although Gristhorpe was even smaller than Filey, Matt lived next to the A165, and the cameras there picked up his house and car. The tall man got out of the car and stepped into his own vehicle parked on the road. Rizwan froze the screen and they zoomed into his face.

The man had a beard and he wore a hoodie, so his features weren't easily visible. Rita frowned.

"Stop the tape. Show him from another angle."

The other angles didn't give a good view of the man's face. But for some reason, he looked familiar to Rita.

He got into his car, and drove off. CCTV had picked the car's registration through ANPR, and tracked him again. Rizwan speeded up the tape, and the car moved to Bridlington. It parked in the Sea Front, and Rita recognised the boatyard she and Richard had visited earlier. The name – Bridlington Chandlery and Boat Engineering, was written in big yellow letters across the front. The man got out of the car and went inside, although it was late at night. He had keys to a side gate next to the massive doors of the warehouse.

As Rita watched the man, she suddenly realised where she had seen him.

"He's the main engineer at the boatyard. The man we saw this afternoon," she exclaimed. She looked at Richard, who was still fixed on the screen.

"David," Rita whispered. "That's his name."

Richard nodded slowly and glanced at her.

"I think you're right, guv."

CHAPTER 25

Melanie Salford was putting Carla to sleep. The toddler was unusually quiet and Melanie's heart ached with sorrow. Carla missed her dad. Melanie didn't know what to do about it.
She had told Carla daddy's not coming back, and Carla didn't understand. Her question had made Melanie weep, which Carla didn't understand. Then she too, was upset.
"Why isn't he coming back?"
"I don't know."
There was no way she could tell Carla what happened. Maybe one day, the little one would understand. Melanie had also made up her mind to leave Filey. She had only settled here because of Andrew. Life in Runswick Bay left a lot to be desired. It was far and remote. At least here they were between the towns of Scarborough and Bridlington. Bridlington was better for shopping and days out with Carla. But their time here was now at an end. Melanie had spoken to her mother. They would move up to Edinburgh, at least for a while. Mel needed support with Carla. Besides, she didn't feel safe out here anymore.

Melanie read Carla her night time story, and the toddler held her mother's hand tightly. As Carla's eyelids fluttered shut with sleep, Melanie went on reading. Then the grip of her little fingers loosened, and the baby was fast asleep. Melanie never tired of looking at her sweet baby's face. She was the picture of cuteness. Perfect in every way. She would do anything for Carla.

Melanie kissed Carla's cheek softly, then pulled the blanket over her. She made sure the windows were shut, then pulled the curtains back. She set the toy camera next to the small bed, then shut the door softly.

It was then that she heard the noise. It sounded like a door being opened.

Melanie froze. It came from downstairs. They lived in a terraced house, two up and two down. The kitchen was at the rear extension, at the back. Had she locked the kitchen door that led to the garden? She never used to, but since Andrew started doing his new job, she had grown more careful.

She crept down the stairs. The front door was shut and locked, like she'd left it. Melanie strained her ears, but she couldn't hear anything else. She went down two more steps. She couldn't hear anything more.

She felt for her phone. She took it out of the back pocket. She had spoken to the detective constable, Rizwan Ahmed, earlier today. He said a patrol car would be around her house, keeping an eye. Melanie hadn't seen the car.

She came into the landing, phone in her hand. She pressed 999 and kept a finger on the green call button. She would press it at the first sight of danger.

The narrow landing and the front door looked fine. Lights were on in the kitchen as well, where she'd heard the sound. She thought of calling her friend, Sarah. But she didn't want to alarm her. She crept down the hallway. The lounge door was open, as was the dining room door behind it. The kitchen was empty. The back door to the garden was shut, the key dangling where she had left it, on the latch.

Melanie relaxed. She'd heard a car, maybe. Or one of her neighbours in the garden. As the houses were terraced, all the properties shared walls on either side. Yes, her mind was playing tricks on her.

She went into the lounge and made sure the windows were locked. They were, and she pulled the curtains close. Then she went into the dining room at the back. The lights were on, and the dining table was as she had left it.

She stepped inside. A hand clamped over her face, curling round from behind. Her head was thrust back and the hand was strong, suffocating her. She smelt stale sweat on the fingers. Fear bulged in her chest and she tried to scream, but only a muffled shout came from her mouth closed by the fingers.

"Be quiet," a man's voice growled in her throat. "If you make a sound I'm going to hurt you."

CHAPTER 26

The grip tightened around her mouth. Melanie couldn't breathe. She squirmed trying to get free. The man had been hiding behind the door. She cursed herself for not checking the kitchen door first. That had to be the way he came in. Her phone had fallen on the ground, and she couldn't see it.

"Did you hear what I said?" the man growled again. "Nod if you want to say yes."

Melanie did so. The man said, "If you don't listen to me, things will turn bad. I know your daughter's upstairs."

Melanie stopped moving. "That's better," the man said. His grip on her face loosened a fraction.

"If you move, I'll slit your throat, then take your little girl. Got that?" Melanie nodded, her heart pumping, bile rising in her throat. The man kept hold of her, but he was trying to get something out from his pocket. Soon, Melanie felt his other hand back on her wrists, and she felt the touch of something else. A rope?

"I'm going to let go of your mouth. Scream, or shout, and your daughter will be gone. Do you understand?"

Melanie nodded. The man's hand moved from her face. Swiftly, he pushed her forward a fraction, then she felt the rope sliding over her hands. She whimpered with pain as the tight knot burned into her wrists.

"I don't have any money," she whispered. "Please leave my child and me alone."

The man didn't answer. He finished tying her hands, then she felt a piece of cloth go around her mouth. He tightened it, then turned her around. For the first time, Melanie saw her attacker and she gasped as fear slammed against her spine. He was wearing a mask, and she could only see his eyes and mouth.

"Make a sound and you're dead," the man said. She didn't recognise him, but the voice sounded familiar. "I'm going to lower the gag so you can speak. Don't raise your voice."

Melanie nodded, shivering with panic. She took in a deep breath when the gag loosened.

"Where did Andrew hide the gear?" The man's lips moved as his eyes stared at her without blinking. It was a strange, fearful sight.

"I…what gear are you talking about?"

"Don't play games with me," the man said between clenched teeth. "The gear he collected when he was out at sea. It was in the boat, but its not there anymore. It will be in at least two bags. Big duffel bags. Where has he hidden them?"

"I haven't seen them," Melanie couldn't stop her voice from shaking. "Honestly, I don't know." She stifled a scream of horror as the man gripped her throat and pushed her against the wall.

"Don't lie to me, you bitch. I've checked the garden shed already. It's not there. Has he dug a hole in the garden? Have you seen him do that?"

Melanie tried to think, forcing her frozen mind to work. "N…No. I haven't seen him digging. He's not a gardener."

The man stared at her, then he blinked once. "He got those bags inside the house. You must've seen them. Tell me where they are."

His accent was northern and local. Suddenly, through the fog of terror, Melanie knew where she'd heard that voice. It was the big man who came to see Andrew. The guy who came with Matt.

She gasped. "I don't know. I've not seen him with the bags. But then, he comes home when I'm sleeping. If he's put them somewhere I don't know."

The man thought about this. "Where are the hiding places in your house?"

"There are none. It's a small house. I...I don't know."

The man gripped her throat again, and his face pressed close to hers. She could smell the cigarettes on his breath, and the sweat. It was nauseating.

"Don't. Lie. To. Me."

"Honestly, I-

"Shut up," the man hissed. "Do you want to see his daughter die?"

"No, please, no. I'll do anything. Please don't-

"Then tell me. Where could Andy have hidden two big bags?"

Melanie tried to think as fast as she could. "There's a loft. You could try there."

"What about the floorboards? Have the carpets been lifted recently?"

"No. Not that I know of."

"What about the wardrobes and cupboards? Any hidden space behind them?"

"No. This place isn't big, there isn't much space here."

The man considered that. Then he tied the gag tight around her mouth. He sat her down, then tied her ankles together.

"Sit still and don't make a sound." He rummaged around on the floor, then found her phone. "I'll keep this." He put the phone in his pocket. He frisked her once, quickly and efficiently. Then he went out, and shut the door behind him.

Melanie heard him go into the kitchen. He was quiet, she had to give him that. Maybe he didn't want to alarm the neighbours, or wake up Carla. She heard him knocking on wood, and moving around. Then she heard a drill, and the sound of screws being removed. He moved through the ground floor., checking everywhere. Her heart sank as she heard him go upstairs.

Panic mushroomed in her belly. She threw caution to the wind as her maternal instincts took over. She squirmed and crawled on her belly, the best she could. She got to the door, and shimmied up the wall, grunting with the effort. She tried to open the door, but it was impossible with her hands tied behind her back. She turned, and tried to use her hands to depress the handle. Her hands kept slipping.

She could hear the man upstairs, opening and closing drawers. Her heart froze with fear when she heard him step across the landing, to Clara's room. He was going in there. What if Clara woke up?

Adrenaline spiked in her veins. Her hands moved feverishly, and she was able to depress the handle and open the door. She wanted to shout, but she had the gag in her mouth. She fell to her knees, then crashed on the floor. Tears sprouted in her eyes.

She heard steps again, but they were at the front door. Then there was a loud knock.

CHAPTER 27

Melanie couldn't speak due to the gag on her mouth. She leaned her back against the staircase and pushed herself upright. Her ankles were also tied. She couldn't move very well. But the ties around her ankle were looser than those around her wrists. She could take baby steps. Frustration, and anger, mounted inside her as she shuffled her way. The knocking came again, louder this time.
The sounds upstairs had stopped. Melanie knew the man had also heard the knocking. Through the glass panel on the front door, Melanie could see a man's shape. But the man had a cap on his head…could this be the police? With renewed strength, Melanie forced her legs to move. She was close to the door when she heard steps charging downstairs. She flinched as the man rushed down the stairs. He brushed past her. She caught a terrifying glimpse of his masked face. Then he was gone, through the kitchen back door, into the garden.
Tears bloomed in Melanie's eyes. Somehow, she managed to get to the door. But she couldn't open it easily. By now, the man outside had realised something was happening. Melanie heard him call out her name.
"Mrs Salford? Are you okay?"

Melanie mumbled, then kicked the door with her foot. There was a knocking on the lounge window, but Melanie couldn't reach it, there was a wall between her and the lounge. She tried her best to jiggle the keys in the lock. But it was incredibly difficult with her hands tied around her back.

Then she heard a sound at the rear again, and shrank back in fear. The back kitchen door was opening again. Panic surged in her chest, but then a uniformed policeman wearing a chest rig and peaked black cap entered. He rushed to her. Melanie fell to the floor. The man worked quickly, removing the gag from her mouth, and freeing her legs. He opened the front door and a policewoman stepped inside. She was already speaking on her radio, asking for back up.

"My daughter," Melanie sobbed. "Please check on her. Help me upstairs."

As soon as her hands and legs were free, Melanie ran upstairs. The policewoman came with her. The door to Carla's room was wide open and Melanie gasped. She turned the light on in the landing, and crept inside.

Her heart was hammering wildly, a freezing fear claiming her limbs. She could barely move as she approached the small bed, her eyes getting used to the dark. She heaved a sigh of relief, and fell to her knees when she saw the little shape on the bed. Carla was there. Incredibly, the child had slept through all the commotion.

Melanie rested a hand on the blanket, feeling Carla's warmth. Tears ran down her eyes. She was alone, the policewoman was checking the other rooms. Melanie checked Carla quickly. The child was unharmed and alright. She stirred as Melanie stroked her head once, then went back to sleep. Melanie made sure the window was shut. The man had been here. He had pulled the drawer from under the bed and flung the clothes out. The desk drawers had also been opened. The policewoman came in. She had a torchlight which she turned off.

"Is your child alright?" she whispered.

"Yes, thank god," Melanie whispered back. "He was here, as you can see. The man who attacked and tied me up."

"Let's go downstairs where we can talk."

When they were outside and the door was closed, the policewoman said, "Your child will be fine, don't worry. I'm sorry we were late. We had orders to check on you earlier. From now there will be a permanent patrol in front and behind your house."

They went downstairs. Two more policemen had arrived. Blue and white flashlights were revolving in a patrol car outside.

"Please turn that off," Melanie said. "I don't want my neighbours to get alarmed."

"No problem." The policewoman spoke to her colleague. Then the two of them sat down with Melanie in the lounge. Melanie made sure the little remote TV was working, which showed Carla sleeping upstairs. The tiny screen was dark, but Carla's outline was visible and her breathing was audible.

"Tell us what happened," the policeman said. They were both uniformed officers. Melanie hadn't seen them before. She wrapped her arms around herself as if in protection, and told them.

"You didn't lock the kitchen back door when you went up?" The female officer asked.

"No. That was a mistake."

"Not your fault," the woman reassured her. "Most people keep the back door unlocked. You weren't to know. But be more careful in the future."

There was a knock on the door, and her friend and neighbour, Sarah came in. Melanie got up and hugged her, then they sat down close to each other.

"Did you recognise the man?" The male officer asked.

Melanie froze. Her eyes closed as she cradled her head in her hands. Sarah's comforting arm rested on her shoulder.

"Yes," Melanie whispered. She didn't want this to look bad on Andrew, but he was no more. There was nothing here for her and Carla anymore.

"It was the man who came to our house once, with Andy's friend, Matt Yardley. I don't know his name. But I recognised his voice. I think so, anyway."

"How many times did you see him?"

Melanie thought for a while. "Three times, I think, in total. Once he stood outside and spoke to Andy. The other times he came in. He never spoke to me. But I heard his voice when they talked here, in this room."

"We need to treat this area as a crime scene. We need to take fingerprints." The woman's voice was gentle. "Is there somewhere you can stay for a couple of days?"

Melanie's head sank, but she also thought it might not be bad to be able to leave this house. Yes, it was her home. But the memories had rusted like the hull of a derelict boat. Melanie needed to get out of here.

"You can stay with me," Sarah said. "I live next door," she said to the police officers, who nodded. Sarah gripped Melanie's hand. "It's alright, love. No problem. Bryn can live in his flat for a few days." Bryn was Sarah's partner, but he had his own place.

"Are you sure?" Melanie asked.

"Positive."

The policewoman said, "That would be great for us to collect evidence. Instead of a week, we could finish up in less than two days." She glanced at her partner, who nodded.

The policeman asked, "Do you know what the man was looking for? He clearly searched your house, didn't he?"

"I don't know what he was looking for, but yes he did search. He had checked in the shed, and also in the garden."

"And you never saw your husband hiding anything, or acting suspiciously?"

Melanie now noticed the two police officers watching her closely. There was a slight shift in their attitude. A new tension in their eyes as they stared at her.

"No, of course not. Again, I would've noticed something like that. Our house is small. He had to keep them in the hallway outside. I would've asked him to move it. Unless he kept the bags in his car. That's possible."

The policewoman nodded, and they both made notes. "Do you mind if we have a look in the garden?" The male officer asked. Melanie agreed. When they left, she turned to Sarah.

"I can't stay here anymore," Melanie said. "These people can come back again.

"Come and stay with me. Honestly. For as long as you like."

"I can stay with you, but only for a while," Melanie shook her head. She wiped her face and sniffed. "I need to keep Carla safe. I can't live here anymore."

CHAPTER 28

Rita was back at home, sitting with her feet up on the lounge, cradling a glass of wine in her hand. She didn't have any dinner, and didn't feel like it. The demons of her past had been let loose, and she'd lost her appetite. She kept wondering if this was a coincidence. She thought she'd seen the last of the Salt family, but she'd been wrong. Edward might have gone from Scarborough, but his brother remained. And with Damien, Rita felt Edward malevolent presence.
She suspected Edward was still active in the businesses the family ran – shipping, fishing, real estate – but now he stayed in the background. The investigation that Rita ran when she discovered her mother's remains, and the scandal that ensued, had forced Edward into leaving Scarborough, but Rita knew he lived in Harrogate now. That wasn't far, and from there she was certain he managed his businesses. Damien might be the front man now, but Edward still lurked in background.
The bitter bile of anger and regret returned in the back of her throat.
The cracks were appearing again, the long fingers of the ghosts she had laid to rest were returning.

Her mother, Clara's birthday was next week. She celebrated it always, lighting candles under photos she had. Last year, with Angela and some more of Clara's friends, they had a little party. Angela told Clara's stories, and they laughed and cried. It made Rita realise she wasn't alone.

Next Tuesday, which was now six days away, she would light candles for Clara again. Visit the grave and put flowers. She did that often, in Christmas and Easter as well. But Clara's birthdays were special. It was the day Rita reflected on how life might have been for her, if Clara had been alive. She would still have left Scarborough and gone to university, then perhaps gravitated to another big city. Maybe London. But she might have returned to this small town sooner. Or settled in Leeds or York, to be closer to Clara.

Past regrets clouded her mind, and then the present returned. With it, thoughts of the evil bastards who had escaped justice for so long. A resolved strengthened like steel in the forge of her mind – she wouldn't let Damien or Edward escape. She had no evidence against Edward. But Damien had slipped up when he ordered the Merigold to be returned to the boatyard. Rita was going to make him pay.

Her phone rang, and it was Jack. She decided to answer.

"Hello stranger," Jack's warm voice came down the line. "Let me guess. Sitting on your own after a long day and nursing a glass of white wine?"

"Predictable, aren't I?"

"Only doing the same as millions of othesr, including me. How about going out for dinner? My shout."

Rita felt guilty. Jack was beyond generous and she didn't want to make it a habit. She enjoyed his company, and it was getting harder to hide the attraction she felt for him. She knew he felt it as well. Things were reaching a tipping point, she knew that. But did she want Jack as a lover, and thereby lose his friendship? They had been lovers once, but that had been so long ago. What would happen if they became lovers again? Would they disappoint each other? Perhaps she needed to let things take their own course. Thinking about it too much didn't help. Rita had always been an instinctive person. She would go where her heart led her to. Like a river flowing to the sea, she would find her direction in the stars, flowing with the currents. That's what life was like. She just had to trust herself.
"Okay," she said. "Pick me up in fifteen?"
"Your wish is my command."
Rita washed her face and applied some new make up. Her hair was straggly, and she did what she could with the brush and spray. When the doorbell rang, she drained her glass of wine. She didn't drink any more than a glass a night on weekdays. Given the revelations today, she might make an exception. Jack was waiting on the doorstep, in his dark blue jacket and brown shirt. He looked handsome as ever, and his dark eyes roamed over her face.
"Are you okay?"
"Why wouldn't I be?"
He shrugged, but she could tell he knew otherwise. He knew her too well. She locked the door, and they drove out in his car.
"Where are we going?"

"There's a new restaurant on Oliver's Mount, near the War Memorial. Nice views over the bay. Might be worth a try."

Views over the bay…that gave Rita an idea. She looked at Jack's silhouette as he drove. "How hungry are you?"

"Reasonable. Why?"

"Well, we could go up Oliver's Mount, but I want to check out something on the bay first. You know they car park and viewing area?"

"Yes. Why?"

Rita sighed. "Well, the HMCG has seen a lot of boat traffic recently. And I know our victim's boat was one of them, as he was often gone at night." She told Jack about Andrew Salford, and his connection to the Salt brothers.

"Damien Salt?" Jack whistled. "He's one of the big donors to the harbour regeneration plan. Are you sure he could be mixed up in this?"

"How did you know he's a donor?"

"Our firm did the contract for the North Yorkshire council. The council wants to be safe if the donors put their money in, but the plan doesn't make the money they're hoping for. Basically, if the investors don't get make a profit, the council doesn't want them to sue."

"And you saw Damien Salt's name as donor?"

"Yes. He's putting down almost five million, in cash."

"What about his brother?"

"Edward Salt?" Jack slid his eyes towards Rita. He knew the significance of the name. "No, he wasn't mentioned." He paused. "Is he connected to the victim in any way?"

"Edward? No. But Damien is, through his company. He recalled that boat, and it was kitted out with heavy surveillance equipment. It wasn't an ordinary fishing trawler."

They arrived in the car park. It was empty. There was a viewing point that looked out over the bay. There was also a telescope, which worked when coins were inserted. Rita walked over to it, the fresh salty breeze from the sea whipping at her jacket.

"What're you hoping to find?" Jack asked.

"Not sure." Rita fed two pound coins into the slot, and adjusted the telescope. The view out to the sea was better than she expected. It was a clear night. The moon was big and round, and a silvery sheen fell across the water. Rita kept her eye on the dark sea, and after a while, her vision adjusted. Slowly, she scanned the horizon. Her neck ached, and her hand was freezing on the cold metal of the telescope.

But her patience paid off. She thought saw small shapes moving across the water. They were not on the horizon, she could only see the big tankers there. And the big tankers had their lights on so they were easily visible.

Were the smaller shapes boats? They were closer to the shore. Still far out, and way beyond the harbour, where the cliff fell away to the North Sea. Far enough to not be visible from the harbour, especially without lights. But not so far that they couldn't make it to shore quickly.

"Have a look," Rita said, straightening. She was surprised to see Jack standing there with binoculars in his eyes. They had funny eye pieces that were square and big. They had a purple colour, and they wrapped around Jack's head with a strap. It wasn't like any binocular she had seen before. They looked like ski glasses.

"What the hell is that?"

Jack took the strap off the back of his head. He came closer, and looked sheepish. "When I decided we were coming up here, I decided to get my latest gadget. I use it sometimes to watch over the water."

Rita eyed it curiously. "What's those eye pieces for?"

"These are built in night vision goggle. Here, try them on." Rita did so. Jack helped her to put them on and adjusted the strap at the back of her head. She could barely see anything. The night outside was now dimmer than anything she had seen through the telescope.

"What's going on?"

"Hold on," Jack said. His hands moved to the binoculars, and Rita heard him press a switch. A sudden green glow appeared, and everything – the car park, the hills, the sea, came into a sharp and vivid focus.

"Oh wow," Rita said. She held the binoculars with her hand, and moved them around slowly. "I can see so clearly."

She could now make out the harbour to her left, on the South Beach. She could see the fishing boats in the marina, and the larger commercial boats farther to the left. She zoomed out, and panned back to the sea.

"Good, isn't it?" Jack said.

"Amazing, really." She focused on the small black shapes crawling on the water. Just beyond the cliffs. Now she could make out the boats, which were just obscure shapes before. None of them had their lights on as she had noted.

"Have you seen the boats?" Jack asked softly.

"Yes." Rita removed the strap on her head and lowered the binoculars. They were heavier than she had expected.

"Is that what the HMCG reported?" Jack asked.

"Yes, I think so. The boats are small enough to escape the radar system, aren't they?"

"Yes, I think so. Some of them are also standstill, like they've put down anchor."

Rita looked again. Jack was right. Two boats were standing still. They were not far from a set of rocky cliffs. Rita knew they wouldn't get too close to the rocks for fear of capsizing. What were they doing out there now? The fishing trawlers went far out, way beyond the cliffs.

Then she thought of the surveillance equipment on Andrew's boat, and her mind started spinning. She took the strap off her head and lowered the binoculars. She looked at Jack, who was standing next to her.

"What if the boats are picking up other stuff?"

"Like what?"

"I don't know. It could be narcotics, weapons. Anything illegal."

Jack looked thoughtful. "Possible. Our coast has always done narcotics trade. Maybe there's a new wave of it."

Rita was going to speak when her phone buzzed. She had ignored it before, but she didn't like the persistent ring. She handed the binoculars back to Jack, and answered. It was Richard.
"Bad news, guv. Melanie Salford just got attacked in her home."

CHAPTER 29

Rita spoke to Melanie on the phone as Jack drove. "Are you sure you don't want me to come over?" Melanie sounded hesitant. "It's been a long night already, although it's not that late. I'd rather be left alone to be honest."
"Of course, I completely understand," Rita said. She felt awful. She should've foreseen something like this might happen.
"Are you staying in the house tonight?" Rita asked. "Officers will remain on guard outside and back."
"Yes, I am. I don't want to move my daughter, who's still asleep."
Rita was quiet for a beat. "I'm sorry this happened to you. I think tomorrow you should move somewhere else. We can help you with that."
"No need. My neighbour Sarah will put us up for a few days."
"I'll see you tomorrow morning."
Rita hung up. She rested her head on the seat. Jack spoke softly. "Not your fault."
"I don't know," Rita sighed. "I'm wondering why this guy came back. They must've looked for the bags they knew Andrew had. They were on the boat, the man said. And Melanie thinks he's the same guy who came earlier – the boatyard engineer, David. I saw him earlier today. I should've arrested him then. I knew he was dodgy."

"Stop blaming yourself," Jack said. They stopped at a red light. "How did this guy know about the bags Andrew had on the boat?"

Rita glanced at him. She had thought of the same thing. "They must've been in touch. Maybe Andrew confirmed the pick-up. But then he died. So they took the boat back to search for the bags. When they didn't find the stash, they raided Andrew's house."

"They knew his wife and child was there," Jack shook his head. "Pretty desperate if you ask me."

"Aye, we're dealing with desperate people alright. I don't know why they would kill Andrew though, if he had picked up their so-called *gear*. Surely it made more sense to pick it up from him first?"

Jack nodded slowly. "Unless Andrew hid their stuff and threatened to expose them or whatever, if they didn't pay him more money."

Rita's eyes met Jack's. Rita spoke slowly. "Andrew might've been playing a high stakes game. He needed the money, that's for sure."

"Or he could be selling to a rival gang. If it's uncut drugs, the street value for something that big will be millions. Andrew might've been tempted."

They were both silent for a while. Dinner was forgotten, the evening marred by the news of what happened to Melanie.

"I'm sorry," Rita said, touching Jack's arm. "We should have dinner some other time. Maybe tomorrow."

"No worries," Jack smiled. He was relaxed, and she knew he was being genuine. He wanted to spend time with her, and she felt the same way. It was good to have Jack around.

They stopped at a kebab shop and picked up two wraps. They went back to Rita's place and sat at the kitchen table, eating the wraps with glass of red wine.

"Nice healthy dinner," Rita said, grinning. "Beats the romantic meal you had planned."

The words had slipped out without her understanding, and she cursed herself immediately.

Romantic dinner? Really, Rita?

Jack watched her speculatively. "I guess we're still having dinner now. What's not romantic about kebabs and wine?"

The awkward moment was avoided. But did a part of her feel disappointed that Jack didn't admit that he had planned a romantic dinner? The place looked romantic enough, but she had to spoil it with her work.

Nice one, Rita.

But Jack played along with her, because the truth was he cared about her. He was a shoulder she could lean on. The familiar conundrum reared its weird head. Would she lose Jack as a friend if they became involved in a romance?

Jack was watching her, his expression serious. "Who else do you know in the gang that hired Andrew? Matt is still on the run. And now this boatyard engineer. Anyone else?"

Rita swallowed her food and wiped her mouth. "No. But I bet you Damien Salt would know."

"But you don't have anything on him. And he's got a good reason to reclaim the boat like he said – Andrew had defaulted on the lease."

"I know he's guilty," Rita said. "So do you."

"I agree with you. But how are you going to prove it?"
Rita smiled. "When I find the boatyard engineer. Damien can't deny that man works for him, can he? "
Jack grinned. "No, he can't."

CHAPTER 30

Rita had a restless night's sleep. Jack had gone home shortly after their impromptu dinner. She had been exhausted, and Jack was understanding. He kissed her goodbye and left.

"Don't stay up late thinking about the case," He cautioned, lingering on the doorway. "Or trying to work on it."

"Says the man who manages four offices in three cities."

"I still get my downtime. I mean it. Look after yourself." He blew her a kiss and walked down to his car.

Rita had that familiar, warm fuzzy feeling as she watched him drive away. A part of her wished he stayed…she didn't ponder that for too long, as she fell asleep soon. The dreams woke her up – the same dreams as before. Clara at the mouth of a windswept cave, crying for her help. She startled awake, rivers of sweat pouring down her head, white knuckles clutching the bedsheets. Rita fell asleep again, but it was restless and broken.

She was up before the alarm.

She wanted to go for a run, but didn't have the energy. She dragged herself into the shower.

After a strong coffee she was feeling a little more human. She decided to walk the twenty minutes to town. The bracing air from the sea was nice – gusts of cold and salty wind that helped to clear her head.

It was seven in the morning when she walked into the canteen. The duty uniforms team were handing over to the day team over cups of coffee. Rita spotted Inspector Steven Bennett. He waved at her, then came over where Rita was buying her coffee.

Steven looked tired. Rita guessed he had been up at least some of the night. "Ey yup," Steven said. "Thought you'd like to know what Eastfield and Filey PC's sent us last night. It's about the wife of your victim, Andrew Salford."

"I know, I heard," Rita said. They sat down with their coffees.

Steven opened up his phone and scrolled to the report. "I didn't go there myself. But the woman was shaken up. She'd been tied up and assaulted – not sexually, and no physical injuries. But he threatened her daughter."

"And I think we know this man's identity. He's the main engineer at a boatyard in Bridlington." Rita told him about her meeting with Damien and then visiting the boatyard, where they met the engineer.

Steven whistled. "That Damien Salt's a big dog, ain't he?"

"He's in trouble now. His engineer's going around breaking into our victim's homes. We've got CCTV evidence of this man visiting Andrew's house when he was alive. Traffic will do a facial recognition search on HOLMES today, and we'll get you his name and details."

Rita smiled. "But you go home now. Not your concern. Anything else from last night?"

"Uniforms did a prelim search of the house and garden. Nothing in the house, which was also searched by the attacker. To think he even looked in that child's room. It's lucky the child was unharmed." Steven shook his head.

"And nothing in the garden?" Rita asked.

"Not that they saw. But it was night. Shola should be down there today, right?"

"Yes. She's been busy lately. I'll go down there myself to speak to Melanie. Thanks for your help."

"I hope you get this bloke. He was desperate. Anything could've happened last night. It's lucky the uniforms knocked on her door." Steven pointed a finger at Rita. "That was your orders, I heard. Well done."

Rita thanked him, and left the canteen. The CID office on the first floor was empty. Rita went to her desk and opened her laptop. She had received a report from HMCG. They had found a boat on Cloughton Wyke, a tiny coastal village north of Scarborough. The boat matched the description of the one that Matt Yardley had escaped in. HMCG found the boat in the early hours of this morning.

Rita had never heard of Cloughton, but she looked it up on the map. Cloughton was indeed tiny and the beach looked exposed to the sea. It was rocky. Although it had a sheltering cove it looked dangerous, like much of the open coastline around Scarborough. Rita called the number on the report and spoke to a HMCG sergeant called Kilpatrick.

"It was a black RIB, Inspector," Kilpatrick said. "The registration number on the hull, and the engine sizes matched what we were given. We got that data from CCTV, which caught the boat as it was leaving the harbour.."

"Cloughton Wyke looks very open to the elements. Was the boat wrecked on the rocks? Did you find a body, or anything else?"

"Whoever drove that boat knew that place well. Cloughton doesn't have a landing spot and yes, it is dangerous. But in low tide you can get out and drag the boat up to the rocks. I think that's what this man did. The boat was reasonably intact when we boarded it. We have it in our boatyard in Whitby."

"And there was no sign of the man who drove the boat? His name is Matt Yardley and he's a murder suspect."

"I'm afraid not. He would've taken the path leading up to the village from Cloughton beach. It's a wild beach, so he would have to walk for a while. Cloughton Newlands is the nearest camp site area. The actual village is a little distance to the south. You might have some luck asking around in the camping site or village. It's small, so the residents might remember a stranger."

"Thanks, we'll do that. Do you have forensics department?"

"Yes, we do. We can take fingerprints, swab samples, and anything else we collected and send them to you as evidence."

"If you could please." Rita thanked the man and hung up.

She looked at the map again. From Cloughton Wyke beach, the campsite of Newlands was indeed the closest. It was a remote place, and there was a waterfall nearby, called the Hayburn Wyke Waterfall. The area might be popular with ramblers and hikers. Could any of them have seen Matt? But finding a witness in this remote region would be next to impossible, Rita knew. Her best hope was a door to door in Cloughton village, and the forensic evidence from the boat.

Matt had chosen his spot well. But once on land, he would need a car. From the map, Rita could tell it was time consuming and difficult to get anywhere on foot from Cloughton. Matt either had a car here, or he hitched a ride. He certainly wouldn't stay in Cloughton, because he could be found there easily. Rita made some notes, and called the duty uniforms team. Sergeant Cleverly had taken over the day team. Rita gave him the details of Cloughton Wyke and Matt.

"Is he the geezer who took off in the boat from the harbour? Rizwan told me about him," Cleverly said.

"Yes, that's him. He's dangerous, a potential murder suspect. He's got a partner, and I need his details too. Tall, slim chap. Clean shaven. Blue eyes and blond hair. I'm about to send his CCTV images back to Traffic. But they should have him on file already."

"That's right, they should. Do you think Matt might have met his partner and got a lift from him, in Cloughton?"

"Definitely a possibility. We could look for the same car that Matt drove to Andrew's house, right?"

"Exactly. Not that we've seen it as yet. It could be off road. But now that HMCG have found the boat, there's a chance we might find the car if the men used the same car to escape. Leave it with me."

"Wait. This partner of Matt's, he could be dangerous. His name is David, and we think he's the same guy who broke into the victim's house last night. He assaulted the victim's wife. He thought there's stuff hidden in the victim's house. We need to find this guy today."

"Alright, guv. We're on standby."

Rita hung up and called Traffic. She gave them David the boat engineer's description, and mentioned the CCTV footage where Matt had driven him from Andrew's house back to his.

The traffic sergeant Maddy, or Madeline, was on duty. She was a bubbly, cheerful blonde with whom Rita got on well. Maddy couldn't stop talking.

"Gosh, I was wondering what you were up to? Do you know what my Troy did? He got sent home from school for disrupting the class. I mean, not again, you know? Honestly, Rita. I don't know what to do with that lad. He's so good at home though."

Troy was Maddy's twelve year old son who had ADHD. Rita said, "Let's meet up and talk about him later. He's going to be alright, don't worry. ADHD improves with age, and there's always tablets he can go on."

"Really? I can't get a doctor's appointment. He needs to be referred to a specialist, don't you think?"

"Yes, he probably does. Maddy, I'm sorry, but what I just told you is urgent. We need to get hold of this guy."

"No worries," Maddy said briskly. "Hold on." She loved to chat, but she was also excellent at her job. Rita heard Maddy's fingers clicking on the keyboard. She was no doubt switching screen, zooming into the man's face and checking the facial recognition software.

Rita waited, drumming her unpainted fingernails on the desk. The door opened and the lads came in. They saw Rita and wished her good morning in silence. They knew she was on an important call, so they didn't make a sound as they sat down.

Rita put a hand over the receiver and spoke to them. "I'm on the line to Maddy in Traffic. She's tracing the identity of the man who broke into Andrew's house last night."

When Maddy came back on the line, she put the loudspeaker on. "I've got a hit on HOLMES. Facial recognition software did the job. His name's David Foley. He's got a list of offences, and he's served prison sentences twice. Both times for armed robbery. I'm sending you his details now."

CHAPTER 31

"I recognise that name, guv," Rizwan said, when Rita hung up. He was busy searching his screen.
"I should've taken his full name when I saw him," Rita said. "But he might well have given me a fake name."
"Here we go," Rizwan said, leaning back in his chair. "He was interviewed briefly by Uniforms yesterday morning at the harbour. He was seen loitering around the Merigold. He didn't say much. Denied knowing Andrew. We didn't follow him up."
"Let's do it now," Rita said. "I just spoke to Sergeant Cleverly. Can one of you please update him with David Foley's details? I want his house checked, and put out an All Points Bulletin for him."
Rita's phone pinged and she looked at it. A groan escaped her lips. It was her boss - Detective Superintendent Nicola Perkins. Rita and Nicola had a hate hate relationship. Rita didn't know why and she had stopped thinking about it. The less she saw of Nicola, the better it was for both of them. She had sent Nicole the report on Andrew, but it seemed Nicole had questions. She had asked to see Rita asap.
"I'm going to see the boss. Won't be long," Rita said.
"Take your umbrella in case she unleashes a storm," Richard said.

"Left that and my raincoat at home," Rita said as she closed the door behind her. As she walked down the corridor, then ran up the stairs, an ominous feeling was settling in her guts. She knocked on Nicole's door, then pressed down on the handle.

The diminutive figure of Nicola looked even smaller in her high backed armchair. "Come in," she said. Her blonde hair was pulled into a ponytail, and the horn-rimmed spectacles on her eyes had slipped down to her nose. She pushed it up with a forefinger. She wore a perfectly pressed anthracite suit. Her table top was as immaculate as her appearance. Two pieces of paper on the left, a folder that she was examining in the middle, and a laptop to her right. The rest of the table was empty. On another desk, to her left there was a printer and fax machine.

"Sit down," Nicola said. Rita did as told. Nicola dead cold eyes rested on Rita.

"You went to see Damien Salt yesterday?"

So that's what this was about. Rita should've expected it. "Yes, I did. His staff disobeyed orders to remove the victim's boat from Scarborough Harbour."

"He's a civilian not a policeman. He doesn't have to obey orders. In addition, he doesn't have any links to the victim, apart from owing his boat. And Mr Salt has a large company that owns hundreds of boats."

"And one of his boatyard engineers broke into the victim's house last night and terrorised his wife."

Rita allowed a note of satisfaction to creep into her voice. "The same man who's been to the victim's house before. His wife heard them speaking to Andrew about joining them for supplying goods and making drop offs. Then this man terrorises the victim's wife, asking her about *gear* that Andrew has hidden." Rita raised an eyebrow. "Do you still think Damien Salt is not connected?"

"So, your evidence rests on a boatyard mechanical engineer who visited the victim's house? How do you know this engineer is not the member of an OCN? He might not have anything to do with Mr Salt whatsoever." OCN was the common acronym for Organised Crime Network.

"Then why did Mr Salt order the boat to be towed back to the boatyard in Bridlington?"

"As he explained to you," Nicola said, "Mr Salford had fallen behind on his lease payments. Mr Salt needed to repossess the boat."

"Spoken to you, has he?" Rita said. She couldn't hide the anger in her voice. "A man like him would have connections, I suppose."

Nicola's jaws ground together, and her eyes flashed. "DI Gupta. I'd watch what you say."

"HMCG says hundreds of boats are going up and down our coast at night. A marked increase from before. Chances are Andrew Salford had joined that trade. He was enticed into it by David Foley, the man who broke into Andrew's house last night. Matt Yardley also visited Andrew – and like Mr Foley, he also works for Damien Salt."

"So what? Like I said, his employees could be a part of an OCN. How does that get Mr Salt involved in the case?"

"His employees are using his boats, and you're saying he knew nothing about it?" Rita was getting tired of this.

A sneer rippled across Nicola's face. "He can't control his employees any more than any other employer. If you want to bring Mr Salt into this, you're going to need a lot more than that."

Rita tried to calm herself. Her chest was heaving, and her pulse raged against her eardrums. She couldn't let anger disrupt her thoughts, but Nicola was goading her, almost as if she was aware Rita would fall for it.

"He was rattled when I went to see him. He tried to remove himself from the enquiry. I know he's guilty."

Nicola sucked her cheeks in, then narrowed her eyes. "Do you think that because of who his brother is?"

And there it was.

Nicola knew very well who Edward Salt was, and his connection to Clara Winters, Rita's mother. It was a low blow, and Nicola knew it. Her expression didn't soften. Her eyes drilled into Rita's. The slow fury unleashing in Rita's heart was close to tipping her over into blind rage. With a huge effort, she controlled herself. She spoke slowly.

"Edward Salt is a convicted criminal now on release. Does that have any bearing on hi brother, Damien Salt? Given that Damien has now taken over the family business, which was dodgy to start with, what conclusions can we draw?"

Nicola spread her hands. "Conclusions don't stand up in court. You need hard evidence. And you don't have that on Mr Salt." Nicola ground her teeth together and her eyes flashed a warning.

"You are not to disturb Damien Salt again. He's a valuable member of the community. The CC called me this morning. You are hereby ordered to stay away from Mr Salt."

So, Mr Salt's reach was deep indeed. The Chief Constable was Alistair Grant, and Rita had met him a couple of times. He was the highest authority in North Yorkshire Police. If he had called personally, Rita had no hope of collaring Damien Salt again.

Or that's what they thought.

"I need to keep my lines of enquiry alive," Rita said. "We should be able to apprehend Matt Yardley and David Foley soon. If they mention Mr Salt we need to investigate him." Rita stood. "I can clear that with the CC himself, if you wish?"

Rita knew Nicola would be furious about reaching up beyond her rank. She wanted to give back as good as she got. Nicola looked like she was about to come apart at the seams. Her hands were fists, and the sneer on her lips was now an angry snarl.

"Watch your step, DI Gupta. Do not disobey a direct order."

"Understood, ma'am," Rita said. "All I want to do is catch the killer who probably is still terrorizing the victim's family. I'm sure you can understand that. I'll report to you later today."

Without waiting for a response, Rita turned and left the room.

CHAPTER 32

Rita was at Melanie's house in Filey. Melanie was still there, but she'd spend the night at Sarah's. Melanie had told Rita everything about last night.
"It was the voice. And those eyes." Melanie shivered and looked away. "I never want to see him again."
"You won't, I promise," Rita said. "We're going to hunt him down. We know who he is now. His name's David Foley. Does that ring a bell?"
Melanie thought for a while. "No."
"And you are totally sure you never saw any of those bags he mentioned?" Rita watched Melanie closely. They had been through this already. She didn't think Melanie was lying but she had to be sure.
"Positive. You didn't find anything in Andy's car, did you?"
"Nope. We took it apart, obviously. It's such a small car anyway. Nowhere in it to hide three large bags."
"Well, I hope you find it. Is this what Andy died for?" Melanie's face crumpled, and she lowered her head to her hands. Rita put a hand on her shoulders.
"I don't know," Rita said softly. "But there is a chance, yes. Thanks for letting us look in your garden."

Scene of crime and uniforms were digging up Melanie's garden. They had made small survey holes, and fed ultrasound machine probes underground to see if the ultrasound waves encountered anything the size of the bags.

Rita went upstairs and checked the rooms. She had shoe coverings on and a mask, along with hair covering. With gloved hands, she checked Melanie's wardrobe. David had chucked most of its contents on the floor, and he had turned dressing table upside down. How would he find a bag in there? Rita shook her head. She took some samples from the floor in an evidence bag.

Little Carla's room was relatively unscathed. Although David had been here, Rita could tell. The clothes in the drawers had been messed around, a couple of the child paintings on the wall were on the floor. Henry was on the floor, dusting for prints. Rita said hello to him. She took photos of the room and the stick paintings that Carla had done. They had Andrew in them, Carla standing between her parents. Rita's heart ached when she thought of the little girl who would now grow up without her father.

She went downstairs, and found Melanie still in the living room. Carla was on the floor, eating from a packet of crisps, and Melanie was holding out a drink for her. Carla took the drink and chugged it noisily before handing it back to her mother. Rita smiled at them and sat down opposite.

"There's something I forgot to ask you," Rita said to Melanie.

"These are just routine questions. I've asked you this before, but just wanted to check again. Where were you on the night Andrew didn't come home?"
"I was at home with Carla."
"Was anyone else here?"
Melanie frowned. "No. Why?"
"We always ask for an alibi, that's all. But it's okay, don't worry. My team told me you lived in Runswick Bay before you came here. Is that correct?"
"Yes, that's right. I used to work as a receptionist in the Runswick Bay hotel. Andy and I met there. After Carla was born, we moved down here."
"When was that?" Rita had her notebook out.
"Two years, but it seems longer. So much has happened since."
"Of course. How long did you live in Runswick Bay by yourself? While you were working at the hotel, I mean."
"I'm originally from Middlesborough." She smiled. "Not a Yorkshire lass, as Andy used to remind me. But I stayed in Runswick Bay for a good two years. I commuted at first, then decided to move when my job became permanent."
"Then you lived with Andy after you met him?"
"Not immediately, of course," Melanie smiled but Rita could tell the strain of the questions was beginning to tell on her. But Rita needed the answers. "We moved in after six months, I think. Yes, about that."
"So, you were in Runwick Bay for two years, then you met Andy and moved in with him," Rita said, scribbling in her notebook. "How long did you live with him for? And when was Carla born?"

"She was born two years ago. We moved shortly after." Melanie looked at the floor, seemingly lost in thought. Her fingers scratched her knuckles.

"How long did you live with Andy for?" Rita repeated.

"About two years as well."

"So you lived in Runswick Bay for about four years, is that correct?"

"About that, yes."

"Does Andy still have family up there? Do you feel like moving back?"

"Aye, he does have family there. Not his parents though. His dad's died and his mother's moved to Kent, where her sister lives. He's got paternal uncles and aunts. My parents are still alive and they've moved up to Hartlepool. I want to live closer to me mum. So that's where I'm going, like."

Rita had to agree that made sense. Melanie needed to be close to family. Besides, Filey wasn't the sort of town where jobs were easily available. Most people here commuted to the cities of Hull or York for jobs.

"I understand," she said. "But please stay here for a couple of days more while we bring our investigation to a conclusion. I think there is an organised crime network or OCN operating here. Andrew might have joined them. I don't want the gang members to think that you know where the bags are located. Which you don't, obviously."

Melanie locked eyes with Rita. "I've said this repeatedly. No, of course I don't. My child's safety is the only thing I'm concerned about."

"I know." Rita didn't think Melanie was lying. Carla got up and gave Melanie the bowl of fruits that she had finished. It was a little plastic bowl coloured with rainbows. Carla wanted a hug and Melanie put her daughter on her lap and put her arms around her, as if protectively. She kissed the top of her head.

Rita smiled at them. "There will always be police protection around this house and in front of your neighbour's. There will be no repeat of what happened last night."

Melanie's face clouded over, and her lips trembled. "I went shopping this morning. Everyone knows and they offered support. But on the way there, and back, I kept looking over my shoulder. Carla was in the pram. I can't dare to leave her out of sight for one second."

Tears squeezed out of her eyes and she wiped them. Carla looked up at her mother, and twisted in her lap, trying to face her. In a sweet and tender gesture, the little one tried to wipe her mother's tears.

Rita looked down at her hands and sighed. She was furious with herself, and at David Foley, who had done this to Melanie. Was David also the killer? There was no evidence to implicate David at the castle rampart crime scene. But it was still early days. David's DNA was on file, and Dr Das would be doing a match without delay. David's boot prints would also be checked with the prints found on the ramparts.

Most importantly, if there was an OCN hunting for their stuff, Rita needed to find who they were as soon as possible. Melanie didn't know where the bags were. And if they had been in the boat, would David not have found it when he towed the Merigold back to the boat yard?

Hence, the bags were somewhere else. If David didn't know where they were, then how about Matt?

Rita stood. She gave Melanie her personal number. "Call me anytime, night or day. We will sort this out, once and for all. You have my word on that."

Her phone buzzed and it was Rizwan. "Guv," he said quickly. "You need to see this."

CHAPTER 33

Rita was back at the station, standing behind Rizwan's chair, with Richard next to her. Rizwan played the CCTV film on his screen. It showed Scarborough Harbour's fishing marina. The date was four days ago, and the time was half past ten at night. The yellow streetlights gave scant light, but bright halogen lights were preset inside the harbour.

"The HMCG took their own time in getting these to us," Rizwan said. "We didn't have footage from inside the harbour until now."

The film showed a row of fishing trawlers, moored at the marina. They saw a man on the deck of a boat, and Rizwan zoomed in. It was the Merigold, and the man on board matched the description of Andrew Salford. Rizwan stilled the image, focusing on the man. He wore a dark blue windproof jacket, and Rita could just make out the grey jumper underneath. Blue jeans on his legs, and black trainers on the feet. Exactly what Andrew Salford was wearing when he was found. The face was similar to that in his passport and driving licence.

"No doubt that's Andrew," Richard said.

"Yes," Rita agrees. "I think even the CPS will accept that, without further proof." CPS – Crown Prosecution Service.

Rizwan played the film again. They saw Andrew come off the boat. He had two large black duffel bags in his hands. He put them on the ground. Then he went back on the deck and got another identical bag. A car pulled up by the boat. A man with a white beard got out. He had a slouching gait, and he wore a blue cap.

"Jonty Stanforth," Rita whispered softly. Jonty helped Andrew put the bags into the boot of the car. It was a blue Fiat, the car that Andy drove. Rizwan checked the registration number. It was the same. But the person who got behind the wheels was Jonty.

"He also drove the car up there. The car that we took apart," Rizwan said. After Jonty drove away, Andrew got back on the boat. He remained there for the next half hour, and Rizwan speeded up the tape.

They saw the blue Fiat, driven by Jonty, leave the main harbour gates. It took a right, heading towards North Beach.

"Where does the car go?" Rita asked.

"Traffic followed it after I informed them. Do you want to see it now?"

"No," Rita said. "Keep it on Andrew for the time being."

They watched as Andrew got off the boat. He spoke to a couple of fishermen who were the doing the same. Andrew walked to the entrance of the marina. He slipped through the side gate, as the main entrance was closed. The harbourmaster's cottage was shut, and there was no on in the kiosk. There was no sign of Jonty.

The camera on the south beach main parade picked up Andrew again. He waited at the bus stop till the bus for Eastfields and Filey arrived. He boarded the bus and was gone.

"The cameras at Filey bus stop show him arriving forty minutes later," Rizwan said. "But there's no other cameras at Filey, so we don't exactly see him walking home."

Rita folded her arms across her chest, her mind abuzz like a swarm of bees around a hive. She had already checked the date and time on the top right hand corner of the screen. 4th April, 22.10 hours.

Rita said, "So this was two days before we found Andrew's body." It was a statement, not a question.

Richard nodded. "Yes, guv."

"Show me where Jonty went with the car."

Rizwan switched the tape and clicked play on his keyboard. They saw the blue Fiat meander through Scarborough town and then get on the A171. It was night, and the A171 was not particularly well lit in places, despite it being the main road artery heading up north. The car took the exit at Cloughton.

"That's where Matt's boat was found," Rita said. "In the beach at Cloughton Wyke."

"Wyke means wild beach, guv," Richard said.

"Tell me summat I don't know," Rita rolled her eyes and Richard grinned.

The car had vanished from the screen.

Rizwan pulled up another file.

The A171 went through the sleepy village of Cloughton. Jonty had taken an exit off the main road, and they watched the red tail lights of the car as it disappeared down a road an unmarked road called Salt Pan's Road. The turn off didn't have any directions.

"That road leads to a blind end near Cloughton Wyke," Rizwan said. "Cars can travel on it. But it stops abruptly on the hills that slope down to the beach."

He pulled up a map and showed it to Rita. "The end of Salt Pans Road offers easy access to the Cloughton Wyke beach. We don't know what Jonty did there. But we catch him again, an hour later, going back on the A171 to Scarborough."

"Show me," Rita said. They watched as the blue Fiat appeared again, coming up Salt Pans Road and joining the A171. The car went down to the harbour car park and Jonty got out. He went back to the harbour master's cottage. Rita saw the lights go on inside the cottage, and then turn off.

"He doesn't come back out till the next morning," Rizwan said. "And that's where we finally found the car."

"Where is Jonty now?" Rita asked.

"I called him," Richard said. "But he didn't answer."

Rita pressed her lips together as she thought. "Where was Jonty the night of 6th April?"

Rizwan said, "He came out of the harbour at seven pm. Then he went to the George Inn and he was seen coming out at nine pm. He got on the bus and went in the direction of Barrowcliffe, where he lives."

"And we don't see him after that?"

"There's no CCTV on his street. Unfortunately, we don't know if he was at home or not."

Rita frowned as she thought. "That means Jonty is now a clear suspect in Andrew's murder. He needs to provide an alibi for his movements on 6th April evening."

"I've tried to contact him, but he's not responding to calls."

Rita tapped a fingernail against her chin. "Jonty's got the bags that David, and I think the OCN, are looking for."

Rizwan asked, "Are you sure an OCN is involved?"

"I think so. I need to speak to my contact in the NCA." National Crime Agency.

Rita continued, thinking aloud. "Where did Andrew pick the bags up from? He came from the sea, didn't he? Which means he picked them up from another boat…

"…Or he found them on a wild beach," Rizwan said. "Maybe like Cloughton Wyke. He would know when the tides would be lower, just like Matt did."

"But at night the tide would be up, right?" Rita said. "That's why the fishing trawlers go out to sea then."

"That's correct. I meant a beach that allows landing even at high tide. Maybe one with a jetty or small harbour."

Richard spoke up. "There is another option. This is going way over our heads – but if we are considering an OCN, then they can use submersibles to transfer narcotics. I mean things that float, have lights on them, and can be picked up by radar."

Rita stared at him, thinking of the surveillance equipment on the Merigold. "That could be why Andrew's boat had state of the art instruments. The OCN invested heavily into that boat. The stuff that Andrew picked up was expensive."

Richard nodded. "Hence they had to repossess that boat without delay."

"Okay." Rita bent her head and inspected the floor as she thought. "Do we have patrols in Cloughton? Did the door to door reveal anything?"

"Nothing so far," Richard said. "And Cloughton Wyke is a tiny village, guv. It's remote. If Matt and Jonty came and went at night it's likely that no one saw them."

"Keep the patrols there," Rita said. "If those bags are hidden somewhere on the beach, we need to keep searching. Jonty took the car down that road that led to the beach, and he might well have hidden them there. Maybe that's what Matt came to pick up when he escaped, and HMCG found his boat on the beach. But where did Matt go?"

"Door to door found nothing. CCTV on the main roads haven't shown his car as yet."

"He's got to be somewhere around there," Rita said, "or someone helped him escape."

Rizwan said, "Do you really think an OCN is involved, guv?"

"Hang on." Rita went to her desk and took out her handbag. From her personal phone, she rang the person she knew at the NCA. His name was Inspector John Sturridge, and he had worked in the London Met with Rita. When Rita broke up the human trafficking gang recently, John had helped her with information.

"Hi John, this is Rita Gupta. Not a bad time, is it?"
"Long time," John barked down the phone. "I heard you moved out of the Met and headed up North. Is that correct?"
"Yes, it is. Listen John, I need a favour. I think we're investigating an OCN up here, who are trafficking narcotics or whatever, up and down the north east Coast line, using private boats. HMCG has seen increased maritime activity, and we have a victim who I suspect was one of the traffickers."
Rita told him the case details to date, and John listened without interrupting. "Let me do a search of the names. Can you text them to me, and I can call you back?"
"Sure."
He called Rita back in ten minutes. "Of the names you sent me, we have records on two – David Foley and Matt Yardley. David was arrested twice for armed robbery, but Matt has escaped justice so far. But he has been caught on camera on undercover surveillance operations. Both of them are low ranking OCN members. They do the driving and pick ups. But we have shut down a lot of the land routes in the North East."
"So it makes sense they are using the sea now," Rita said, growing excited. "Besides, the terrain here is difficult. A lot of hills and moor land, and there's only one or two A roads. No motorways."

"Exactly. Road links are not great. Like you said, the OCN might well be using the sea. They're called the Hessle Gang. They originate from a village called Hessle, near Hull. They're big in the ports – Hull, Immingham, Grimsby. They also have operations in Teeside and Middlesborough."

Rita thought about that. "Who are the top boys in the OCN?"

"They are shadowy figures as you can imagine. The truth is that we don't know. They work through subsidiaries. In fact, they ran a human trafficking ring. You dismantled them last year."

Rita frowned. "Thanks for your help that time. I didn't realise an OCN was behind the gang. We caught the ringleader, didn't we?"

"You're welcome. As for the ringleader, yes you did. But he was like the CEO who was employed by a board of directors. As you know, that's how OCN's function."

A slow thought was circling round in Rita's brain like a seagull moving over the sea. "Where did you the say the Hessle Gang operated from?"

"From the village of Hessle, near Hull. They have their hands in everything, from narcotics, weapons, human trafficking and prostitution, you name it."

"Has the name of Edward or Damien Salt ever come up in connection with them?"

"Not in a big way," John said slowly. Rita heard him clicking on a keyboard.

"But it's interesting you mention the Salt brothers. They are known as big businessmen in the North East, obviously. They have a lot of real estate investments – night clubs, warehouses, factories, residential property, all of that. And one of their warehouses in Hull was found to be used by the Hessle Gang. But the warehouse was derelict and empty by the time the local police force arrived. The Salt family denied any connection, and the investigation was dropped. The family is also from Hull."

"The Salt family is from Hull?"

"Yes."

"I didn't know that. I put Ed Salt in jail, as you know. But Damien Salt is now in charge, and he has a boat mortgage firm called Poseidon Ventures."

John was silent, and Rita could almost hear his brain clicking into gear. "Right, I see," he spoke finally. "Is that relevant?"

"Given that our victim worked for Mr Salt, and the victim was more than likely a narcotics trafficker, and that he knew Matt Yardley and David Foley very well – I would say it is very relevant. Oh, and guess who was very defensive when I went to question him?"

"Mr Damien Salt?"

"You got it."

John's voice was measured and slow. "This could be very big, Rita. I know the Salt brothers have connections. We have no evidence against them, which is a measure of how careful they are. You need to be careful of how you approach them."

"Yes, my boss has already told me to lay off him."

"There you go. Make sure you have concrete evidence if you're going after them."

CHAPTER 34

Edward "Kyle" Warren was facing his sister, Luna, in the visiting room of HMP Full Sutton. Luna had got him a flower vase. The bouquet looked pretty, but Ed had no time for it.

"Thanks, sis," Ed said. He raised his eyebrows. "A bit over the top, ain't it?"

"Oh, shush you. I think a bit of colour in your room will be nice." She winked at him and smiled; her lush red lipstick smeared all over her filler filled thick lips.

"Cell, you mean, not room. And definitely not mine." He looked at her closely. His eyes scanned in both directions without moving his head. The guards were standing at a safe distance, their eyes on the inmates in the room. No one could hear Ed and Luna.

Ed whispered. "Did you tell Rafik?"

Luna dropped her voice as well, which was difficult for her. "Aye. He's now got Rita Gupta's address, and he also knows where Maggie Long is. He's seen them both, in fact. Maggie's going to antenatal classes with her mother." Luna shook her head, and a smile appeared on her traffic light red lips.

"You'll be a daddy soon, bro. And I'm going to be an aunt. I can't wait."

"Neither can I."

Luna's smile faded. "But you need to be able to see your child. We have to make that happen."

"One step at a time. What else did Rafik say?"
Luna looked around carefully. Ed wished she wouldn't do that. "Stop that," he hissed. "You look suspicious. The guards are watching you. There're also cameras on us all the time. Just look at me, okay?"

Chastened, Luna patted down her hair and cleared her throat. "Doesn't hurt to be careful. Anyway, Rafik's told me something interesting. His old boss also knows about Rita Gupta. He says she's been a pain in his neck for a long time."

Ed frowned. "I thought his boss was in jail, and the gang was busted."

"No. His boss on the ground was the operations guy. The actual head is someone else. There's a few of them. They're like a group, and they have businesses everywhere. Rafik says they're big, but he won't tell me who they are. It's for my own safety, he says."

"An Organised crime network," Ed said slowly. He couldn't stop the smile that appeared on his face. "Rafik's gang leaders are still alive and well. And they've got a score to settle with Rita Gupta. This is great news."

"I know. Anyway, Rafik's spoken to them and they want to get in touch with you." She stared at Ed till he understood. He nodded slowly.

"Say no more," he whispered. "Do they have contacts here?"

"Not in this prison. Rafik said it's a shame you're not in a less secure place. They could actually have met you, or sent someone. Would you like to see them? The men at the top of his gang, I mean?"

"Yes, of course. If they can help me get out of here. Do you know any names?"

Luna shook her head. "Rafik wouldn't tell me. He said it's for the best. Their identities are completely secret."

"Does he know who they are?"

"Well, he's met them, so I guess he does."

Ed rubbed his cheek as he thought. Rafik had to be high up in the gang's pecking order, otherwise he wouldn't be meeting the top brass. Is that how Rafik had stayed out of jail? Everyone else in that trafficking gang had either been caught or was dead, thanks to Rita Gupta. But Rafik had survived. And he hadn't ratted out the top boys because the police hadn't come after them. They probably respected Rafik for that.

Therefore, it made sense for Ed to be close to Rafik. For revenge on Rita, but also to make Ed's own life easier. If Ed made it of prison, he could definitely use Rafik and his gang boss's help.

It was such a stroke of luck that Luna was going out with Rafik. He looked at his sister.

"Keep Rafik happy. It's important for both of us. Do you understand?"

Luna read the look in his eyes, and inclined her head. "Don't worry. He's a good man anyway. Looks after me."

"Glad to hear that."

They chatted for a while, then it was time for Ed to leave. He grabbed the plastic flower vase which had already been searched once– no other material was allowed. Outside the visiting chambers, he was searched, and handcuffs were snapped on his wrists.

For the second time, a guard looked inside the flower vase. He took the flowers out and looked at the water in the vase, shining a torch inside it. Then he nodded and handed it to one of the two guards escorting Ed back to his cell.

Ed watched the guard carry the vase and walk in front of him and the other guard, who walked next to him. Ed had the mouthguard around his face, which was a real pain. He couldn't speak, and even breathing was a chore. He was glad when they reached his cell. He was taken inside, and the two guards searched the cell and bathroom thoroughly.

Ed watched as one of them put the flower vase on the table. He was made to sit down in the solitary chair. A guard stood behind him and unhooked the mouthguard. The other stood a safe distance away. Ed sighed in relief and took a deep breath. His handcuffs were released.

"Sit here," the guard in front said.

"I know the drill, don't worry." Ed smiled at them.

He remained seated till the guards filed out. The door locked and the eyepiece snapped shut. Ed waited till the guards' footsteps faded away.

He got up and went to the flower vase. He picked out the rose in the middle. Unlike the others, the rose was not a real flower. It looked like the real thing, but it was made of plastic. He took it into the bathroom and shut the door. When he pulled at the middle of the stalk, it separated on gentle pressure. Inside, there was a rolled-up scroll of paper.

Ed stretched the paper out on the bathroom floor and started to read.

"You are going to ask for a psych evaluation. Ask for the psychiatrist because you are feeling depressed. His name is Dr Curtis. He will recommend you to a ward with less security. Do this tomorrow."

CHAPTER 35

Rita knocked on the door loudly and stepped back. Richard stood behind her. They were at Gristhorpe, at Matt Yardley's home. The door opened, and a woman with a baby in her arms opened the door. She looked pale, her cheeks sunken, eyes red rimmed. Her dark hair was straggly and fell in clumps around her face. Her arms and legs were very thin, even behind the skinny jeans and vest she wore.

Rita had seen drug addicts before. This woman looked like she had a habit of some sort. Her suspicions were increased when the woman put the baby down and pulled the vest down over her arms. Was she trying to hide needle marks on her elbows? The woman's eyes darted all over Rita, then to Richard. "Are you the bizzies?" She had a Liverpool accent.

Rita showed her warrant card, but the woman waved it away. Rita asked, "Are you Sharon Matson?"

"Why you askin' if you know already, like? Who else gonna be 'ere? The Queen of England?"

Rita asked, "Is there anyone else here?"

"Not that good for nothing bloke of mine who ignores his family. And you bizzies have scared him off, ain't yer?"

"Can we come in please?"

"What for? Tell me what you have to now, like."

"This would be easier if we're indoors."
Sharon grimaced and pulled out a tissue from her pockets, then wiped her nose. Her fingers shook as she put the tissue back in. She turned her head to check the baby was alright. He was crawling on the floor, right behind her. Sharon turned back to Rita, her dull grey eyes watery.
"I don't know where Matt is. So don't even waste yer time."
"It's important we find him, Sharon. Do you know which pub he went to? Where did he hang out?"
Sharon grimaced. "It's *important* for me to feed my little bairn!" Her voice rose and she pointed at the crawling baby. The boy stopped and looked up at his mother, snot running down his nose.
"That lousy bugger's pissed off and left me with fuck all," Sharon snarled. She pointed a finger at Rita. "All because of you."
"The neighbours are watching," Rita said. "Do you really want to do this out here?" She raised a hand. "We're not here to make trouble for you. We just want to talk."
Sharon grit her teeth together, then stood to one side. Richard and Rita walked in.
There was a smell of cigarette smoke inside. The floor was littered with toys, coloured paper and magazines.
The boy had crawled to the coffee table and was now standing, holding on to the table.
Rita realised he was pulling papers off the table, and making a mess. He blew a raspberry at Rita and belched loudly.

The baby looked healthy; Rita was glad to see. But the living room was dated, and she saw mould in one corner of the ceiling. The leather sofa looked second hand and old, with one of the side bars broken.
The kitchen door was open, and a smell of bacon came from inside it. A back door at the kitchen led to the small outside garden.
"How long have you lived here for?" Rita asked. The baby cried and Sharon picked him up, bouncing him in her arms. She sniffed and wiped her red nose on her sleeve, then caught the baby's hand as he tried to grab his mother's nose. Rita looked again at Sharon's skeletal arms and legs. There was a lighter and ashtray on the bookshelf above the TV, where the child couldn't reach.
Sharon said, "Last five years. We were in Hull before that."
"Where in Hull?"
"Near the docks. Matt worked in the fishing quay there."
From her attitude Rita guessed things weren't going well between Sharon and Matt. "Has Matt been out of work?"
"Aye, for long periods. And he stays out all times of the night, saying he's out fishing." She scowled. "He don't smell like the sea when he comes back. I'm from the Mersey and I know fishermen."
"So where does Matt go at night?"
"If I knew I'd go look for him, wouldn't I? Hardly a week's food money left. The bugger doesn't answer his phone, or care about his son. What sorter man is he, like?"

Sharon glared at Rita. "Enough of your stupid questions. Now leave us alone. It's the bairn's sleep time."

"Did anyone come to see Matt here?"

"No."

Rita suspected Sharon was hiding something from her. She wanted her husband back home after all, if only to pay the bills. He couldn't do that if he was under arrest.

Rita glanced at Richard. "Go outside."

Richard looked surprised. "Are you sure, guv?" His eyes scanned the ceiling. "Who's upstairs?"

"The Mafia with machine guns," Sharon snarled. "Who do you think?"

"It's alright," Rita said to Richard. "Go outside and check with Rizwan. See if he found anything at the harbour. I'll be out in a minute."

After Richard shut the door, Rita pointed at the sofa. "Sit down."

Sharon didn't budge, so Rita made herself at home. Sharon remained standing, the boy in her arms. She looked at Rita suspiciously.

"What do yer want?"

"Where was Matt on the 6th April? That's four nights ago."

Sharon lowered her eyebrows as she thought. "He was 'ere, strangely enough," she gave a short, mirthless laugh.

"He was here the whole evening and night?"

"Aye. He came home in the later afternoon. Went out for a bit but was home before dark, for sure."

Rita had her small red notebook out and she scribbled. That meant Matt was at home the night Andrew died. Ergo – Matt didn't kill Andrew. If she could trust Sharon, of course. But Sharon didn't have a reason to lie about this. She didn't know about Andrew's death.

"You're sure he didn't leave the house at night?"

"Yes. I got up a couple of time as Kay was cryin'. Matt was fast asleep." She frowned in irritation again. "Is this what you came to ask about? Why don't you find out where Matt is now?"

Rita closed the red notebook and put it back in her pocket. She looked at Sharon.

"How much are you using?" Rita asked quietly.

Sharon blinked. "Don't know what yer talkin' about."

"You've got needle track marks in your elbows. I've seen one and it's old. That means you're not a heavy user. But I can see some silver foil on the bookshelf. Do you smoke the heroin?"

Sharon had turned paler and she took a step back. She clutched her baby tighter and the boy squirmed in her lap.

"I think yer should leave now."

"If the social service finds out they can take your child from you," Rita said gently. She raised both hands to placate Sharon. "But I won't do that, don't worry. If you were a real junkie, you would be passed out now. But you're looking after your child, which is good. You've not been using long, have you?"

Sharon flexed her jaws, and seemed to swallow a heavy weight in her throat. The tip of her nose turned a bright red. She sniffed loudly.

"It's bad, isn't it?" Rita whispered. "The stuff destroys you. It takes over your life. You're fighting it, aren't you?"

Sharon sat down cross-legged on the floor as the baby wanted to be let down. She kept a hand on him as he crawled around her.

"What's his name?"

"Kay."

"That' a nice name."

Sharon stared back at Rita without speaking. "I love my son," she said. "I won't let anyone take him away." A teardrop escaped her eyes. Rita felt a strange pain twist inside her like an old rusty knife in her guts. She too, had lost a mother when she was eleven. She could feel Sharon's agony.

"I can help you give up the stuff. Would you like that?"

Sharon looked to the floor, then nodded in silence. Rita sighed in relief. "Good. I'll speak to someone. Now, where did you get the heroin from?"

She could guess already, but she had to ask. Sharon didn't answer. Her fingers drew a pattern on the carpet.

Rita said, "Did Matt get it for you?"

Sharon looked up then. Her eyes were red with unshed tears. She wiped them quickly. "Aye. He sells that stuff. Brings back loads sometimes. Doesn't touch it himself, though."

Rita could see what sort of a man Matt was. A drug peddler and a vile human being who was turning his own wife into a junkie.

"You need to get out of here," Rita said. "Find yourself and Kay a new home, in a different town."

"Aye, I know. But I ain't got no money. No folks I can rely on."

Rita wasn't the social service, neither was she a good Samaritan. But something about Sharon's plight touched her. Sharon was essentially a single mother who was struggling to make ends meet, and her heroin habit was nibbling away at her sanity.

"There are charities that can help. You can apply to the council for housing if you're a single mother. You can put Kay in nursery and get a job. But you need to move to a bigger city or town for that."

Sharon gaped at Rita. "I can help you," Rita said. "I mean that. You don't owe me anything."

She let the silence drag on for a few seconds more. Kay crawled over to her, and gripped her trousers, then stood. He stared at Rita, then offered her a lego block that was wet with his saliva.

"Thank you," Rita smiled, not sure if she should take the lego piece with saliva dripping from it.

"I'm sorry," Sharon said. She pulled Kay back gently and into her lap.

"No problem," Rita said. She tried hard not to think what it must be like to have a child, to hold one's own offspring in one's own hands. It wasn't worth thinking about now.

"Sharon. Does Matt live anywhere else? Or does he have a place he goes to?"

Sharon closed her eyes and touched her forehead. Then she seemed to make her mind up.

"He's got a cottage in Cloughton Wyke. It's on the hills, not far from Salt Pan Road. That's like a country lane…"

Sharon gaped in surprise as Rita jumped to her feet, pulling out her radio as she dashed out the door.

CHAPTER 36

"Near Salt Pan Road, yes," Rita shouted on the radio. The black car was screaming down the A171, heading north towards Whitby. Cloughton was on the way. Richard was driving, his knuckles white on the steering wheel.
"We have the area covered," Rizwan's voice crackled on the radio. "Do you have an address?"
"Sharon didn't know the street name or house number. But she said the cottage was small, and it faced the sea. She's never been there. Matt's parents used to own it. Matt could see the sea, and maybe watch boats at night if they came to drop off on the Cloughton beach."
"Uniforms are searching the beach, guv. We stopped pedestrians from approaching. It's an isolated beach so no tourists, thankfully."
"Good. Keep up with the door to door. Block all exits from Cloughton village. ETA 10 minutes," Rita read from the dashboard sat nav.
"See you soon, guv."
Richard was forced to slow down as they went through the narrow lane that led to Cloughton Wyke.
 The views of the brown cliffs, the gorse and heather rolling down to meet the vivid blue of the sea was breathtaking, but Rita didn't have eyes for it.

She held on to the overhead rung as the car shuddered and rattled through the lane. The road leading up to the village was shut down by two police cars. A man walking his dog was speaking to a uniformed constable.

Rita waved at the uniformed officers as she got out of the car. She ducked under the blue and white crime police tape, and ran down the lane, heading from the last road on the cliff. Houses on either side clung to the slopes. Old stone cottages, with red flower pots in the windowsills and white shutters. The lanes were narrow, just wide enough for a car to get through but it was quicker on foot.

Rita went round the bend of one street and emerged on a wind-swept stretch of road. The land sloped down further to a set of fences. After that, the wind tousled heather and bracken reached the cliff edge, where it fell off sharply.

Rizwan was standing outside a cottage door. This building had closed windows, and the stone surface of the wall was ravaged by wind and rain. It's dereliction was in sharp contrast to the other cottages on either side which were well maintained.

"This is the only door that's not opening," Rizwan said. "The neighbours haven't seen anyone come or go. But an old lady said Mrs Yardley used to live here, before she died last year."

"That must be Matt's mother," Rita said. She went up the three steps and rapped on the door. The heavy, wind battered oak door remained immovable. The house remained silent.

"Anything round the back?" Rita asked.

"Nope. The garden's overgrown. The kitchen's at the back and there's a patio door."

Rita went around the side alley, ignoring the inquisitive neighbour at the side window, trying to get her attention. The garden had waist high grass and smelt of animal waste. At the rear, there was a fence, separating the cottage from the house beyond. Rita tried the patio door. It was old fashioned, made of thick wood, but the door wobbled on the frame. It was locked from inside.

"Break it down," Rita ordered. Rizwan spoke on the radio. Two uniformed constables arrived, holding the portable battering ram between them. They swung the heavy device and slammed it against the door. After two heavy crashes the lock snapped and the door smashed open, rocking against the back wall.

The constables barged inside, followed by Rizwan, Rita and Richard. The smell inside was awful. It was putrid and humid, hanging like a cloud inside the house. Rita put a hand over her nose. She had a horrible feeling already.

The smell got stronger as they went through the kitchen. There were plates in the sink, and an empty pizza packet on the table. In the hallway there was a door to the left and a staircase to the right. The constables went upstairs with Rizwan, while Rita poked the lounge door cautiously.

The stench hit her like a sledgehammer. Seconds later a swarm of flies buzzed around her. Rita covered her nose, waving her hand to get rid of the flies. Her eyes fell on the floor. A man lay face down, with a hole in the back of his head. Blood and brain tissue had leaked out of the hole, caking the back of head with dark clotted blood.

Rita put on a mask and gloves, trying not to retch at the smell. Behind her Richard was doing the same. He moved past her and entered the room. He went to the window and drew apart the curtains. Daylight flooded inside, making the ghoulish scene clearer. The man had been dead a while. His face was swollen, tongue protruding, eyes bulging.

Calmly, Rita knelt on one knee to take a good look at the face. She waved a hand again to get rid of the flies. She recognised the man. There was no doubt. It was Matt Yardley.

CHAPTER 37

Rita was at Scarborough harbour. The harbourmaster's cottage was empty. Uniformed constables had broken the lock. Rita stepped inside to find a small desk and chair, with a single bed behind it. The bed was slept in. She knelt and had a look under the bed. It was empty. There was no sign of Jonty's clothes or any of his belongings. But behind the door, she did find a coat hanging from the hook. It was a dark blue moleskin coat, with round brown buttons.

Rita lifted the coat up with gloved hands. It was the buttons that interested her. They were round, with yellow threads on them. And one of the buttons was missing. She touched the empty space, feeling the yellow threads.

She looked through the table top and the drawers. The papers on the table dealt with shipping forecasts and weather reports. Rita didn't find a laptop or an iPhone.

Outside, Richard was helping the uniforms to ask about Jonty. So far no one had seen him this morning. There was an APB out for him and David Foley. Rita had gloves on, and she looked in the small toilet behind the bedroom. She found a toothbrush and shaving kit, and took them in evidence bags.

As she looked around the room, she thought about the connection between Jonty and Matt, and her mind returned to how Matt was killed.

Matt Yardley's killer had done a professional job. A single bullet to the back of the head, from close quarters. The front door of Matt's cottage was not broken in. He had let the killer in. Unless Matt was killed outside, then brought in. Rita doubted that. Although Cloughton Wyke was a quiet village, there was a risk of leaving blood drops or a trail that led to the front door.

Who would Mark have let in? Someone he trusted. Someone like Jonty. Or maybe David. Dr Das was on the scene now, and Rita would know the time of death soon enough. Matt was killed at least twenty-four hours ago, Rita knew that. Otherwise, his face wouldn't be swollen the way it was. That meant Matt had died shortly after he escaped, which was yesterday. HMCG found his boat on the beach this morning. What time did Matt get to Cloughton Wyke?

Rita stood in the middle of the small room, the wooden planks creaking under feet as she moved. Matt wouldn't have waited till nightfall to get to Cloughton Wyke beach, as the tide would be up. He wouldn't be able to see the rocks. He needed daylight, and low tide, to be able to navigate to the beach without fear of hitting the rocks and the boat capsizing.

Jonty had driven to Salt Pan road two days before Andrew died. He had the bags with him. The same bags that poor Melanie had been terrorised for. Jonty had dropped those bags off somewhere…on the beach?

A search of Matt's cottage didn't reveal the bags. Uniforms were combing the beach now. Did Matt come to Cloughton to pick up the bags? He must have, Rita thought.

He found the bags, but he couldn't leave because the tide was up, and perhaps he was worried about saw the police finding him on the street? Hence he decided to stay until dark? That meant someone had to give him a lift.

That could be Jonty, because he had a car. David's records didn't show he owned a vehicle.

One thing Rita knew for sure. Matt didn't kill Andrew, because Sharon had confirmed Matt was at home the night of 6th April. Jonty was seen coming out of the harbour and driving to the Salt Pan Road. But then he returned, dropped the car at the south beach car park, and disappeared. Where did he go? Rita stared at the moleskin coat she had now laid on the bed, and the missing brown button. She had picked up a very similar round, brown buttons with yellow threads from the castle rampart crime scene. There were no witnesses from that night, no one was seen walking down the road that Andrew had walked, up to his fateful trip into the castle.

Did Jonty come back, and then go up to the castle? But why would he want to kill his friend, Andrew? The questions kept revolving in Rita's mind relentlessly. She was here to look for Jonty, but the mystery of Andrew's death was slowly revealing itself to her. Now she knew for certain that Jonty was connected to Andrew's death.

Rita didn't think the bags were the reason Andrew had died. She thought there was something more at play here. Andrew's death didn't seem like a gangland killing. Gangs didn't throw someone off a cliff or castle. They shot them – like someone had shot Matt.

If Jonty killed Andrew, what was his motive?

The thoughts continued to ping off the interior of Rita's skull like little silver bullets, the ricochets like voices whispering to her.

The door of the hut opened and Richard came in. "No one's seen Jonty this morning. He was here last night. He left in the evening around eight pm. Not been seen since then."

"What about CCTV?"

"Rizwan's spoken to Traffic. They have the images and they show Jonty leaving last night at eight oh five. He didn't go back home to Barrowcliffe."

"Did CCTV show Jonty here the whole day?"

"No, he went out several times. He was out for more than one hour at midday. If he had a car, then he kept it in a street which doesn't have CCTV. The cameras track him going past Foreshore Road, but then he vanished down a side alley."

"He could've gone to Cloughton in a car or bike, killed Matt, then returned to his duty," Rita reflected.

"That's what I was thinking."

"Any sign of David Foley?"

"Not yet. We have the Bridlington boatyard under lockdown. Human Resources from PV got back to us, but they haven't seen David since he didn't turn up for work yesterday."

"And they're denying knowing anything else about David? Like why he broke into Melanie's house?"
"Exactly."
Rita went outside the hut. Two uniformed constables were speaking to some fishermen. There was a heavy police presence now. Inspector Botley and his men had taken over the harbour gate, and they were stopping any vehicles trying to enter.
Richard said, "I went to the George Inn, where we saw Jonty and Matt. They haven't seen Jonty." Richard patted his coat pocket. "I checked their cameras, and have got the footage here. Jonty's not been in there today."
"Right," Rita said. "Let's head back to the station for now. Tell Rizwan to stay at Cloughton Wyke and help with the search on the beach."

CHAPTER 38

Rita was surprised to see Maggie Long at the office when she walked in. Maggie was at her usual desk, checking her phone as if this was another day at the office. The fact that she was obviously pregnant was the only difference this time.

"What're you doing here?" Rita asked.

"Just thought I'd drop by." Maggie rose and gave Rita a hug, then Richard.

"Look at you," Richard said. "Absolutely blooming."

"And getting heartburn, swollen feet, finding it hard to sleep," Maggie grinned. "The joys of being pregnant."

"It goes by quickly. You'll be absolutely fine."

"So," Rita said, eyeing Maggie. "What *are* you doing here? I didn't have time to speak to the boss about a research job. You're meant to be on maternity leave. I'd enjoy the break if I were you." Rita paused. "Has anything happened?"

"No, I'm fine," Maggie said quickly, to reassure Rita. "Like I said, I'm getting bored at home. There's only so much baby clothes shopping I can do."

"How far gone are you now?" Richard asked.

"Seven months tomorrow," Maggie said. "Can't wait for him to arrive." She stared at her tummy and rubbed a protective hand over it. Richard looked at Rita and they exchanged a smile.

Maggie said, "So where's Rizwan?"
Rita knew Maggie and Rizwan were close. They had gone through detective entrance exams together and had worked as uniformed officers prior to that. Maggie stayed in touch with Rizwan.
"He's at the crime scene. Things have heated up here," Rita said.
"Is this about the fisherman's death? I heard he might be…" Maggie stopped, realising she had given the game away.
"How do you know this?" Rita made a mock severe expression and wagged her finger at Maggie. "Did a little bird tell you?"
"Yes, a little bitty blue bird," Maggie grinned. Rita knew it was Rizwan. She shook her head and sighed. "Keep it to yourself Mags, I don't have to tell you that."
"Of course, guv. Now if I had that job as a researcher, I could be helping you, even work from home." Maggie winked as the smile remained on her face.
Rita had to admit that made sense. Maggie would be ideal as a home working research assistant. No, Maggie was not at work, but it wouldn't take Rita long to arrange paperwork to employ Maggie as a researcher. She didn't think Nicola would mind. They needed all hands on deck right now.
"Alright then," she sighed. "I'll speak to the boss about keeping you as a researcher."
"Thank you, guv," Maggie grinned.

Rita sat down at her desk. "So, we found Matt Yardley, who was a suspect. He's been shot in the head, left to rot in a cottage in Cloughton. That's were Riz is now. We think there might be a narcotics or weapons haul somewhere there, too." Rita told Maggie the latest developments, with Richard filling in.

Maggie's face clouded over. "Gosh, I feel sorry for that woman, Melanie. What an ordeal to go through."

"Yes, indeed." Rita said, narrowing her eyes as a thought struck her. "How did you get here?"

"By car, I drove."

"Can you drive to Runswick Bay and meet some people there?"

Maggie's eyes lit up. "I love Runswick Bay. Been there a couple of times in the summer. Nice beach when the tide's out."

"Our first victim, Andrew Salford, lived there. That's where he met Melanie, his wife. She used to work in the Runswick Bay hotel."

"I know where that hotel is." Maggie said. "It's on the hill overlooking the bay, on the left, as you're looking at the sea. When that place was built, the locals were up in arms. They said it would destroy the place and the construction was bad for the environment."

Richard said, "And it was a chain hotel. People here hate that."

"Aye," Rita agreed. There was one thing all Yorkshire folk disliked – their precious countryside being tarnished by big business. But business also created jobs in a region where jobs had shrunk in recent decades. It wasn't an easy decision by any means.

"So, you don't mind?" Rita raised an eyebrow. "I'll clear it with Nicola." Rita raised a hand to stop Maggie from speaking. "But remember, this is your maternity leave, and ideally, I want you to go home and rest. You shouldn't even be here, to be honest."

"I want to, guv. Please." Maggie looked at Rita sincerely. "I wouldn't be here if I didn't want to. Medically, I'm all okay. Blood tests, scans, all normal."

"Okay," Rita sighed. She knew that Maggie wouldn't be in any danger in Runswick Bay. It was a quiet fishing village, after all. The hordes of tourists wouldn't arrive till July. "Don't spend too long there. I've got the addresses of Andrew's relatives. Speak to them, and to the hotel staff where Melanie worked." Rita glanced at her watch. It was half past three already. "I want you back here in two hours."

"Thanks guv," Maggie said, grinning. "You won't regret this."

"Just be careful. Don't go to the beach and stay on the main streets where you can park and not walk too much."

"I can look after myself, but thanks." Maggie slung her handbag over her shoulder.

"And I'll send Rizwan over to help you. You have his number, right? Give him half an hour, then liase with him."

Maggie nodded, and left. Rita sat at her desk and made some calls to the council about Sharon Yardley. The poor woman was a drug addict, and now a single mother. Rita knew it was easy to be judgemental about women like Sharon. She had fallen into hard times, but she was doing her best to turn her life around. Rita knew the news of Matt's death would be devastating for Sharon, but it also offered her the glimpse of a new life.

From the Council's health department, Rita got the number of the drug and alcohol rehab centre, and sent the details to Sharon via text. She also arranged a time to meet Sharon later today, to give her the news of Matt's death.

"Shall we go, guv?" Richard asked. Rita nodded as she rose from her desk. They drove to Marton, a small village near Bridlington, where David Foley lived. Marton was a nice and picturesque village, not far from the sea, and basking in the sunlight. A uniformed constable stood guard outside as the house was now a crime scene.

It was a bungalow, the low roof hanging over the porch as Rita climbed the two small stairs that led up to the front landing. Inside, the house had been searched already by the uniformed officers. Scene of crime had not been as yet, they were busy at Cloughton Wyke, from where they would have to visit Jonty's house in Barrowcliffe, before they came here.

Rita put on gloves and shoe coverings, like Richard. The front lounge was unremarkable, a TV in one corner with two three-seater sofa sets arranged around it. The lawn was visible from the patio door behind the TV.

Richard checked out the lounge and kitchen while Rita headed for the bedrooms at the back. The hallway led to two bedrooms at the rear, and a bathroom in between. The master bedroom was larger, and the bed was slept in. Rita checked the bedside cabinets, and the ensuite bathroom. The cabinets, wardrobes, and the ensuite bathroom had already been stripped clean. There were no clothes in the wardrobe, no toothbrush or shaving kit in the bathroom. The bedside cabinets, and the desk and chair next to the window – were empty of all contents. No loose papers, laptops or phones.

Rita checked the other bedroom which was smaller and probably used as guest bedroom. This room also had been cleared out. In the main bathroom it was a similar story. Not even a hair follicle left in the bathtub.

She joined Richard in the kitchen, which was opposite the open plan lounge, separated by the hallway.

"Somone got here before us," Rita said. "They did a good job here."

"No cups or plates in the sink," Richard said. He was standing by an open cabinet. "But cutlery and plates in the cupboards. Dish washer is empty though. Nothing for us to get prints or DNA from."

A bad feeling was churning in Rita's guts. Someone was trying to erase David out of the picture. Was he still alive?

■■

CHAPTER 39

Ruth Hodgson gripped the little pink pony tightly in her hand. The pony had pink down fur, and colourful sequins were pasted on its little forehead, and on its legs. Its tail was lighter coloured, but still pink and furry. The toes were brown. It was a distinctive toy. Her knuckles were white, breathing harsh. Like a manic camera, the snap shots fired in rapid succession, blinding her with the painful flashes, drowning her ears with the screams. She turned away from the window, and the tranquil view of the sea. She closed her eyes and pressed her hands to her temples.

As Dr Patel had taught her, she forced herself to breath slowly in, then slowly out. She could do the breathing yoga later, the *Pranayama*. First, she needed to control herself.

As her breathing returned to normal, she relaxed her hands. Then she did the yoga exercises which calmed her further. She checked that she didn't hurt the pony – a silly thought, because it was a toy. And yet, it was a lot more. She stared at it, and then closed her eyes. There was a knock on the door. Ruth opened it to find her mother Carol standing outside.

"Is it true?" Carol asked, as soon as she came in. Ruth took a deep breath.

"Yes." Ruth watched as Carol's eyes flickered down to the pony in her hand. She gasped. Her wide eyes gazed at Ruth's.

"Is that….
"Yes, it is. There's no doubt. I've not seen another like it. Look at the initials underneath."
She showed it to her mother. Carol had to sit down. She had taken the pony from Ruth, and she moved her hands across it tenderly. She sniffed, and wiped tears from her cheeks.
Ruth opened the drawer of her desk and showed Carol the letter. Carold hands were bent with arthritis and age. The skin on them was wrinkled. Her hands shook as she read the letter. Then her hands fell on her lap and a thunderstruck look appeared on her face. Her fingers loosened and the white piece of paper slipped to the floor.
Ruth picked the letter up, and put it back on the envelope with her name on it. Carol was staring ahead like she couldn't focus on anything. Her sunken, lined cheeks were gaunt, and her face was colourless. Ruth wondered if Carol had lost weight. She knew that she had. The events of the last eighteen month had certainly not helped her appetite.
Ruth watched the shafts of sunlight slant in through the window. The dahlias were starting to bloom in the garden. The other flowering plants would follow soon. Just a few feet after the garden, the steps began. They descended down to the beach. The sea unfurled to the distant horizon. A beautiful view, but Ruth couldn't dwell on it. She saw it every day – familiarity bred contempt. The sea had never been her friend.
It was her worst enemy.
Carol dragged her eyes slowly back to Ruth. "Is this true?"

"How can it not be," Ruth asked, pointing to the pony that now on the sofa, next to Carol. "That came with it. And did you read the details he provided?"
"How do you know it's a he? You said the letter was left on the doorstep."
"People in the village saw a stranger. A man who was asking about me. I showed the letter to Dr Patel, by the way."
Carol raised her eyebrows. "Really? Why?"
"Because I need to find out, mum. I need his help. And I didn't think Dr Patel would believe me unless I showed him the letter, anyway."
Carol's eyes rested on Ruth's. "How are you feeling?"
Ruth pulled up a chair and sat down. A breeze ruffled the curtains, bringing in the saline smell of sea spray. Her little cottage faced the rocks and the sea. She heard the surf smash against the rocks. The tide was coming up.
"I didn't imagine this, if that's what you mean," Ruth said. She turned and held her mother's eyes. "The letter and toy arrived on my doorstep, like I said. It's been a week now, and I can't stop thinking about it."
Carol sat still, thinking. "Who saw this man?"
Ruth nodded. "Mrs Herrington next door saw him. A bloke in blue jeans and a dark coloured jacket, she said. Her eyes aren't great, as you know. She doesn't remember what he looks like. He wasn't old, didn't walk with a stick."
Carol shook her head and her face became animated. Her feet tapped the tiled floor. "Love, you look so calm. You didn't even tell me until this morning. Just tell me. Is there anything else going on?"

Ruth rose and sat next to her mother. "I didn't tell you because I wanted to make sure it wasn't a prank or a hoax. I asked around at the shop, and with the neighbours. Derek at the shop also saw this man. He stopped to buy an envelope. I showed the envelope to Derek. It's from his shop, he confirmed it. The man put the letter in the envelope and left it outside." Ruth indicated the front door.

"Derek said he was a stranger, and he had blue jeans and the dark jacket that Mrs Herrington described. I think it's the same man."

Ruth squeezed her mother's hand. "I didn't write it myself, if that's what you're thinking."

Carol closed her eyes. She looked troubled, and her eyelids fluttered. A teardrop coursed its way down her cheek.

"Oh, come on, mum, it's alright." Ruth gave Carol a hug.

It was Carol who had stood by her. If it wasn't for her mother, Ruth would now be somewhere very different.

But the events had taken their toll on Carol. She wasn't the woman she had been. And Ruth blamed herself for that. True, Dr Patel always said no one could be blamed for what happened. But Ruth felt the burden of guilt.

She carried a lot of guilt.

Carol asked, "What're you going to do about it?"

Ruth stared at her mother. "What we're trying so far isn't working. I'm going to the police."

CHAPTER 40

Maggie had taken the coastal path of A171, the long and winding road that went up to Whitby. The sea flashed blue and green in the sun, to her left. She enjoyed the drive as usual, glad that she was out of the house.

As much as she loved her parents, it was stifling at times to be in the house all the time, when her parents were both retired. When Maggie was working, she spent most of her time on the job.

She had friends in Bridlington and Flamborough as well. One of her close university friends from York, Cathy, now worked for the Leeds United Football Club and Maggie visited her too. But she couldn't keep visiting her friends just to get out of the house. She needed a vocation – and what better way than to return to her job for a few weeks? Besides, she could do with the money. Maternity benefit only gave her full pay for three months, then she had state maternity allowance, which wasn't much. She could get more if she left home, but she couldn't bear the thought of living in council housing, away from her family, while raising a child.

Maggie drove through Whitby, that quintessential charming town of North Yorkshire, clinging to the side of the hills that descended to the sea. The derelict cathedral loomed to her left, the sea unfurling all around it as she drove past.

Soon, she was taking the exit to the right on the A174, a narrow road called Ellerby Lane. Open grassland undulated on both sides, the hills rising and falling in waves till they dipped to the snippets of water in the distance, the North Sea playing hide and seek with the land.

Runswick Bay appeared in the distance, a tiny village in a picturesque, sheltered cove. The village had red tiled pretty houses, most of them detached and well maintained. Runswick, like Staithes above it, used to be a village of rich fishermen – back in the days when fishing folk made good money. Those days had long gone, but Runswick had been lucky. Its picture postcard cove was still a magnet for the summer crowds.

Maggie drove down to the High Street. It was an average main drag, with a post office, grocery stores and cafes. Maggie was glad to see the absence of a supermarket. People here still shopped in local stores which was great for the community.

She parked and walked to the church, as Andrew's aunt lived in the street behind the church. Andrew's house was the road after that, closer to the bay, with a view of the sea, according to Maggie's map. No one lived there now, it was rented out.

Andrew's dad had passed away, and his mother was down in Kent. But Andrew had another uncle who lived here. They were on holiday; Maggie wasn't able to contact them. She wondered why Andrew and Melanie had moved with a little baby when they had so much support. Perhaps for Andrew's work, which made sense.

Maggie had made phone calls before she set off from Scarborough. She parked her car in the church yard, then walked down to Andrew's aunt's house. The cottage was white washed with black framed windows, and green ivy growing down the walls. Maggie knocked on the door. She heard a dog barking inside. The door opened and an elderly, white haired woman peered out into the sunlight.

"Mrs Jackson?" Maggie said. She held up her warrant card.

"Yes, that's me." The woman stepped forward and looked at the card carefully. "You must be the policewoman who called earlier."

"Yes. I'm DC Maggie Long. May I please come in?" Maggie walked into the narrow hallway, whose walls were laden with photos and mementoes of holidays like small plates and flags. The dog was a Russell terrier, which bobbed over and barked at first, but then settled down when he heard his mistress shout at him. Maggie gave her hand to the dog's nose, and he sniffed, then licked it enthusiastically.

"Don't encourage him," Mrs Jackson said, sitting on a hard backed rocking chair. "Would you like a cup of tea by the way? Kettle's just boiled. I'm having one." She pointed at the steaming mug next to her seat.

"No, I'm fine, thank you," Maggie said. She noticed Mrs Jackson was wiry and thin, but with a firmness in her step. Age had not diminished her movements. Maggie thought she was in her mid to late seventies.

"So, tell me," Mrs Jackson sighed. "Is my nephew Andrew really dead? How?"

"I'm very sorry. His body was found on 6th April, under the castle ramparts." Maggie told Mrs Jackson what she knew. She left out details of the investigation.

"And you think someone pushed him from the castle ramparts? Why?"

"We don't know. When Andrew lived here, was he ever in trouble with the police?"

"No. His dad, my brother, was a fisherman and Andrew was his apprentice. That's been the way of this village as long as I can remember. Yes, I know things are different now. But many lads here still follow in their families' footsteps of fishing."

"Where did Andrew work?"

"In the sea, obviously. The port in Staithes is bigger, and that's where James, that's his dad, had his boat. They sailed around from here down to Bridlington, like most of the trawlers."

"Did they moor their boats in Scarborough Harbour?"

"Not as far as I know. Staithes is cheaper, and the sea is colder, which is good for lobsters and cod. Hence most of the fishing folk from here moor their boats in Staithes – which isn't far up north from here."

Maggie scribbled in her notebook. "Yes, I know where Staithes is. So Andrew and Melanie had a baby, didn't they?"

Mrs Jackson was surprised. "Not that I know of. They left these parts, and I haven't heard they had a baby. Mind you, I don't speak to Jody – that's Andrew's mother – that often. She can be a little funny sometimes."

Maggie frowned. "But I was told they had a child, and then left due to Andrew's job."

"That they did. But they didn't have no child, as far as I know." Mrs Jackson stared at Maggie with a strange expression. "After my brother James died, Jody went down south to Kent. I don't really speak to her much anymore. So Andrew and Mel had a child, did they? I didn't know that."

Maggie's eyebrows lowered as she thought, staring at the open notebook. Rita had mentioned that Melanie and Andrew moved after their daughter was born. She was six weeks old at the time? Maggie thought hard. Maybe she was making a mistake, she had to check again with Rita.

Why had Rita missed this? It must be a mistake in the statement that Melanie provided. Melanie's state of mind wasn't exactly great at the moment. Maggie made up her mind to clear it up with Melanie when she returned to Scarborough.

"Do you remember when Andrew and Melanie left?"

"It was two years ago, wasn't it? I can't remember the exact date. Andrew came to see goodbye." Her eyes moistened and her lips quivered with motion. "He was such a sweet little boy. He had lots of freckles on his nose. I can't believe he's dead. Do you know why he died?"

"That's what we're trying to find out."

Mrs Jackson narrowed her eyes. "But you must think his death was suspicious, don't you? Or you wouldn't be here."

Maggie tried not to smile. Mrs Jackson might be old, but she didn't miss a trick.

"That's right. We think he was pushed from the ramparts. That's why he need to find out about his life here. Did he have any enemies? Or did anyone bear a grudge against the family?"

"Not that I know of. Fishing folk tend to be simple. They don't have feuds. The sea is their biggest adversary. Some get lost at sea and don't return."

"So, Andrew was never in any trouble with the police, or with anyone else, as far as you know?"

"That's right. He was an honest lad. I never saw him get into trouble."

"How did James, Andrew's father, die?"

"Natural causes. He had a heart attack four years ago."

"Was Andrew close to his parents?"

"He was, yes. James taught him how to fish. Jody was, well, she was just Jody. A quiet person. We got on okay as long as we didn't see each other much."

Maggie wondered about the family dynamics. She would like to interview Jody was well, but it would have to be a telephone call.

"What did you think about Melanie?"

Mrs Jackson shrugged. "She was alright, like. Quiet lass, didn't talk a great deal. Didn't really see her much." The elderly woman frowned. "She couldn't fall pregnant, I remember that. She had a couple of miscarriages."

Maggie wrote that down in her notebook. "Do you have children?"

"Aye," Mrs Jackson smiled. "Two girls. They're married with children. Both live down south. I go down to see them a couple of times every year. They come up here as well."

"Thank you. Do you know if Andrew had friends who might still be around?"

Mrs Jackson downturned her lips. "Sorry, I wouldn't know."

"Thanks," Maggie said, and rose. She gave Mrs Jackson her card. "Please call me on this number if you remember anything else."

CHAPTER 41

The boatyard near the lighthouse on the Bridlington Sea Front had a police car parked outside. Rita parked the car, and got out. With Richard, she walked to the front gates, which were shut. The small door to one side was open. A uniformed sergeant walked up to them and nodded in greeting. It was sergeant Cleverly, and he greeted Rita with a smile.
"Afternoon, guv."
"Good afternoon, glad you're here. Any sign of David Foley?" Rita asked.
"Nowt, and none of this lot inside know about him, either. You checked his house, didn't you?"
"It was cleaned out," Rita said. "Someone got there before us and took David's stuff. I think there was incriminating evidence there. Have you taken statements from everyone here?"
"Yes. No luck so far."
Rita thanked Cleverly and went inside with Richard. The huge atrium of the warehouse had several boats getting repaired. The sound of machines, knocks of hammers against metal, and pop tunes on the radio filled the air.
"Business as usual, eh?" Richard said. "Mr Salt's still making his money."

"Aye, that he is," Rita said. She watched the men carefully as she walked down the middle of the space. Several heads raised to watch her, then swiftly returned to work. Rita went through the middle partition, which opened up into the second section of the warehouse.

The Merigold was still in one corner, but now there was a blue and white crime scene tape around the boat and none of the engineers were allowed near it. It was quieter here, with fewer but larger boats being tended to by a small group of engineers. Rita caught a man looking at her as she walked past a boat. Something about the man was familiar. He ducked behind the boat he was working on and vanished from view.

Then she caught sight of him again, walking across the sides, heading for the rear exit. The warehouse sloped down as a concrete jetty to the harbour where the lighthouse stood. The waters were sheltered and calm, and a couple of boats were moored to the jetty. Rita saw the man walking down the steps that led to the jetty. She could see the side of his face, and suddenly she remembered who he was. Daniel Ashman. The man she had seen with Matt Yardley, the first say she went to Scarborough Harbour.

Rita set off in a sprint. She could tell Richard was following her, his steps quick behind her. Daniel looked back and saw her. His eyes widened, and he froze.

"Stop, Daniel," Rita said, waving her hand. Daniel looked around him.

He was in blue overalls that had grease on them. The jetty and water lay behind him, but there was a path that snaked around the rear of the warehouse, going out to the main road. Rita knew he could run for that path, and she moved as fast as she could.

Daniel didn't run. He watched her warily as she got closer, his eyes flicking to Richard.

"I need to speak to you about Matt," Rita said. She was out of breath and waited for a few seconds, breathing fast.

"Why?"

"Matt is dead. We found his body in Cloughton Wyke, a small village."

Daniel gaped at her. His weather-beaten face was pale, and the shock was clear in his eyes.

"He was shot to the back of his head," Rita said, watching Daniel closely. "You knew Matt, didn't you?"

"Only through work. I didn't mix with him socially."

"Why not?"

Daniel scratched the back of his neck. His eyes moved past Rita and Richard to the warehouse. Rita didn't glance back but she could tell Daniel was feeling awkward. And also scared?

"Tell us what you know about Matt," Rita said. "We can speak somewhere else, if you like."

Daniel cleared his throat and nodded.

They let him go first. Rita went down to the moored boats and had a look to see if anyone was on them. The boats were empty. Then she went back up the path, and to the front of the warehouse.

Daniel was waiting at the mouth of an alley, opposite the boatyard entrance, but partially hidden so no one could see him from across the street. They walked up to him.

"Get in the car and we can drive somewhere," Rita suggested. Richard brought the car around and they drove to a side street nearby. Richard parked up, and Rita remained in the back seat, with the two men in front.

"Now talk," Rita said. "Two men are dead – Andrew and Matt. The harbourmaster, Jonty, is missing. Let's stop this before others are killed. Do you agree?"

Daniel sat very still, watching the quiet road through the windscreen. Then he looked down at his hands.

"You were scared at the boatyard, weren't you," Rita said. It was a statement, not a question. "What happens there, Daniel?"

Daniel sighed, but didn't speak for a while. Then he said quietly, "You asked me about Matt. I told you."

"You barely told us anything. You didn't mix with him socially. Why not?"

"I wasn't his type. They…they can be a difficult sort."

"Who's they? Men like Matt?"

"Yes."

"You need to stop talking in riddles, Daniel and spit it out. Did Matt mix with criminals? Was he a part of an organised crime network?"

Daniel squirmed in his seat. "I don't know, okay? Look, this was a mistake. I shouldn't be talking to you. I need to go."

"No one knows you're in the car with us," Richard said. "Don't panic. No one's going to find out."

Daniel half twisted in his seat to look at Rita. His chest rose and fell rapidly as he breathed.

"You don't understand. They can find you no matter where you are."

"Tell us who they are," Rita said. "Was David Foley one of them? The foreman at the boatyard? We can't find him either."

Daniel gaped at Rita. "David? What's happened to him?" he whispered.

"We don't know. He's missing. He's not at his home. Do you know where he might be?"

Daniel looked unsure. Rita said, "You're not going to be in any trouble. You're not a suspect. We just want some more information."

Daniel licked his lips. "David's not been to work the last two days. I was wondering what's up. He's got a boat, and that's also missing. He kept it by the jetty at the yard."

Richard exchanged a glance with Rita. "Tell us what the boat looked like."

"It was a thirty feet grey Vanguard. He kept it here sometimes. But mostly, the boat was at the main harbour at Bridlington, where it was moored."

"Do you know where the main harbour is? And where the boat is moored?"

Daniel nodded. "Yes."

It took them fifteen minutes to get to Gummer's Wharf in the south beach of Bridlington. It wasn't far from the Spa, which Rita had been to many years ago. Rita spoke on the radio, asking Cleverly to send a unit as back up.

She let Daniel go back to work. She didn't think he was capable of cold-blooded murder. But she also needed to keep an open mind. The most dangerous individuals looked like the person who lived next door. Daniel could still be a suspect.

Compared to Scarborough, the Bridlington harbour was small. The harbourmaster gaped at Richard's warrant card as he held it to the man's face. He was old, in his late sixties, Rita thought, with a bald scalp boasting just four strands of hair.

"Have you seen a thirty feet grey Vanguard boat?" Richard asked, as they walked quickly towards the quay side, the harbourmaster struggling to keep up with them.

"There's a couple of those, like. Do you know the name of the boat?"

"No. But it belongs to a man called David Foley."

They were at the waterside now, and Rita scanned the boats bobbing in the water.

"David?" The harbour master said. "Aye, I've seen him, like."

Rita whipped round and the old man took a step back, startled. "Where have you seen him?" Rita snapped.

"La…last night. He came in to the harbour late, about ten at night. I was leaving, and bumped into him. He didn't say much, but I recognised him."

"Show us where his boat is."

"Around the corner," the harbourmaster said. He led the way, understanding the urgency. He hobbled on his left foot, trying to run. Rita hoped he wouldn't fall down, but the old man seemed as sure on his feet as a mountain goat. They moved across a pile of fishing nets and boxes stacked high. This section of the harbour was deserted, and it was also secluded from the road. The harbour building stood in the middle, blocking any direct views of the marina from here. Rita saw the boat immediately. It wasn't as long as other boats she'd seen, but the grey colour was distinctive. Richard got on it, and Rita spoke on her radio again, asking for back up. Then she got on the boat herself, trying to make as little sound as possible.

CHAPTER 42

Maggie walked slowly up the hill to the top of the road. Runswick Bay was divided into the upper and lower hills. The slopes got progressively steeper down the hill. Pretty red roofed and white walled houses clung to the slopes, and the old thatched houses were Grade II listed buildings.
The half-moon of the bay unfurled below the hills, waves drawing the sea to the sandy beach. Maggie stopped for a while to catch her breath, and admire the view. It was a lovely day, with the sun playing peek a boo with the clouds. The seagull swooped and swirled, gliding in the air above the waters.
Maggie got to the Market Street, where the few shops, post office and bank were based. She walked into the post office, where a woman was putting up a poster on the front window. Maggie read the poster's sign and paused.
It was about a missing baby, who was lost at sea two years ago. There was a photo of the little newborn in her cot. She had a fluffy pink blanket, and a toy pony rested by the baby's feet, on the blanket.
The mother was appealing for help.
Maggie looked at the pale, drawn face of the young woman putting up the sign.

She finished sticking the edges to the glass and stepped back. She was dressed in a cardigan and jeans. She was skin and bones, face without make up. Her dark brown hair was combed straight back. Despite that, she was naturally attractive, her dark eyes deep and soulful. When she looked at Maggie, her eyes dipped down to Maggie's belly, and she smiled. There was a sadness in that knowing smile that broke Maggie's heart.

"How many weeks have you got left?" The woman asked, getting closer to Maggie.

"Ten weeks and counting," Maggie smiled back, placing a hand over her protruding tummy.

"It goes by so quickly." The smile faltered on the woman's face, and was replaced by a harrowing, forlorn look. The face of a woman who has lost all hope and has nowhere to turn.

Maggie said, "Are you alright?"

The woman looked at the floor and nodded. Maggie pointed at the poster. "Is that your child?"

"Yes."

"What happened?" Maggie looked around the post office. It was quiet, and there were two chairs by the entrance. "Let's sit down."

"What's your name?" Maggie asked.

"Ruth Hodgson." Ruth looked at Maggie curiously. "Who are you?"

"I'm a detective constable for North Yorkshire Police. I'm here on a police matter, but don't worry about that," Maggie smiled.

Maggie asked her about what happened, and slowly, Ruth spoke. She stopped several times to wipe her eyes. Instinctively, Maggie reached for her hand. By the end, Maggie also found her eyes wet with sadness. Ruth's heartbreak was like a shockwave, sending tremors in her soul. Maggie couldn't imagine what this poor woman had been through.

"So, this happened in Staithes?"

"Yes. That's where I live, still. It's hard to stay there, and if I don't find Jenny soon, I'll have to leave. My mother will too. But first, I need to try to find Jenny. We're going up and down the coast, putting up posters. We're on the missing person website, and I've also spoken to the police. They didn't want to get involved as there was no crime committed, they said."

Maggie thought for a while. "And no charges were brought against anyone, right?"

"That's right."

"Okay. If you want, I can make some enquiries. But you're doing the right things so far. Local knowledge and witnesses can be very useful in cases like these. If I were you, I would make the posters bigger, and also write your contact phone number in larger letters. If you don't get any joy, offer a reward. It doesn't have to be much, anything you can afford. You'll be surprised how much people care when there's money on the line."

"Thank you," Ruth said. "I'll do that. We're checking the coast by boat as well, but it's a thankless task as you can imagine. My uncle's a fisherman, so we're using his boat."

Maggie considered this. "Did your uncle know people in Runswick Bay? Or did you, for that matter?"

"No."

"This man who dropped off the letter and the toy pony at your doorstep, can you describe him to me again?"

"Middle aged man, weather beaten face. He wore blue jeans and a dark brown jacket. The shopkeeper in Staithes, Derek, said the man looked like a fisherman."

Maggie narrowed her eyes. "Does Derek's shop have CCTV?"

CHAPTER 43

Rita steadied herself on the deck of the boat, planting her legs apart. Then she moved to the foredeck, trying to keep the sound of her steps as soft as possible. The harbourmaster had gone. There was no one else in this section of the marina, and apart from the whisper of a gentle breeze blowing in from the sea, it was quiet.

Richard had stopped, and was looking down at something. Rita couldn't follow his gaze because the cockpit was in the way. She checked out the engine and steering wheel of the cockpit cabin. She stepped inside the cabin, then froze as she heard a sound. It came from under her feet. It was a soft clunk, but she didn't imagine it. She remained still and listened hard. There was no sound anymore, but it was clear she needed to head below deck. She waved at Richard till she got his attention. She indicated down with her finger and mouthed *I heard a sound.*

She moved out of the cabin slowly. Her senses were on fire. Richard was behind her as she took the first step down to the cabin below. She looked behind and raised a hand, telling him to stay where he was. He wasn't happy, but he knew she wanted him to stop anyone if they came charging out.

Rita put her gloves on, then depressed the door handle. It opened with a creak. The lounge room was visible, with the sofas, dining table and chairs, all screwed to the floor. It was empty, like the kitchen behind it.

Rita moved inside, leaving the door open. She could see the narrow corridor that led to the bathroom and bedroom behind. The corridor was right under the cockpit cabin. That's where the sound came from. Rita suspected someone was here.

She moved slowly, flicking out her extendable baton. It made a snapping sound as it extended to its full height. It wasn't a gun, but she had used it stop men in their tracks. A crack to the head was all it took.

She looked around the kitchen, opening the cupboards with one hand. They were well stocked. There was a plate and cutlery in the sink. She touched the kettle, it was warm. This kitchen was being used. Holding the baton tightly in her right hand, but holding her wrist loose so she could snap it if necessary, Rita moved slowly ahead. She nudged the bathroom door open with a foot. There was no one inside. She noted the toothbrush and man's shaving kit on the shelf in front of the mirror.

Then she moved to the bedroom. The door was closed, and she had to reach for the handle. She opened it a fraction, then stepped back. She kicked the door open with her foot, holding the baton in front of her. A quick glance showed her the double bed was empty, as was the rest of the bedroom. There was a wardrobe that was large enough to hide a man inside. Its doors were shut. Two round oculus windows let in light, but they couldn't be opened from inside.

Rita dropped to her knees and looked under the bed. Apart from cobwebs and a gym bag, she saw nothing. She heard steps behind her, and whirled around. It was Richard. She put a finger to her lips and he nodded. He tapped the radio on his left chest pocket. Then he mouthed *backup*. Rita understood. Sergeant Cleverly and his men had arrived at the harbour. Rita gave him the thumbs up sign, and went back to her task. She needed to clear this room quickly. She went inside, holding the baton in front of her like sword, raised and ready to strike. She got to the wardrobe and took a deep breath. Then she yanked it open. It had some clothes inside, and a shoe rack. But no hiding human being.

But she did hear something when she was up on the deck. And it came from down here. She didn't imagine it. Rita removed all the clothes from the wardrobe and dumped them on the bed. She reached out a hand, and roamed it around the rear wall of the wardrobe. It was fitted to the wall, as expected. Then she stilled. She had moved her hand carefully, in case there was a nail poking out. But she didn't feel a nail. She went back to the spot. There it was. About waist height. A shallow, soft depression. Almost as if there was a hole here. Only it wasn't a hole, and she would've missed it if she didn't feel for it.

"Richard, give me your light," Rita said over her back.

Soon, the bright beam of the pencil torch illuminated the dark rear of the wardrobe.

Rita handed her baton to Richard, then reached into the soft depression with both hands. She could now grip the sides of what was clearly a carved-out compartment. And now she could hear something else. The sound of breathing. Either a human, or an animal. And Rita knew who it was.

She didn't push any further, in case he caught her hands. "David," Rita shouted. "Come out of there. You're surrounded, don't even try to escape."

Silence greeted her, but the faint sound of breathing was now stronger. Richard shone the light into the hole, and they could now see a shadow moving inside.

"Make it easier for yourself, David. Come out now," Rita called out again.

There was a slight scuffle, then the rear panel of the wardrove moved. It bent outwards like a folding door, and then slid to one side. A man stood there. It was David Foley, the engineer she had seen in the boatyard. His teeth were bared in savage fury, and his eyes were blood shot red. He held a hunting knife in one hand, the blade long and dangerous.

He held up the knife, pointing it at Richard and Rita. "You came to get me? I'll cut you to bloody ribbons." He moved swiftly, lunging at Rita with the knife in his hand.

CHAPTER 44

Rizwan was glad he had the earbuds on otherwise he would've missed Maggie's call. He was on the beach, and he turned away from the sea, cupping hands over his ears as he answered his phone.
"Now then, our kid, how are you, like?"
"Fine and dandy. Listen Riz, I'm up in Staithes. The guv sent me to Runswick Bay to speak to the victim's family there and see what I could find out. I spoke to his aunt, and a couple of the villagers. He seems like a clean skin, no trouble."
"What're you doing up in Staithes, though?" Rizwan was confused.
"Well, I met this woman in Runswick Bay. Her name's Ruth Hodgson, and she was lookin' for her missing baby. It's a long story; I'll tell you when I see you. But I came up to Staithes to help her. You see, someone dropped her a note to say her baby was alive and well. The baby's name was Jennifer, or Jenny, for short. She disappeared in her cot, and she was wrapped in a pink rug. The rug had her name on it, and in the cot, there was also a toy pony. The pony and letter, bearing the child's correct name, was left on Ruth's doorstep."
"Right," Rizwan said slowly, more confused than before. "Why are you tellin' me this?"

"I'm getting to the point, hold on. A shopkeeper saw the man who dropped the envelope at Ruth's house. His shop has CCTV inside. This man was caught on camera and I've just seen him."

"Are you still getting to the point? 'Cos I can't see one." Rizwan frowned.

"The man's photos on CCTV match the description of our victim. Andrew Salford. Now, I never saw him obviously. But the guv sent me his file, and I've seen his passport photo. By heck, he looks like this man in the shop."

"Whoa, whoa, hold on," Rizwan said. He sat down on a rock. The surf rolled a distance behind him, and he had walked away from the water. "Can you send me the video footage?"

"That's why I called. Have a look at it then call me back. Hold on." Maggie hung up.

A moment later, Rizwan's phone pinged with the video file. He was glad he had reception out here. He clicked on the file, and the video played. The man looked down at the counter all the time, and the back of his head was visible. But when he went out of the shop, his face was caught on camera.

Rizwan's breath stilled as his hands tightened around his phone.

That was Andrew Salford.

Rizwan pulled out the files on his phone and checked Andrew's passport and driving licence photos. There was no mistake. The man in the shop was definitely Andrew Salford. Riz rang Maggie back.

"That's him all right. Our victim. What the heck was he doing there? You said he left a note at this woman's door, about her missing baby?"

"Aye. Ruth says he's correct about the baby's name, and that pink toy pony is exactly the same toy she had left in the baby's cot. The pony had the baby's initials in it. He also mentioned the pink rug the baby was wrapped in."

"But how did Andrew…" words failed Rizwan as numerous strands of thought roped around his mind like knots in a fishing net.

Maggie spoke softly. "He could've seen another woman, or a family, with the baby in the pink rug, and heard them call her name. At close quarters. Like in a church, or wherever, I don't know. But how did he get the toy pony?"

Rizwan thought hard, shaking his head. "This is surreal. Even if we can figure this out, what does it have to do with Andrew's murder?"

"I don't know. But this happened a week before Andrew died. I can't help thinking it's important, somehow."

"What about the baby's father?"

"He's in jail, doing time for armed robbery. I called and checked – he's in HMP Rotherham."

Rizwan massaged his forehead. "How did the baby disappear?"

Maggie told him and Rizwan's eyebrows rose as a space cleared in his chest, leaving him vacant.

"My god," he whispered. "That's unbelievable."

"And yet true. Police were involved at the time, but no criminal charges were made."

"Have you told the guv?"

"I can't get hold of her," Maggie said. "Anyway, I'm heading back soon. I'll see you back at the nick? Any sign of that old bugger, Jonty?"

"Not as yet. But the tide's coming up now, and it's not safe here anymore. So we're calling off the search for today. HMCG will do patrols around the beach to see if anyone tries to land. See you soon."

CHAPTER 45

For Rita, time had slowed down. She saw David jump towards her, the knife flashing, a wild gleam in his eyes.
He swiped up with the knife, and in slow motion, Rita leaned back, letting the knife slash past her torso. Then her hand was raised, baton striking David's wrist, the impact a bone jarring shock that rattled up into her shoulders. David screamed and fell to his knees.
Richard kicked David in the head, making him sprawl to the side, then jumped on top of him. Rita had her radio out, shouting into it. David was fighting back. His right hand was out of action, but he could still swing with his left. Rita tried to help, but there wasn't much space.
She jumped on the bed and tried to hit David with the baton, but the chances of striking Richard were too high. Then the room was suddenly swarming with uniformed officers. Rita went out as a scuffle ensued. She waited in the deck with Sergeant Cleverly, as his men dragged David out, kicking and screaming.
His hands were cuffed behind him, and he was held down on the deck when he spat at one of the officers. Rita knelt on the floor to speak to him.
"You are under arrest for suspicion of murder, breaking and entering and grievous bodily harm. Do you understand?"

"Fuck you," David said.

"Charming," Rita said, rising. "That attitude isn't going to help you."

"I didn't do anything," David bellowed as he was pulled to his feet.

Rita eyed him. "Where's Jonty Stanforth?"

"I don't know."

"If you cooperate this become easier for you, David. I can put in a good word to the right people. You know how it works. Help us and you get a lighter sentence."

David snarled, but didn't say anything. Rita gestured at the uniforms to leave her and Richard alone with David. He remained on the deck floor, hands cuffed. The uniformed officers climbed out of the boat and stood on the marina, watching them.

Rita lowered her voice. "You didn't kill Andrew, did you?"

David narrowed his eyes. "No, I didn't. And you know it."

Good, Rita thought. She was getting him to talk without a lawyer.

She nodded. "Does Jonty have the bags?" David looked away from her.

Rita pressed on. "Andrew had the bags first. He picked them up from another boat at sea or from a beach. Then Jonty took them down to Cloughton Wyke beach. Matt was supposed to meet him there, wasn't he?"

"No comment," David said. Rita feared he might ask for a lawyer soon. She dropped her bomb.

"Matt's dead, David. And the person who killed him might be after you now. Is that person Jonty?"

David clenched his jaws hard, and then opened his mouth to breathe. Slowly, he turned to look at Rita. Rage burned in his eyes.

"You're lying about Matt."

Rita took out her phone and scrolled to the right image. Then she showed David the photo of Matt's face with the bullet hole in the back of his head. David's jaws went slack.

"I think Jonty did that, so he could keep all the stuff in the bags. Where is Jonty, David?"

"You're the police, why don't you bloody find out," David snarled. But his attitude was different now. The steam was going out of him. Rita knew seeing Matt's photo had made a difference. He averted his face, grinding his jaws together.

"They cleaned out your house, David," Rita said softly. "Your clothes, car, even your toothbrush – all gone."

David kept his face turned away, but he snapped his eyes shut once. He was an armed robber. A hardened criminal who was used to violence. But Rita could tell she was getting under his skin.

"You're lucky we got to you first. This boat was the next place they would've searched for. Who are they, David? They don't want you alive, do they?"

David shook his head. Then he looked at the ground, between his legs. He looked up at Rita, then at Richard.

"I want a lawyer," he said.

Rita tried not to show her disappointment.

If David had talked, her work would be a lot easier. But David was a veteran of the justice system. He knew how to make life difficult for the police. He could use a number of tactics now to stall Rita. Rita sighed and rose to her feet. "Alright. Let's get him into custody."

***

At the office, Maggie and Rizwan were already present. Maggie was pink cheeked and blooming, with a smile on her face. She looked tired, Rita thought, and she wondered if she had done the right thing by giving into Maggie's demands for a job. On the way back from Bridlington, she had received a text from HR that said Maggie's job role was accepted. She would get a salary as a researcher, on top of her maternity benefits.

Rita told her now and Maggie clapped her hands happily. "Thanks guv, I knew you'd come through for me."

"Don't get too excited," Rita cautioned. "I don't want you to go traipsing around everywhere. You need to take it easy."

"I was careful," Maggie said. "I drove everywhere, walked slowly, didn't go up and down hills. Well, a few steps in Runswick Bay, but that's it." Maggie looked around her. "The three R's are back." That was her nickname for Rita, Richard and Rizwan.

"Aye," Rizwan said. "Tell the guv what you found."

Rita and Richard sat down while Rizwan went to get coffees for them. He wasn't happy about it, but Maggie couldn't help him. He grumbled as he left and Maggie blew him a raspberry. Then she looked at Rita, getting serious. Her face changed like a cloud had gone over it.

"I tried to call you," Maggie said. "But you were after the suspect. I found out something very strange."

Rita listened as Maggie told the story of Ruth, her baby and how Andrew was involved.

"How weird," Rita frowned. "How did Andrew get hold of the toy pony?"

"That's exactly what I thought. He might've known what happened to the baby, but to get the pony he had to be in the house where the baby was. But there's something else, guv. Melanie's daughter, Carla, wasn't born in Runswick Bay. They moved before the baby was born. I think she must've been pregnant at the time, and gave birth in Filey, or Scarborough General Hospital to be precise, as there's no maternity unit in Filey Community Hospital."

"Good," Rita nodded. "Have you checked the birth's register at the hospital to see when Carla was born?"

"Not yet. But I'm sure we'll find it. I called Melanie, by the way, and introduced myself. She was out shopping, with Carla. She said to call back in a couple of hours."

Rita stood, and paced the room, hands clasped behind her back. There was a knock on the door, and she opened it to let Rizwan in with a tray of coffee mugs and biscuits.

"Glad to see you being useful, Riz. That's a good lad," Maggie chirped.

"Shut up," Rizwan said, sitting down and reaching for his coffee.

Rita didn't take her coffee. After hearing Maggie's story, an uneasiness had settled on her like a heavy cloak. She turned to Maggie.

"Did Ruth say if Andrew tried to contact her again?"

"No, it was just that one time. When he left the letter and the pony."

"Show me the CCTV footage from the shop," Rita said. She went to Maggie's desk and took her phone, where the video was playing. She nodded.

"That's Andrew there's no doubt. The fact that his happened a week before his death…that bothers me. I think Melanie knows about this baby. I want to speak to her."

"I'll call her soon."

"Have you got Ruth Hodgson's PCN from when she first called about the missing baby?"

"It was her mother, Carol, who called and filed the PCN, but yes, I do."

Rita sat down at her laptop and looked through the PCN. It was a harrowing read. She couldn't imagine what Ruth had gone through, and how Carol, the grandmother had also suffered.

Rita looked at her watch. It was almost six pm. It had been a long day, and she had skipped lunch. Hunger gnawed in her belly, and a pressure behind her eyes was growing. She pressed her palms to her eyes, rubbing them slowly.

She still had to interview David. He might know where Jonty is, but she doubted he would talk if he now had a solicitor. She looked up at Maggie and Rizwan.

"Is Ruth here, or in Staithes?"
Maggie answered. "She's staying in Scarborough tonight. She came back with me. Baby Jennifer is up on the missing person unit already, but I promised her I'd raise this with you, to see if we can open an investigation."
Rita rose, her tired brain fighting against the tide of a new concern surging in her mind.
"I want to speak to Ruth."

CHAPTER 46

20 months ago

Staithes

Ruth woke up with a fire burning in her brain. It was pitch black dark. A wind howled outside, matched by the distant thudding of the surf against the rocks. But all sound was drowned out by the shrieks of Jennifer crying.
Ruth was paralysed with fear. She could hear the crackling of the dry heat, branches splintering in a wild forest. A fire was raging, red, red, yellow orange and the flames were licking up the walls, scalding her skin. The voices were whispering in her mind again. Sharp jabs of a needle, piercing her peace, perforating her sanity. The flames went higher, crashing through the roof.
Above that, she heard the howl of Jennifer's loud cry.
"No!" she screamed, clasping hands over her ears. She drew her knees into her chin, and squeezed her hands between her head till she thought her skull would crack.
"NO!" She screamed again. "Leave me alone. Go away!" She sobbed, beating her fists against the side of her skull.

But the voices didn't go. Like the flames licking higher, they grew stronger. The whispers were louder, like lashes of a whip on her mind.
"The devil is waiting. She's waiting next door…"
A horrible vision emerged in front of Ruth's eyes. Jennifer crawling towards her, on the floor. But she wasn't a little baby anymore. She had the body of a large dog, like an adult Staffordshire bull. She had long teeth, drooping with saliva. Her eyes were red and they gleamed like hot coal. She bared her teeth, growling, staring at Ruth.
"No," Ruth whispered. Sweat had drenched her body, clothes sodden wet. "Go away," she shivered, her body now shaking. "Leave me alone."
The menacing creature said nothing. It had Jennifer's angelic face, but the eyes had changed, the teeth were sharp, long….it was a hideous, macabre sight.
The creature growled again, and came closer to Ruth's bed.
"No!" Ruth screamed. She flung the covers off, jumped off the bed, and ran out of the room. The baby's room was adjacent to her. She had moved the cot here when she couldn't tolerate the cries anymore. It was dark, but she could still see cot. When she looked inside, the shock hit her like a hammer blow to her guts.
That creature was inside the cot. It had Jennifer's face, but the burning eyes were red and gleaming, the fangs dripping with saliva. Then it changed again, and became the sleeping baby. Her peaceful, angelic baby who was in perfect repose.

Only, now Ruth knew the truth. Her chest heaved and breath tore in her lungs as she stared down at the baby's cot.
Jennifer wasn't Jennifer anymore. She wasn't a baby any longer. The devil had infested her soul.
The devil was that creature with the scissor sharp teeth and burning eyes, and it would come for Ruth again, whispering the voices, attacking her while she slept.
Those sharp teeth would sink into Ruth's flesh, tearing her muscles from her bones.
"No," Ruth whispered. Her body was shaking like a leaf in a storm. Her ice-cold hands were fists by her side. She put the bedside lamp on. She picked up Jennifer. The baby was swaddled in a pink rug with her name on it, and the pink pony toy was inside the rug. She looked around the room wildly and her eyes fell on a shopping bag.
Ruth put Jennifer in the bag, then ran out of the house. The gale force wind shrieked into her face. The voices were louder, clamouring in her skull.
"Get rid of the devil," they screamed. "Save yourself."
Ruth didn't know what she was doing. Her legs moved of their own accord. She went down the deserted street, and took the alley where she saw the steps that went down to the beach. She could hear the surf smashing against the rocks in the distance.

There was a wooden jetty at the end of the steps. It was relatively protected by a shallow, rocky cove. A small boat was tied to the jetty. As if hypnotised by the voices inside her, Ruth walked on the jetty. She was barefoot, and the wet wood was freezing against the soles of her feet. She crouched on the jetty, the wind howling in her ears, brushing hair into her face. "Give the devil away," the voice whispered. "Do it now."

Ruth leaned over the jetty. She put the shopping bag with Jennifer in it on the boat. Jennifer didn't make a sound. She had fallen asleep. Ruth untied the rope that held the boat to the jetty.

She gave the boat a push, and watched the boat moved out into the sea.

Then she stood, her body numb with cold, mind like a block of ice. With frozen feet, she walked back up the steps, into the alley, then higher up into her street. She walked up and down the street, her feet wet, toes like icicles. Then she stumbled into her house, and collapsed on the floor, leaving the front door open. That's how Carol found her when she arrived the next morning.

CHAPTER 47

Ruth wiped the tears in her eyes and lowered her head.
Rita and Maggie stared at her. The clock ticked on the wall. They were in the family room of the police station, which had sofas, and was nicer than the interview rooms in the custody cells downstairs.
Rita felt the room was in a vacuum, all air sucked out of it. She could barely breathe. She forced herself to think. There was a link between Andrew's death and Ruth's missing baby. She felt it in her bones, but the link remained just beyond her reach and it was frustrating.
"What happened after that?" Maggie asked. "Tell us everything."
Ruth sipped from the glass of water on the coffee table in front of her. "I was admitted as an inpatient to the Cross Lane Psychiatric Hospital in Scarborough. For a week, I was in the Psychiatric Intensive Care Unit, or PICU. It was basically a prison. I had a matron who watched me constantly, and I was in a private cell. I was sedated on heavy drugs. I barely remember that week."
Ruth sighed and passed a hand over her face.

"After that I was moved to the general psychiatric ward in Cross Lane, and I stayed there for the next four months. That's where I met Dr Vik Patel, my psychiatrist. I think he felt sorry for me. With his help, I was able to reduce the heavy sedating medications. I couldn't even think straight on those meds. I just wanted to sleep. They also made me very hungry, and I put on weight."

Rita noticed Ruth was now skin and bones, her hands skeletal. The cardigan was loose on her thin shoulders. She was a pretty young woman, but her sunken cheeks and gaunt looks made her look sick.

"Eventually, I was allowed to go home. A community psychiatric nurse and her team attended twice every week to see me. I also had to go and see Dr Patel every week. It took me a year to feel normal again."

"What was the diagnosis?" Rita asked. "Some sort of psychosis?"

Ruth looked at Rita. "Yes. I suffered with depression before, and I was on medications. But I didn't take any during the pregnancy. That made my post-natal depression worse. That led to what the doctors called post-natal psychosis."

Rita nodded. "When did you start looking for your baby?"

"I was tormented, as you can imagine.

After what happened, I was barely allowed to step outside the house without my mum, or my case worker.

I was deemed a risk to others.

But after one year, Dr Patel helped me to reduce the restrictions on my social life.

I was allowed to go shopping. I still suffered with the depression. I'm still on medications. It was about fourteen months from the incident that I finally started looking for Jennifer."

Maggie said, "There was a case, wasn't there? You were not charged due to diminished responsibility."

"That's right. Social services and the Yorkshire Polie safeguarding teams were involved. I wasn't called to the tribunal. My mum and Dr Patel testified on my behalf. I was in cloud cuckoo land, to be honest, at that time. Heavily sedated and barely functioning."

"And what now? How far have you got in your search?"

Ruth sighed and looked down at the table. "The boat left Staithes and went out to sea. No one found it again. My uncle's a fisherman, and he looked around at the other coves and beaches. So did his friends. They didn't find the wreckage of the boat. It just sailed away and I lost my baby."

Splotches of colour appeared on her face, and tears budded in her eyes. She wept, shoulders shaking. Then she composed herself.

Maggie said softly, "But you kept searching, and HMCG were also aware of the situation. But they didn't find anything either, did they?"

"No, they didn't. But then I got the message on my doorstep. And I knew immediately that my Jenny was alive and well. The person who wrote the letter didn't sign his name. But now we know who he is."

"Yes," Rita said softly. She glanced at Maggie. "Thank you."

"No problem," Maggie said. She also looked emotional – all of them were. "The key thing now is to find Jenny."

"Andrew knew," Ruth said. "It had to be someone whose house he went to regularly." Then a hardness glinted in her eyes, her posture changing as she sat up straighter. "Or he had the child."

The suspicion had revolved in Rita's mind from when she heard Maggie's story. But she wanted to hear Ruth's opinion.

"What do you mean?" Rita asked.

"I mean Andrew and his wife found the boat. Then they kept my baby. I don't know how Andrew discovered Jennifer was mine. Maybe he saw a poster in Runswick Bay, or someone told him about me. Maggie said he was a fisherman. He put two and two together."

Maggie said, "Melanie didn't have her daughter when she lived in Runswick Bay." Then she exchanged a glance with Rita. "And I checked before coming down here. There is no record of Carla Salford – her daughter's – delivery in the birth record of Scarborough Hospital. However, we do have the birth record of baby Jennifer to you," Maggie looked back at Ruth, who nodded.

Ruth said, "Jenny's father wasn't present at the birth. It was an accidental pregnancy, and while I regret being with him, I'm also glad I could raise Jenny on my own." She held eyes with Rita. "But I just know Andrew found Jenny. Don't ask me how. I feel it in my bones."

Rita felt a coldness seeping into her limbs. She looked at both of the women, and the realisation was clear on their faces. But she had to be rational. She asked Maggie.
"Carla could've been born in another hospital."
"I looked in Bridlington, Hull, York and Leeds," Maggie said. "Then in the national directory. Melanie's name was never registered as the birth mother of a child. And Andrew has never registered as the father."
With cold fingers, Rita took her phone out. She showed Ruth the photos of Andrew and Melanie. Ruth shook her head.
"No, I've never seen them."
Rita's pulse was cannon balling against her ribs as the shock spread through her limbs. She too, knew it was the terrible truth. Melanie and Andrew had raised Ruth's baby as their own.
She showed Ruth the photos of Jonty, David and Matt. Again, she shook her head.
"No, I don't know these people. But my uncle was a fisherman. He helped me to search and also spread the word. He might know Andrew, to be honest. He's from Runswick Bay, but lives in Staithes now."
"Did you show your uncle the letter?"
"He knew about it, yes. But until Detective Long," Ruth indicated Maggie, "asked me about the CCTV in the shop, we didn't know who he was."
Ruth continued. "My mother and uncle told their friends, and the news spread in our community. We took out ads in local papers. I'm sure Andrew came to know by speaking to someone."

Rita nodded. She asked Ruth for the note, and the woman took it out of her coat pocket and slid it across the table.

Rita read it carefully.

"Your daughter Jennifer is well and happy. She's in a good home and very well looked after. She will have a good life, don't worry. I will stay in touch and let you know how she is. Jennifer started to walk when she was twelve months old. She babbles a lot and is trying to talk.

I'm leaving the pony that she came with. I also have the pink rug she was wrapped in, that had her name sewed in the bottom right corner. Jennifer is happy and thriving. One day, I hope we can all meet up. I will send these notes to you often, telling you how she is.

Jennifer sends her love."

Rita found it hard to stay focused and professional as she read the words. She wasn't a mother herself, but she felt the pain that Ruth must've felt when she found the letter. Rita blinked away tears, swallowed a heavy weight at the back of her throat, and handed the letter to Maggie.

She told Ruth, "We need to keep this as evidence, if you don't mind."

"I have a copy," Ruth said. "Detective Long already told me I need to submit it, and the pink toy pony."

Rita opened her mouth to speak, but there was a knock on the door.

CHAPTER 48

Rita and Maggie were back upstairs. Ruth had gone back to the hotel she was staying overnight with her mother, Carol. Rita leaned over Rizwan's desk, who had knocked on the door.

"It's not a coincidence," Rizwan said, pointing at the screen. "Look at the father's name on Melanie's birth certificate."

Rita couldn't believe it. But the words were there in black and white. There was no doubt.

Melanie's maiden name was Stanforth. Her father's name was Jonty Stanforth. Rita stared at the screen in shock, her mind rumbling like thunder clouds. There was a storm coming, and the dark clouds were getting more ominous by the second.

Richard put a hand over his mouth and stifled a yawn. "Unless there's another harbourmaster called Jonty Stanforth, which is highly unlikely, I think it's safe to conclude Melanie is Jonty's daughter."

"And it's entirely possible Andrew and Melanie found baby Jennifer, and decided to keep her," Rita said, looking up at Richard. The shockwaves were still echoing in her mind. Could this be possible? Had Melanie planned this with her father, Jonty, all along? Rita's mind was running helter-skelter, but out of the chaos, a pattern was emerging. Pieces of the jigsaw were finally slotting into place.

Maggie discovering that Melanie had not been pregnant while she lived in Runswick Bay had been the trigger. Rita owed Maggie the crucial breakthrough. Thank goodness she came back to work.

Richard said, "We don't know how exactly Andrew got Jennifer, and the only person who will know is Melanie. Have we got in touch with her?"

Richard and Rizwan shook their heads. Richard said, "A uniformed unit from Filey and Eastwick are at Melanie's house. She's not there and her car is also gone. Her friend Sarah doesn't know where she is. Uniforms have done a door to door, but no one knows."

Rizwan said, "Melanie's not answering her phone. It's switched off. I've asked Traffic to triangulate her last call. Let's see if we can get a location hook."

Rita massaged her tired forehead. The pressure behind her eyes was like a knife now, piercing into a sharp point. She shook her head, trying to dispel the exhaustion. She pointed a finger at Maggie.

"Go home, now."

"But-

"No," Rita said firmly. "You've been a great help, but now you need to rest. You can't just think about yourself anymore, correct?"

Maggie sighed, but she didn't look too unhappy. "Alright, guv. But keep me posted, yeah? I want to know what's happening." She glanced at Rizwan, who nodded.

After Maggie left, Rita excused herself and went to the canteen. She had to eat something; her stomach was creating a hunger cavity in her abdomen.

Evening food at the canteen wasn't exactly inspiring. There was still some leftover from lunch, and she picked up some lasagne, and sat down to eat. She closed her eyes as she chewed. Her mind was firing again, synapses reigniting.

With it, came a wave of anger. She had believed Melanie, but Melanie was the person who had carefully stage crafted this entire show. Right from when she drove to Scarborough Harbour, to search for her missing husband. To meet with Jonty, the harbourmaster. Her father, Jonty. Melanie knew the CCTV cameras would show her at the harbour. She was the worried wife, searching for her husband.

Did she kill Andrew?

Andrew clearly had a conscience. He wanted Ruth to know her baby was safe and sound. Did he also threaten to tell Ruth the whole story? If that happened, Melanie would lose her baby.

Melanie didn't have an alibi for the night Andrew died. But would she really leave Carla at home, drive to Scarborough, then walk up to the castle ramparts on a windy night?

Maybe not. Maybe she got someone to do her dirty work for her.

Her father, Jonty.

Rita's jaws clamped tight as her nostrils flared. She didn't feel like eating, but she needed the energy. Her instincts told her Melanie was with Jonty now, and they had fled. They had taken Carla with them – and Carla was actually Jennifer, Ruth's lost baby.

There was no other explanation for Melanie not being around. The implications spread tentacles around her brain. She finished eating, then pushed her plate away and stood. She had paid for her meal already. She went down to the custody centre, where the sergeant was surprised to see her.

"I want to see David Foley," Rita said. "Now."

The custody sergeant's name was Whitaker, and he scratched his head. "But guv, we need to call the duty solicitor."

"There's no time," Rita grit her teeth together. "Take me to his cell, now. Don't worry, I'll sign the book."

"Guv, I-

"Put it down as an unscheduled visit," Rita said. She knew the law. Prisoners had all sorts of protections. Rita couldn't speak to a suspect without their lawyer being present. She knew she could get into trouble for this. But she didn't care.

She signed her name on the log book, and Sergeant Whitaker reluctantly took her to the steel door that swung open with his fob key. They walked down the corridor of the custody chambers. David was in a cell near the end. Whitaker slid back the viewing box to make sure David was awake and decent.

"Leave us," Rita said. Whitaker was unsure again. "In case he gets violent I should stick around, guv."

Rita knew he was only doing his job. And he was right. She was letting her anger dictate her actions, and she needed to control herself.

"Okay, stand outside, okay? I just want to talk to him. I'll call for you if needed."

Whitaker agreed, and opened the door for Rita. She stepped inside. David was lying on the bed, arms clasped behind his head. Rita didn't give him the chance to talk. She stood over him as he watched her warily.

"Where is Jonty?"

David narrowed his eyes. "You can't be here. I want my lawyer."

"Shut up, you idiot," Rita ground out between clenched teeth. "A baby's life is at stake here. There's more going on than you will understand. If anything happens to that child, I swear to you, I'll charge you with accessory to murder. Your OCN bosses won't save you then."

David blinked at her. Rita knelt on the ground so she was on the same level as him. She thrust a finger at his face.

"The man who killed Matt is going to be after you. Do you understand?"

David's Adam's apple bobbed up and down. His nervous eyes darted around before they settled on Rita again.

David clamped his jaws shut. "No comment. I want my lawyer."

"You get out on the streets and you're as good as dead. The Hessle Boys won't be able to save you. Neither will your boss, Damien Salt."

David looked he'd been punched in the guts. His face was white as a sheet and his lips trembled.

"I want a lawyer."

"And you have one. But your lawyer can't get you a deal with the CPS for good behaviour, I can. What was in those bags? Money?"

David looked down, his shoulders slumping. When he looked up, Rita saw defeat in his eyes.
"Yes."
"Andrew got it, then Jonty stashed it, correct? But Jonty killed Matt, didn't he? Maybe because he wanted the money for himself. He didn't want to hand it back to your boss."
David closed his eyes, then shook his head. "No comment."
But Rita knew she was right. David's attitude had changed. He was close to giving up. He had nothing to lose, and by talking to Rita, he could save himself. She pressed on.
"You broke into Melanie Salford's house and assaulted her while her daughter was sleeping upstairs. You went into her room and you harmed the child, didn't you?"
David's jaws dropped. "What? No way, I don't-
"Whose word will the judge believe? Mine or yours? We have evidence that the child was harmed." Rita was clutching at straws, trying to light a fire under David's bottom, and it was working.
"Hang on! I never hurt a child."
"No one's going to believe you. But you can help us by telling me where Jonty might be. This is your last chance. Tomorrow, I'm going to charge you with physical abuse of a child in addition to GBH."
Rita was snarling, fire and brimstone in her voice, and David's face had paled. Rita suspected he knew where Jonty had a hiding bolt.
"The child is missing, and Jonty might've taken her. Where is Jonty?"

David looked like a cornered rat. His eyes slid sideways, then he seemed to make up his mind. "Okay," he whispered. "But you didn't get this from me. Do you understand?"

Rita nodded. "Tell me now."

CHAPTER 49

Rita ran up the stairs and skidded into the ground floor corridor. Then she ran to the office, smashing the door open, surprising Rizwan and Richard, who were still there.
"Where's Hayburn Wyke?"
Richard said, "Don't know, but let's have a look at the map. Why?"
"David talked. Jonty has a hiding place in Hayburn Wyke. There's no road down to the place, the last stretch is a steep hillside forest, which ends in a boulder strewn beach. But its used by local fishermen. Jonty has a hut in the hills, and he knows a path that leads down to the waters."
Rizwan was busy on his laptop, bringing up the map. He pulled up satellite images as Rita and Richard crowded around him to look.
The wild beach, or Wyke as it was known around here, was indeed remote, with no road route.
However, Rita noted quickly it was very close to Cloughton Wyke.
"Map the distance from there to Cloughton," Rita said, and Rizwan did so.
"Only one point six kilometres. And there's a road that goes past the hills, but it doesn't lead to Hayburn Wyke."

"That makes sense. But there will be country lanes a car can take, and those lanes won't be on CCTV. Like Salt Pan road, which Jonty took to head down to Cloughton Wyke."

Rizwan was staring at the map. "And Salt Pan Road actually skirts alongside Hayburn Wyke. I'm sure there's a path that connects them."

Richard said, "Jonty could easily have gone down to Hayburn Wyke, and not Cloughton, when he dropped off the bags that Andrew had in his boat."

"And that could be where he's hiding now," Rita said, straightening. She pressed the heel of her hand against her temples, massaging them slowly. This was turning out to be a long day, and the end was nowhere in sight. Rita knew she had to act now. This couldn't be left till the morning.

"Look, you two can go home now, and I'll deal with this." She looked at Richard, who exchanged a glance with Rizwan.

"No way," Richard said firmly. "Let's find Jonty and Melanie before this gets any worse."

Rizwan stood. "Do you want us to go up to Traffic and get some eyes on the road?"

Rita smiled at her troopers. She never took her team for granted. "Thank you, lads. Yes please. I'm going to contact Nicola and let her know what's happening. I want Bronze clearance for this, and block some A roads if necessary."

The authority levels in the Police Forces in UK ranged from Iron, Bronze, Silver and Gold. Iron meant there was a local emergency, and all units had to be involved. Bronze upgraded that to a county level serious event. Silver and Gold went higher still, covering wider regions, and Gold represented a massive counter terrorism or nuclear attack scenario.

Richard and Rizwan left, with Rizwan heading for Traffic upstairs, while Richard alerted the duty uniforms team. Alone in the office, Rita rang Nicola.

"I hope there's a good reason for disturbing my evening off," came the first words from the Det Superintendent, Nicola Perkins.

"There is, ma'am. I think I know who killed the two victims, and a child is missing."

"You think?" Nicola said, but the sting had gone from her voice. "I didn't know about the missing child."

Rita told her about Ruth and her missing baby, the connection with Andrew and Melanie.

"We can't contact Melanie, although we're still trying to triangulate her last call. It's possible she's fled with her father, Jonty. She's taken Carla with her, who is Ruth's child."

"But we can't prove that as yet. I know Andrew had the baby's rug and toy, but..." Nicola's voice trailed off. "...I take your point. Andrew knew Carla was Ruth's baby. Okay, what do you need?"

That was different from what Rita had expected. Normally, Nicola kicked up a fuss over the smallest request Rita made. Did robot woman have a soul, after all?

"I need Bronze clearance, ma'am. I want the A171 blocked in both directions. I also want air support over Cloughton and Hayburn in a twenty mile radius. I also want additional units from Bridlington and York."

"You're asking for a lot, Rita. This will take time to organise."

"In addition to the missing child, we also have an OCN at play. I suspect Jonty is deceiving the OCN and running off with their money. The money's in the black bags that Andrew got back with him. If we catch Jonty, chances are if the OCN's after him already, we can catch them too."

Nicola was silent for a few long seconds. Rita forced herself to be patient. Eventually Nicola spoke.

"Very well. I need to speak to the ACC for the Bronze clearance, but I don't think he'll mind. You can authorise air support."

"Thank you ma'am."

Rita hung up and ran upstairs. She spotted Richard sitting and Rizwan standing behind Madeline, or Maddy, the traffic sergeant. Four tv screens rested on her desk, and the wall at the end of the large room was taken up entirely by screens showing various areas of North Yorkshire. Scarborough was a small police station, but it was a technological hub for the North Yorkshire Police Force.

"Hi guv," Maddy said, without turning around. She was a bubbly blonde, her well done hair falling in curls to her shoulders. Rita put her hands on Maddy's shoulders.

"Your sixth sense is working well. Sure you don't want to be a detective?"

"I just know your footsteps, that's all. You're here so often. Not that I'm complaining. Do you know what happened to Troy yesterday?"

Troy was Maddy's teenage boy who had ADHD, and got into trouble at school frequently.

"We'll chat about Troy later. What have you got for me?"

Maddy took a long sip from her coffee cup. Rita's eyes scanned the screens on the table. They showed different sections of the A171 and other local roads. Maddy said, "You're looking for a grey VW, driven by Melanie Salford, is that right?"

"Correct. You got anything on ANPR?"

"We have the grey VW. It was last seen on the A165, coming out of Filey. It went up North, and then we lost it."

Maddy clicked on her keyboard, and the images came up. She pressed play and Rita watched the grey VW appear on the coloured screen, moving in the left lane of the dual carriageway, overtaking other cars. It was going fast. As the car went under a camera, Maddy paused the footage.

They caught a glimpse of a woman clutching the steering wheel with both hands. The passenger seat was empty. Maddy zoomed in and magnified the image, then put it through facial recognition software. It was Melanie.

"Where does the car go?" Rita asked. She read the time stamp. "This was at 19.40 hours. It's 20.15 now."

"I don't know. The car moves up the A165 on the stretch known as Filey Road, then takes a left into Scarborough, and joins the A171. That's all we have so far."

Maddy speeded up the video, and they watched the car streaking down the A171, moving out of Scarborough. An alert pinged on Maddy's screen loudly. She stopped the CCTV and returned to her live feeds.

The central screen showed a dark motorway, the two lanes of the dual carriageway empty. Then the headlights of a car flashed past, and it was the grey VW, the registration number lighting up on the screen, recognised by ANPR.

"It's heading for Cloughton Wyke," Maddy said, tapping on her keyboard, bringing up the map into focus.

Richard and Rizwan were standing next to Rita now, watching the screen with bated breath. The car turned into a road called Newlands Road.

"That leads to the Salt Pan Road," Richard cried out. "She's heading for Cloughton, or Hayburn, where her dad could be hiding."

Rizwan had broken off already, running for the door. "I'm getting the car ready," he called over his shoulder. "See you downstairs."

Rita checked that she had her radio. Her extendable baton was in the office downstairs. She thanked Maddy and ran for the exit, Richard fast on her heels. "Good luck," Maddy shouted after them, and Rita waved her hand in thanks.

CHAPTER 50

Rita was on the radio as the car screamed up the A171. She was speaking to Sergeant Kilpatrick of the HMCG.
"We have Bronze clearance," Rita shouted to raise her voice above the engine's sharp whine. "Can you please inform your patrol boats to monitor maritime traffic in Cloughton and Hayburn Wyke? They are small beaches without harbours. I can send you location details."
"No need," Kilpatrick said. "I know where they are. What are you looking for?"
"Not sure, to be honest," Rita said. "But any boats that are going in or out of those beaches need to be stopped and searched."
"No problem."
Rizwan had reached Cloughton, and he took the turning into Newland Road, then into Salt Pan. The night outside was now plunged into an inky darkness so thick Rita couldn't see anything apart from the road ahead, lit up in the headlights.
The road was made of cement, just wide enough in places to let a car pass from the opposite direction, but it was mostly a single lane. The road rose and fell, sections of it having crumbled into pot holes. Rizwan was forced to slow down.

"Watch out," Richard warned, as a four-legged furry animal ran across the path. It was a fox, illuminated briefly in the headlights before vanishing.

Richard said, "Only drivers who know this road drive on it after dark. Best to go as slow as you can."

Rizwan nodded, his face a mask of concentration as his white knuckles gripped the steering wheel. Rita saw headlights behind them, way back. Her radio crackled, and it was Inspector Botley.

"Now then, Rita. Is that you up ahead?"

"Aye, that's us. Any sign of the grey VW?"

"Nowt as yet. Air support should be with us soon, though."

"Thanks."

Rita hung up and put her window down. The fresh breeze carried sea salt and cold air, mingling with the scent of sage and heather. Rita unhooked the powerful flashlight from the dashboard and pointed it out her side, and Richard did the same from the backseat, to the opposite side, on the left. The car rolled along, moving up and down the uneven road. Rita kept her eyes focused on the grass and trees illuminated in the light beam.

"Stop," Richard shouted. Rizwan slammed on the brakes, and Rita hit her knuckles on the dashboard, holding the flashlight. She rubbed her hand, cursing at the pain.

"There's a car back there. I think it's a car anyway. A machine hidden under the branches of a tree."

Rizwan reversed slowly. Rita jumped out. Richard was already running for the tree, his flashlight sending a beam that jerked across the landscape. There was a thicket with several trees in the middle of a clearing. The land was relatively flat here, before the hills began a few miles out in the distance.

The ground was hard which was good for running. Rizwan ran past her, joining Richard as he disappeared into the vegetation that grew around the thicket.

"Be careful," Rita shouted. Her words were lost in the wind that streaked across her face, loosening strands of her hair.

Panting, and shirt sticking to her chest, she got to the cluster of trees. She waded into the undergrowth, using her baton to clear her way. There was indeed a car under the tree, Richard had done well to spot it.

"The light reflected off one of the wing mirrors," Richard explained as she got closer.

It was a grey VW, and the registration plate matched Melanie's car. The driver's door was open but the car was empty. Rizwan put his hand on the bonnet.

"It's slightly warm," he said, referring to the car's engine.

Rita let the lads search the car while she trained her light beam on the ground and followed it out of the thicket. She moved branches that leaned to the ground, and forced her way through the brush. Then she saw it. A piece of cloth, caught on a twig. It was followed by a child's water bottle.

"Over here," she called out. Rizwan joined her. "Rich is talking to Botley and updating him," he said.

"Look," Rita pointed at the water bottle. She put it in an evidence bag, and they followed a path through the thicket. She found a hair tie on the ground a little further ahead.

Rizwan had the satellite phone and used the GPS to get connection to maps. "Guv, we are close to Hayburn Wyke," he said.

Rita nodded, breath rasping in her lungs as she panted. They came out of the trees, into the clearing again. The path stretched out in front of them, and then dipped down, disappearing into nothing. In the distance, they saw the silver glint of moonshine on water, and heard the thunder of surf on the beach.

"That's Hayburn Wyke," Rizwan said.

"Let's go," Rita said, setting off on a run. Her tired legs protested, but she willed them to move.

CHAPTER 51

Rita's flashlight was on and she turned it off, aware the beam was giving her position away. Her eyes were used to the dark, but she had to be careful not to fall into a ditch now. She slowed down but didn't stop running. If Jonty and Melanie were meeting up here, she had to stop them before they got any further. Rizwan tapped her on the shoulder. "Guv, look to your right."

Rita stopped and peered into the darkness. The light from the moon was faint, obscured by clouds. At first, she only saw the vast shapes of the hills gradually descending to the sea. Then her eyes caught the glint of light in the forest that hugged the slopes. The dull yellow glint was higher than where she stood now. It was stationary.

"That could be a hut in the hills," Rizwan said.

"Jonty's hiding place, that David told you about."

"Yes." Rita did a swift calculation. "It's going to take us some time to get there by foot. Maybe an hour or more. You meet up with the uniforms team, and head down to the beach. Just in case Jonty's already down there."

"They wouldn't leave the light on, would they?"

"Not likely," Rita admitted. "But they might have, if they were in a rush. I don't want them to escape via sea. HMCG will patrol, but they might still miss a small boat."

Rizwan was reluctant, but Rita ordered him, and he nodded. "I'll catch up with you as soon as I rendezvous with the others. Be careful, guv. Jonty will have a weapon. He might be Matt's killer."
"I know."
Rita set off, running gently, then picking up pace as the moon slid past the clouds, showering the land with silvery shine. Sweat poured down her face and neck, soaking her back and chest. Her clothes would now be rinsed like a sponge, she thought. The baton was in her hand as she reached the slope of the hill. To her left, the sea spread out in a wide arc at the mouth of Hayburn Wyke, the surf booming against the boulders below. The tide was coming up. In an hour or so, the beach would disappear. Now was the right time to get a boat ready for sail.
Rita checked the yellow light on the hill. It was still lit, and brighter now that she was closer.
Rita scrambled up the slope, putting the baton back in her pocket. After a while, she stopped behind a tree trunk, to catch her beath. She could see the outline of a wooden hut and the porch now. It was perched on the slope, not too far from where she was now. The porch was lit in the bright bulb that hung over it. She saw a shape move inside the window. It was a woman.
Melanie.
Rita doubled her efforts to climb up the slope.
Her legs screamed in pain, arms heavy like lead. Exhaustion seemed to grow roots and pull her towards the earth.

She clenched her teeth and carried on upwards. She slipped and fell to her knees. The burst of agony in her legs took her breath away, and she stifled a cry. She got up and kept moving, sweat blinding her eyes. When she was about fifty metres from the hut, she went to ground, lying flat on her front. Melanie moved across the window again, and this time she had a baby in her arms. Rita looked around the hut. Trees hung over it, and the dense forest watched in silence. There was no sign of Jonty, or anyone else. Rita got up and ran across the clearing that led up to the hut. She didn't go up the front stairs and into the porch. She tried the back. A wind picked up, blowing dust her way. She heard a sound, and ran across to hide in the shadow of the trees. She saw Melanie open the backdoor, and put a bag on the rear porch. A flight of steps reached the ground from the rear porch. Rita rose as soon as the door shut. She tiptoed up the stairs, and tried the door handle. It was open. She let her eyes get used to the light, then slipped inside, closing the door soundlessly behind her.

CHAPTER 52

Rita heard sounds from the room on her left, which she thought was a bedroom. A hallway lay straight ahead, opening up into a lounge. The lights were on. There was a bathroom to her right, the door open. Another room lay in the front, next to the lounge. Rita crept forward, then peeked in through the ajar door of the bedroom. Melanie stood with her back to Rita. A large black bag rested on the wooden floor. Stacks of bank notes lay inside it, tied with elastic bands. Melanie was picking up the piles of notes and putting them inside a backpack on the bed.
Next to the bed, there was a cot, with baby Carla inside it. She was asleep, resting on her side, a thumb in her mouth.
Melanie was so engrossed in her work she didn't hear Rita come inside. Rita shut the door as softly as she could, but the latch snapped into the lock. Melanie jumped and whirled around; eyes wide. Shock and disbelief battled on her face as she stared at Rita. Her jaws dropped open.
"The game's up, Melanie," Rita said. Her right hand was loose by her side, clutching the butt of the baton. Rita pointed at the bag on the floor. "Your father, Jonty, picked up those bags, didn't he? He took them from Andrew's boat, and hid them out here."

Melanie still couldn't speak. She blinked, her right hand still clutching a roll of bank notes. Rita pointed at the money.

"How much is in the bag? Half a million? More? If Jonty's stealing that cash from the Hessle Boys, don't you think they're going to come after you?"

Melanie found her voice. "I…this is not what you think. This is my friend's place, and she found this bag with money here. We're taking it back to the police."

"Really? Then why do we have your dad, Jonty, on CCTV, taking the same bag from Andrew's boat?"

"I don't know."

"Like you don't know what happened to Ruth Hodgson's baby?"

Melanie's face paled. Breath seemed to freeze in her chest as she went rigid. Rita's eyes slid to the cot where the baby slept peacefully.

When Rita looked back at Melanie, she was clutching the bank notes tightly, her knuckles bone white.

"How did you get Jennifer?" Rita asked softly. "Tell me the truth.

"I…I don't know what you're talking about."

"You didn't give birth to a child two years ago. You never have. Your registered GP surgery documents do not show a pregnancy at any time, but you did have three miscarriages. Ruth wants her baby back. Don't lie any more, Melanie."

Melanie couldn't speak. Rita continued. "Andrew wanted to let Ruth know, didn't he? Well, he succeeded. Ruth found his letter and the toy pony. Was Andrew forcing you to contact Ruth and tell her the truth?"

Melanie's jaws clamped tightly shut and her nostrils flared. Splotches of red appeared on her neck.

"You cannot steal someone's child," Rita said slowly. "How would you feel if that happened to you?"

Melanie blinked, and her neck muscles became taut with tension. Unshed tears brimmed in her eyes.

"The game is up," Rita said softly. "Tell me the truth and I might be able to help you."

Melanie's wild eyes roamed around the room, then rested on Rita. Her voice shook with the weight of her words.

"I wanted a child. The doctor's said I couldn't have one."

"I'm sorry about that. But that doesn't mean you steal another woman's baby."

Melanie whimpered like a wounded animal. "She came to me. Andrew found the boat wrecked on the rocks at low tide. Miraculously, the baby was still alive, and unharmed. God gave us Carla."

Tears coursed down her cheeks. She dropped the stack of notes and wiped her eyes. She flopped down on the bed, her shoulders slumping forward. Rita moved closer, but Melanie didn't seem to notice.

"Did this happen when you were in Runswick Bay?"

"Aye. Andy found the boat and rescued Carla. He brought her up to me. I knew it was a sign. God saved Carla for me. She was mine to look after."

"That's why you left Runswick Bay so quickly. How did Andrew find out about Ruth and her missing baby?"

"Andrew went back to see his aunt and cousin in Runswick Bay after we moved. In the pub, he heard about this woman who lost her baby because she was mentally ill. He realised Ruth was Carla's real mother. He went up to Staithes, and spoke to people there, and found Ruth. Then he wanted me to tell Ruth."

"He had guilty conscience. Unlike you."

Melanie frowned at Rita. "That's not true. I felt bad for Ruth. But I didn't want to lose my child."

"She wasn't yours, though, was she?" Rita paused. "Is that why you killed Andrew?"

Melanie shot Rita a hard glance, and a new light glittered in her eyes. "No. I don't know what happened to Andrew."

"I think you do. The night of 6th April, when Andrew died, you don't have an alibi. Neither does your father, Jonty. Where were the two of you, that night?"

"I was at home."

"I also found a brown coat button on the castle ramparts. Maybe it got torn off during a scuffle. The button has yellow threads. Your father wears a jacket with brown buttons like that. I found it in his cottage at the harbour."

Melanie said nothing. Rita continued. "And I bet you the boot prints on the rampart will show a match with your father's. Isn't that right? Your father went up to the ramparts. He killed Andrew because you told him you would lose Carla. If Andrew spoke to Ruth and she came to us – we could arrest you, and return the baby to Ruth. That's the real reason Andrew had to die. Correct?"

Melanie now stood, her nose flaring. Hatred carved a deep snarl across her face. Her hands were like claws. "You won't take my baby from me."

Rita felt a vague movement behind her. She realised she had been too engrossed in speaking to Melanie and she hadn't locked the door.

She took out her baton and turned in one smooth movement. She caught a glimpse of Jonty, and the flash of a gun in his hand. But she was too late. A loud crack resounded across the back of her skull, and an orange yellow fireball of pain exploded across her head.

Her knees buckled, and the world went completely dark.

CHAPTER 53

Rita heard distant sounds, like the far away cry of sea gulls. The sky was black, thick with strange fumes. She felt movement, like she was shaking. Was she on a boat? The fumes began to clear, and the sky started to change colour at the edges. The cries of the seagulls were louder now. Then she lurched forward, and a sudden, severe pain lanced across her head like a whiplash. She cried out.

The sound of seagulls morphed into a voice. "Guv! Guv! Can you hear me?"

Rita's eyelids felt like they were made of lead. She tried hard to drag them open. The face in front was blurry, like she was looking at them through weird glasses. She blinked twice, and Rizwan's features came into focus.

Suddenly, everything flooded back to her memory. The rug on the floor in which she lay, the wooden walls…and how she got here. She tried to sit up and that was the wrong move. Sudden nausea rose up in her throat and her eyes lost focus. She clutched her abdomen and vomited.

Rizwan helped to sitting, and panting, she wiped her mouth.

The pain in the back of her head was like a spear jutting out through her eyes. It made her sick, and she retched again, but this time it was dry. She rested for a few seconds, then put her hands on the bed, and forced herself to rise. She wobbled as Rizwan held her elbows.

"Guv, you need to go to a hospital."

Rita's vision had returned to normal. She flexed her arms and legs. She could move. She looked around the room. The cot was still there but the baby was gone. So was the rucksack. The empty black bag lay on the floor.

"Where's Melanie and Jonty?" Rita asked.

"I don't know," Rizwan said. His face was ashen and he looked scared. Rita forced a smile on her face and squeezed his shoulder.

"Hey, I'm okay, alright?"

"Okay, guv," Rizwan looked a little more reassured. "I've had a look around. The place is empty. There's a path going down to the beach, I think the water's close by. I can see boot prints outside, and they look fresh."

"Yes, that's Melanie and Jonty. He attacked me from behind while I was speaking to Melanie." Rita winced as she moved past Rizwan and into the hallway.

The lights were still on. The front door was shut. Rita opened it and stepped out on the porch. The fresh breeze from the sea struck her in the face and she relished the sensation. It woke her up further.

She heard Rizwan's radio crackle as he appeared beside her.

"All units alert. Two suspects seen on Hayburn Wyke beach."

Rizwan was moving already, and Rita followed slowly. Rizwan held back for her.

"No, you go ahead," Rita said. She still had her flashlight and she could see Rizwan's beam and his shape in the darkness. "Just keep going, I'll catch up with you."

Rizwan shook his head firmly. "No, guv, I'm not leaving you again."

Rita smiled at his protectiveness. It was sweet of him. "Okay superman," she bumped a fist on his elbow. "Let's go."

Rita didn't have the strength to sprint, but she tried to walk faster. Every step she took sent a jarring pain shooting down her spine. The path sloped down, thankfully. The sound of surf pounding the boulders grew louder.

It didn't take them long to get to the beach. The tide was up, but some of the beach was still accessible on foot. At sea, a long boat with multiple search lights had lit up the beach. It was supplemented by the moving flashlights of the uniformed team, who were splashing through the ankle high water.

A black RIB was bobbing in the waters, tied to one of the boulders. Rita saw Melanie, with baby Carla strapped to her chest. She was on the beach still, and she was stepping over a small boulder, trying to reach the boat. A bearded man was on the boat, at the engine. It was Jonty. He was frantically waving at Melanie, but her progress was slowed by the boulders of various sizes, and the tide that was now moving in.

Jonty couldn't bring the boat any closer for fear of getting wrecked. Rita had delayed them just long enough. She stepped on the rocks herself, aiming for Melanie. She ignored the shouts from Rizwan. She saw two uniformed sergeants, and Richard, splashing over the water, heading in her direction.

"Melanie!" Rita called out. She didn't hear Rita. Rita pressed on, ignoring her pain, driven by pure adrenaline.

She called Melanie's name again. Somehow, the woman heard her. She stopped, and turned.

"Melanie! This is how you found Carla, right?" Rita screamed. For once, the wind carried her words in the right direction, towards Melanie.

"She came to you from the sea. Don't let the sea take her away again."

Melanie said something Rita couldn't hear. Baby Carla was awake, and she was crying. Melanie turned away, and resumed her crawl over the rocks. Rita was fearful she would slip and hurt Carla. She kept moving, narrowing the distance between her and Melanie.

"You won't get far. The Coast Guards are here," Rita shouted. Melanie ignored her this time. Waves crashed against the boulders, sending sea foam and spray into Rita's face.

A uniformed officer arrived from the left, moving faster than Rita. Another arrived from the front. They got to Melanie before she could. Melanie tried to run, but she couldn't. She fell and Rita screamed in fright. But one of the uniforms caught Melanie before she fell. She struggled, but between them, they lowered her to the boulder gently.

"Turn off your engine and return to shore now," a loud voice boomed from the HMCG boat, directed at Jonty. A small speedboat arrived, bearing four officers, who clambered onto the RIB. Jonty stood there, watching them with square shoulders. He raised his arms in surrender as the officers got on the boat. Richard was next to Rita as she reached Melanie. They checked the woman and baby Carla, who was crying, but thankfully unharmed.

"Keep mother and baby together," Rita ordered, surprised by the wobble in her voice. She breathed deeply, regaining control.

Overhead, a helicopter swooped low, the thunder of its rotor blades echoing against the hills. It banked away, rising higher.

"Take them to dry land," Rita said. She glanced down at Melanie as a female officer helped her to stand straight. Melanie held eyes with Rita for a few seconds, before she was dragged away.

CHAPTER 54

Three Days Later

Rita sat opposite Melanie in the children's play area of HMP (His Majesty's Prison) Askham Grange. The prison had a mother and baby unit, and was situated just south of York, the big city closest to Scarborough.
Carla was playing in the soft floored play area, and she picked up a toy and brought it to Melanie. Then she looked at the woman sat next to Melanie.
It was Ruth Hodgson, who sat forward, a big smile on her face, staring at Carla.
Melanie exhaled and clenched her jaws together. Rita stirred in her seat, and so did the female prison officer at the closed door. Both of them scrutinised Melanie carefully. Another woman sat two seats away from Melanie and Ruth watched the proceedings. She was Dr Dixon, the child psychologist who was looking after Melanie, Carla and Ruth.
Melanie said to Carla, "Give it to this lady here." She pointed at Ruth who sat next to her. Carla looked at Ruth with her big eyes. Rita saw the expectation in Ruth's face. This was the moment Ruth had been waiting for.

Carla gazed at Ruth for a long time. Then she stepped over to Ruth and put the toy on Ruth's lap. It was a little toy pony.

"Thank you," Ruth said. "That's a lovely toy. Do you like it?"

Carla was a little confused, and looked towards her mother. Then she walked back to where Melanie was sitting and climbed on her lap.

The three of them had regular sessions with the child psychologist and prison child care worker. Rita had been to one of the sessions, although her presence was not required. Ruth had asked for Rita and Maggie to be there.

Rita and Maggie wanted closure, just like Ruth did. Everyone wanted Ruth to get her child back, but it was a complex matter. It depended on what Carla wanted and how she would cope.

Ruth was starting four weeks of residential stay at the prison, in the mother and baby unit. She would be looking after Carla while Melanie did her voluntary prison work. As Carla got more used to Ruth, the hope was one day Ruth could take Carla to live in her own house.

Carla picked up another toy and took it to Ruth. Ruth slid down to the floor to sit cross legged and took the toy from her. Carla also sat and they played together. Rita glanced at Melanie. The woman was pale and haggard, her sunken cheeks as colourless as the expression on her face. She showed no emotion as she watched Ruth and Carla play.

Rita knew it would take time. Months, maybe even years. But Dr Dixon had assured Rita that Carla, or Jennifer, as Ruth called her, would eventually come to see Ruth as her real mother.

She wasn't even two years old, and the memory of Melanie would fade from her mind eventually. But everyone was concerned about Melanie's frame of mind. Yes, she was guilty of stealing Ruth's baby. But she also saved Carla, and looked after her when no one else did.

A court case was in preparation, and it would take months before they got an actual court date for a hearing. Rita knew by then Carla might well be living with Ruth. Many conflicting thoughts crossed her mind. Would Carla really forget Melanie completely? Or would something remain in her mind?

Would Ruth ever tell her child about what really happened? That was unlikely.

In any case, Rita had done what she could. She put her palms on her thighs and smoothed down her trousers.

"I'll be going then," she said. Melanie didn't look at her, but Ruth did. Carla turned, then got up on her little legs and waved goodbye to Rita. It was a heart-warming moment that made everyone smile.

Outside, Jack Banford rose from one of the green plastic chairs that were fixed to the wall. He wore a blue suit that clung to his wide shoulders, white shirt open at the collar. He saw the look on her face and opened his arms, and Rita embraced him.

Jack smelt of his usual aftershave. It was good to see him. He had been in hospital while she recovered from the head injury. The scan was normal, and she was allowed to go home the next day. Jack insisted on driving her back, and stayed the night in the spare room.

Rita sniffed and wiped the tears in her eyes. Jack took her hand lightly. "Come on, let's go."

Outside, the sun was shining, and the clouds had parted. Rita remembered the date. 10th April. Another five days to go before it was her mother's death anniversary. With Jack, Angela and a few others, Rita would go to the hill cemetery near the castle where Clara was buried.

Meanwhile, Jennifer would be united with Ruth, and the cycle of life continued.

Jack's voice brought her back to the present. "Did Jonty confess to the murders?"

Rita looked up at him. "Yes. He threw Andrew off the ramparts, and then killed Matt, too. He was also going to kill David, I think, so he could run off with the money. He's saying he did it for his family. That might work in his defence. But anyway. His confession makes the case a lot easier."

"And what a rollercoaster ride it's been," Jack shook his head. "I'm sorry I didn't help more. You didn't tell me much, to be honest."

Rita gave his hand a squeeze, then smiled at him. "I know, and don't worry. I'm glad it all worked out in the end."

They got in the car, and Jack started to drive. He angled his eyes towards Rita. "Shall we go to Malton for some lunch? Nice pubs there."

Malton was a picturesque little town, and also the food capital of Yorkshire. "Yes, why not?" Rita smiled. She couldn't think of a better way to spend her day off. She touched Jack's arm.
"Thanks for coming down here."
"It's the least I could do," Jack said. There was a serious tone in his voice. When their eyes met, she saw warmth, affection and acceptance of who she was.
She realised that she felt very close to him, this man who had known and loved her as seventeen year old and then was torn from the page of her life when she moved away. Fate had now brought them back together.
She leaned forward, and kissed him lightly on the cheek. They had stopped at a red light. Her lips lingered on his smooth cheek. She sat back and raised her hand to stroke the side of his face.
The lights changed and Jack drove with his right hand. With his left, he grasped Rita's hand, then kissed it. No more words were necessary.
Rita sat back and watched the greenery of North Yorkshire flicker past the window. It was time for a new chapter in her life, and she was ready for it.

CHAPTER 55

Damien Salt was on the phone to his brother, Edward. "Sixty-eight boats were stopped, searched and the cargo seized," Damien fumed. "Each boat had ten to fifteen kilo's worth of gear. This is nothing but a disaster. How will we recover from a loss like this?"
Edward was his usual calm self. "Did you pay the Peruvians already?"
"Yes - the half they demanded as upfront payment. Now we have to pay the remaining half. They will be hard negotiators. No cargo no pay, but this cargo was seized from under our noses. It's embarrassing."
"How did it happen?"
"Jonty and David were caught. One of them sang like a canary, or both of them did. I don't know which one. We can't get to them now. We have to wait until they're in jail."
"Get rid of them in jail," Edward said, a hint of anger in his voice now. "They should've known better."
"Jonty bought this upon himself. He killed Andrew. I never knew Andrew was his son in law." Damien told his brother Jennifer and Ruth's story.
Edward sighed, and they were silent for a while. Damien said, "This is bad for business. It was going so well even the Albanians wanted a piece of the action. Our supply chain from Dundee to Hull is now disrupted."
"And we know who to blame, don't we?"

"Rita Gupta," Damien said between clenched teeth. "I want to make her disappear."

"Not right now," Edward cautioned. "Its too hot. We kill her and all attention falls on us. We need to ride out this storm."

"She put you in jail. Practically retired you." Damien shook his head. He stared out of his office window, at the sprawling expanse of green that met the sea in the distance. "We can't keep having one crisis after another. Rita's causing us more trouble than she's worth."

Edward said, "What about Rafik? And that man in prison, Ed Kyle Warren?"

"They're both in play. They both hate Rita Gupta. But Warren is in a high security prison. He's more dangerous than Rafik, I think."

Edward was silent for a while. "Warren abducted that child, right? And then killed his step father?"

"Yes." Damien could feel his brother nodding along. agreeing with him.

"You're right. Warren is cold blooded. We can rely on him more. He will do the job for us when the time is right.

Damien sighed and passed a hand over his head. "But first, we need to get him out of prison. I've got a plan for that."

"I'm all ears, bro," Edward said.

…to be continued.

Author's Note

Like a plant, a book is born in silence and isolation. It's air, water and sustenance is you – the reader.

When a reader leaves a review, the little sapling rises in the air, and someday, bears leaves and flowers.

If you can, please leave a review on Amazon, Goodreads, wherever you can. This humble self-published author will appreciate it immensely.

Copy and paste this link on amazon:
https://geni.us/Iknowyoulied

Thank you :)

Sam Carter

WANT TO READ MORE?

Here is the rest of the series - Books 1-4 (all free in Kindle Unlimited):

https://geni.us/forgbones
https://geni.us/deadcoldhand
https://geni.us/littlevoice
https://geni.us/thebrokensouls

Printed in Great Britain
by Amazon